学术顾问
（以姓氏笔画为序）

王　宏　冯智文　李正栓　李丽生　原一川

Academic Advisors

Wang Hong　Feng Zhiwen　Li Zhengshuan

Li Lisheng　Yuan Yichuan

主　编

李昌银

副主编

黄　瑛　彭庆华

General Editor

Li Changyin

Professor of English Yunnan Normal University

Associate General Editors

Huang Ying

Professor of English Yunnan Normal University

Peng Qinghua

Professor of English Yunnan Normal University

云南少数民族经典作品英译文库
Classics of Yunnan Ethnic Groups in English Translation

主编 李昌银　General Editor　Li Changyin
副主编 黄瑛 彭庆华　Associate General Editors　Huang Ying & Peng Qinghua

Meige

梅 葛

整理◎云南省民族民间文学楚雄调查队
英译◎陈萍 刘怡
译校◎[美]包琼

Edited by the Chuxiong Collecting Team
of Yunnan Ethnic Folklore
Translated by Chen Ping & Liu Yi
Revised by Joan Cecile Boulerice

云南出版集团
云南人民出版社

图书在版编目（CIP）数据

梅葛：汉、英 / 云南省民族民间文学楚雄调查队整理；陈萍，刘怡英译. —— 昆明：云南人民出版社，2018.12

（云南少数民族经典作品英译文库 / 李昌银主编）

ISBN 978-7-222-17501-3

Ⅰ.①梅… Ⅱ.①云… ②陈… ③刘… Ⅲ.①彝族—史诗—中国—汉、英 Ⅳ.①I222.7

中国版本图书馆CIP数据核字(2018)第277426号

出 品 人	李　维　　赵石定
项目统筹	周　祥　　殷筱钊
项目组稿	郭木玉
责任编辑	郭木玉　　任建红　　李东华
设计制作	马　滨　　三人禾
责任校对	张齐英　　崔苡菡　　付芳侠　　周桉吉
责任印制	陆卫华　　代隆参

云南少数民族经典作品英译文库
Classics of Yunnan Ethnic Groups in English Translation

梅 葛
Meige

整理◎云南省民族民间文学楚雄调查队
英译◎陈萍　刘怡
译校◎[美]包琼

Edited by the Chuxiong Collecting Team
of Yunnan Ethnic Folklore
Translated by Chen Ping & Liu Yi
Revised by Joan Cecile Boulerice

出　版	云南出版集团　云南人民出版社
发　行	云南人民出版社
社　址	昆明市环城西路609号
邮　编	650034
网　址	www.ynpph.com.cn
E-mail	ynrms@sina.com
开　本	787mm×1092mm　1/16
印　张	18.5
字　数	300千
版　次	2018年12月第1版第1次印刷
印　刷	云南出版印刷（集团）有限责任公司　云南新华印刷一厂
书　号	ISBN 978-7-222-17501-3
定　价	105.00 元

云南人民出版社
公众微信号

序 一

◎李正栓

　　民族典籍英译是传播中国文化、文学和文明的重要途径，是中华文化走出去的重要组成部分。文化与文学的传播，是一个国家提高文化软实力的重要方式，在文化交流和文明建设中起着不可或缺的作用，对提高国家对外话语权、构建国家对外话语体系以及对建设世界文学都有积极意义。

　　中国各少数民族拥有许多优秀的典籍，具有很高的文物价值、文学价值和文化价值。各民族的先人们通过口头流传或用文字记述了他们各具特色的文化。各少数民族几乎都有自己民族的创世史、史诗和神话传说。

　　中国民族典籍独具特色，不可替代。重视民族典籍的翻译和研究工作，对于挖掘各民族优秀文化，保护各民族文明，增强各民族之间的沟通和了解，进一步向世界其他地区传播各少数民族优秀文化，乃至提高我国文化软实力都有着重要意义。不少少数民族聚居地处于祖国边疆，有的处在"一带一路"建设关键部位，有的处在与周边国家进行各种交流的重要位置。

　　中国民族典籍是世界多元文化的有机组成部分，与其他文化共同造就了世界文化的绚丽多姿。世界正因为其文化多样性才变得缤纷多彩。我国各民族典籍中包含的文化多样性极大地丰富了世界多元、特色鲜明的文化。人们对多样性形成全新的认识角度和思维方式。多样性开阔了人们的视野，丰富了人们思考问题的角度。挖掘这些典籍中所蕴含的教育价值和文化价值，对世界其他民族都有指导和借鉴意义，并且有助于建设我国的文化自信。

民族典籍本身蕴含的特殊价值对加强民族文化了解、促进中外文化交流具有重大意义。民族典籍英译具有文学翻译和文化传递之功能，有对外宣传作用，还是一种文学外交。因此，民族典籍翻译和研究对于维护祖国统一、促进民族团结、稳定边疆以及增强国内各民族和中外文化之间的交流都起着极为重要的作用。

中华人民共和国成立以后，中央政府一直十分重视民族典籍翻译和研究工作，提供了强有力的政策支持，并采取了一系列有效措施，加快了各少数民族典籍的抢救、整理、翻译和研究的进程。中央政府多次召开西藏工作会议和新疆工作会议。近年来，国际和国内对于多元文化高度关注，少数民族文学典籍的翻译已然成为业内研究的热点。

近年来，民族典籍翻译和研究迅猛发展，势头良好。国家大力支持，发放国家社科基金课题，教育部和国家民委也发放课题，扶持了一大批研究者。很多民族典籍翻译课题得以立项并顺利开展；为数不少的民族典籍被翻译成汉语、英语和其他语言并出版发行；越来越多的业界人士致力于这个满富生机的学术领域。

在中国文化走出去的国家战略下，全国少数民族典籍英译学术研讨会陆续召开，已经召开三次。

云南是中国民族最多的省份。人口在5000人以上的少数民族有25个，其中有15个民族为云南所特有，分别是：白族、哈尼族、傣族、傈僳族、佤族、拉祜族、纳西族、景颇族、布朗族、普米族、阿昌族、基诺族、怒族、德昂族、独龙族。其中除白族人口占全国白族人口总数的84%以上外，其他14个民族95%居住在云南。

云南还是我国跨境民族最多的省份。在云南的25个少数民族中，有16个民族跨境而居，分别是：傣族、壮族、苗族、景颇族、瑶族、哈尼族、德昂族、佤族、拉祜族、彝族、阿昌族、傈僳族、布依族、怒族、布朗族、独龙族。

云南少数民族创造了辉煌的文化。据不完全统计，云南少数民族文字文献古籍蕴藏量达10万余册（卷），口传古籍4万余种。云南省民委少数民族古籍整理出版规划办公室为了挽救和保护这些古籍，计划在5年内编纂出版100卷《云南少数民族古籍珍本集成》。这是一个令人瞩目的庞大计划。将这些古籍中的珍品翻译介绍给世界，不仅能够弘扬云南省丰富多彩的民族文化，而且有助于增进与南亚东南亚国家的理解与交流，为"一带一路"倡议的实施做出贡献。

云南师范大学外国语学院很重视这一领域的工作。在外国语学院领导支持下，李昌银教授带领一个由教授和中青年学者组成的团队对精选出来的17部云南少数民族经典作品进行英译，计划在5年内（"十三五"期间）翻译出版。这是一项十分有意义的宏大工程。

这17部民族典籍，内容全部为各民族的英雄史诗或神话传说，具有很高的历史意义和文学价值。这些作品涉及阿昌族、白族、傣族、德昂族、哈尼族、景颇族、拉祜族、苗族、纳西族、普米族、彝族等11个少数民族。

云南师范大学这支翻译队伍实力强大，主要由一些多年从事翻译教学、研究和实践的教授和副教授组成，他们是李昌银、黄瑛、彭庆华、孙兴文、吴相如、刘德周、杨慧芳、郜菊、陈萍、包琼（Joan Boulerice）等国内外专家学者。他们在云南翻译界都是风云人物。

在民族典籍英译中，这支队伍异军突起，为我国民族典籍英译壮大了声势，必将为中国民族典籍走向世界而成为世界文学的一部分做出新贡献。

民族典籍翻译与研究事业关乎国家的稳定统一，关乎民族关系的和谐发展，关乎世界多元文化的实现。在中国，民族典籍资源极为丰富，有待进一步挖掘、翻译。因此，民族典籍英译前景光明。同时，我们也应意识到，仍有许多濒临消失的少数民族典籍亟待拯救，民族典籍翻译与研究工作任重而道远。

（李正栓，中国英汉语比较研究会典籍英译专业委员会常务副会长兼秘书长）

Foreword by Li Zhengshuan

The translation of Chinese ethnic classics is an important approach in spreading Chinese culture, literature and civilization. It is a crucial component of Chinese culture going global. The spreading of Chinese culture and literature is a national policy and an important way to improve the cultural soft power of China. It plays an indispensable role in the cultural exchange between China and other countries and the development of world literature.

The ethnic groups in China have countless excellent classics with high anthropological, literary and cultural value. The ancestors of each ethnic group have passed down their distinctive culture orally or in writing. Almost all the ethnic groups have their own story of creation, epics, myths and legends.

Chinese ethnic classics are unique and irreplaceable. It is imperative to attach importance to the translation and research of ethnic classics; to explore the excellent ethnic cultures; to protect the civilization of ethnic groups; to enhance the communication and understanding among ethnic groups; to further spread the outstanding culture of ethnic groups to other parts of the world; and to build the cultural strength of China. Many ethnic groups live in the border areas and thus play an important role in the cultural and economic cooperation between China and its neighbors in the context of the Belt and Road Initiative.

Chinese ethnic classics are an important component of the magnificence and diversity of world culture. It is diversity that makes the world so colorful. The cultural diversity of Chinese ethnic classics has greatly enriched the world's pluralism and its distinctive features. People around the world have formed a new understanding of diversity. This diversity has expanded people's horizon and enriched their way of thinking. Digging out the educational and cultural value in these classics can contribute to the construction of China's self-confidence in culture.

The special value of the ethnic classics itself is of great significance to the strengthening of national culture and intercultural communication between China and foreign countries. The translation of ethnic classics is not just a literary exchange, but also a form of cultural communication. It is diplomacy through literature in that it consolidates the cultural ties between China and other countries.

After the founding of the People's Republic of China, the central government attached great importance to the translation and research of ethnic classics, provided the a great deal of policy support, and adopted a series of effective measures to speed up the process of rescuing, collating, translating and studying ethnic classics. The central government has convened several working conferences on Tibet and Xinjiang. In recent years, both China and other countries have paid close attention to multiculture. The translation of ethnic classics has become a hot topic.

In recent years, the translation and research of ethnic classics have progressed rapidly and have shown good prospects. The government strongly supports and grants the research projects of the national social science fund. The Ministry of Education and the State Ethnic Affairs Commission are also issuing research projects and giving funding to a large number of researchers. Many research projects on ethnic classics have been approved and carried out. Many ethnic classics have been translated into Chinese, English and other languages and published. More and more professionals have dedicated themselves to this new sphere of learning.

In this context, the academic conferences on translation of ethnic classics are held one after another all around the country. And up to now three have been held.

Yunnan is the province which has the most ethnic groups in China. Besides Han people, there are 25 ethnic groups, each with a population of more than 5,000. Among them, 15 ethnic groups are unique to Yunnan, which are the Bai, the Hani, the Dai, the Lisu, the Wa, the Lahu, the Naxi, the Jingpo, the Bulang, the Pumi, the Achang, the Jinuo, the Nu, the De'ang and the Dulong. Among these, 84% of the total number of the Bai people in China and 95% of the other 14 ethnic groups are living in Yunnan.

Yunnan is also the province which has the most cross-border ethnic groups. Of the 25 ethnic groups, 16 live across the border, namely: the Dai, the Zhuang, the Miao, the Jingpo, the Yao, the Hani, the De'ang, the Wa, the Lahu, the Yi, the Achang, the Lisu, the Buyi, the Nu, the Bulang and the Dulong.

The ethnic groups in Yunnan have created splendid cultures. According to statistics, the number of classics of Yunnan ethnic groups is more than 100 thousand volumes and classics in oral tradition are more than 40 thousand. In order to save and protect these ancient books, the Office of Classics Collation and Publishing of Yunnan Ethnic Groups Affairs Commission planned to compile and publish 100 volumes of *A Collection of Yunnan Ethnic Group Rare Books* in five years, which is an ambitious plan. The introduction of the ancient classics via translation can not only promote and develop the colorful ethnic cultures of Yunnan, but also contribute to the understanding and exchange between China and countries in South Asia and Southeast Asia and to the implementation of the Belt and Road Initiative as well.

The School of Foreign Languages and Literature of Yunnan Normal University is paying close attention to this field. With the support of the School and the University, Professor Li Changyin is leading a group of professors and young scholars to do the project of *"Classics of Yunnan Ethnic Groups in English Translation"*, which includes 17 ethnic classics selected carefully from Yunnan's bountiful ethnic classics. These books are the heroic epics or myths and legends of each ethnic groups with great historical significance and literary value. They will finish the translation in five years (during "the thirteenth five-year plan"). After that, all the works will be published by Yunnan People's Publishing House.

The 17 works cover 11 ethnic groups: the Achang, the Bai, the Dai, the De'ang, the Hani, the Jingpo, the Lahu, the Miao, the Naxi, the Pumi and the Yi. All of these groups except the Miao and the Yi are unique to Yunnan.

The translation team of Yunnan Normal University is full of strength and vitality, composed of professors and associate professors who have been occupied in translation teaching, research, and practice for a long time. They are Li Changyin, Huang Ying, Peng Qinghua, Sun Xingwen, Wu Xiangru, Liu Dezhou, Yang Huifang, Gao Ju, Chen Ping, Joan Boulerice and other experts and scholars who are representative figures in the translation field in Yunnan province.

This team is a new force that has suddenly arisen in terms of translating ethnic classics. It is expanding the momentum of ethnic classics translation in China and has made a new contribution for China's ethnic classics to go global and become a part of world literature.

The translation and research of ethnic classics are related

to the development of Chinese culture and the realization of multiculturalism in the world. In China, ethnic classics are extremely rich in resources, which require us to make further exploration and research and translate them into other languages. Therefore, the future of translating ethnic classics is bright. At the same time, we should also realize that there are still many ethnic works which are close to extinction and urgently need to be rescued. We still have a long way to go in the fields of translation and research in ethnic classics.

(Li Zhengshuan, Standing Vice Chairman and Secretary General, Classics Translation Committee of CACSEC)

序 二

◎王 宏

  好友云南师范大学外国语学院李昌银教授来电嘱托我为"云南少数民族经典作品英译文库"的出版写一序言,并随即发来该文库的背景资料,让我"不着急,慢慢写"。我本人从事中国典籍英译及研究,深知少数民族典籍对外传译的重要性,但又是少数民族典籍翻译的门外汉。因此,我是怀着虚心学习的态度来写此序言的。近年来,在中国文化"走出去"战略工程大背景下,在中央和地方各级政府的大力支持下,我国少数民族典籍的对外传译及研究工作顺利开展,取得了很大的进步。请看以下数据:

  2008年,广西百色学院韩家权教授获批国家社科基金项目《布洛陀史诗》(壮汉英对照)。该项目已顺利结项,并于2013年12月获得中国民间文艺最高奖"山花奖"。

  2012年,广西百色学院外语系翻译团队翻译的国家级非物质文化遗产《壮族嘹歌》(英文版)由广西师范大学出版社正式出版。

  2012年,东北大学秦皇岛分校吴松林教授主编的《蒙古族系列:江格尔(汉英对照)》(上下册)由吉林大学出版社出版。

  2013年,河北师范大学李正栓教授英译《藏族格言诗》

由长春出版社出版发行。

2013年，云南财经大学崔晓霞教授撰写的《〈阿诗玛〉英译研究》收入由王宏印教授主编、民族出版社出版的"民族典籍翻译研究丛书"。

2014年，东北大学秦皇岛分校吴松林教授撰写的《满族档案文献研究》申请到国家社科后期资助，他英译的《英雄格斯尔可汗》由吉林大学出版社出版。

2014年，中南民族大学张立玉教授主持的"土家族主要典籍英译及研究"获批国家社科基金项目。

2015年，西安外国语大学梁真惠副教授撰写的《〈玛纳斯〉翻译传播研究》收入由王宏印教授主编、民族出版社出版的"民族典籍翻译研究丛书"。

与此同时，第一届和第二届全国少数民族典籍英译学术研讨会分别于2012年和2014年在广西民族大学和大连民族学院举行，参加会议的院校分布之广、与会代表数量之众、提交论文数量之多和涉及研究话题之细，十分可喜。2016年还将在中南民族大学举行第三届全国少数民族典籍英译学术研讨会。

为什么少数民族典籍的对外传译及研究工作在短短几年就受到译界的青睐，取得众多成果？我认为，这在很大程度上归于典籍翻译界乃至翻译界同仁对"中国典籍"的重新思考和认识。中国典籍浩如烟海，卷帙浩繁，举世瞩目，是全人类共同的精神财富。但对于中国典籍的理解，我们以前较多限于汉民族的重要文献和书籍，而对少数民族多有忽略。在讨论中国典籍时，也较多关注古代文学作品。其实，中国典籍指"中国清代末年1911年以前的重要文献和书籍",这就要求我们从事典籍翻译时,不但要翻译古代文学典籍作品,还要翻译古代哲学、科技、法律、医学、经济、军事、天文、地理等诸多方面的典籍作品,不但要翻译汉民族的典籍作品,也要翻译各少数民族的典籍作品。

民族典籍具有该民族的原型符号的特质,蕴藏着能够"遗传"并不断"再生"的文化基因。民族典籍是中华传统文化的内核,同时还是中华传统文化的符号构成规则。中国是具有56个民族的多民族国家,少数民族典籍是我国少数民族勤劳与智慧的结晶,是中华文明、也是世界文明不可或缺的一部分。少数民族典籍对外传译具有跨文化交流的作用,它不但有助于更多的人了解少数民族的独特文化,而且还有助于保护少数民族文化的独特性、维持少数民族文化多样性、促进各民族团结、提升中华文化软实力等。

中国少数民族典籍涉及宗教、文学、历史、语言、医学、天文历算等领域,内容丰富,版本多样,载体特殊,传承奇特。仅以《中国少数民族古籍总目提要》为例,该书于1997年正式立项,全书总体设计约60卷、110册,目前已出版23个民族卷共20册:纳西族卷、白族卷、东乡族卷·裕固族卷·保安族卷、土族卷·撒拉族卷、锡伯族卷、哈尼族卷、回族卷·铭刻、柯尔克孜族卷、羌族卷、毛南族卷·京族卷、仫佬族卷、达斡尔族卷、土家族卷、鄂温克族卷、鄂伦春族卷、赫哲族卷、苗族卷、侗族卷、黎族卷、朝鲜族卷。该书真实地反映了我国各少数民族古籍赋存的全面情况,充实了中国的历史和文化内容,为后人探索各种文化形式的源流、揭示中国社会文化发展的轨迹提供了极为珍贵的资料，为我国乃至世界各国人文科学研究提供了一套新颖而全面的资料，对于弘扬中华民族传统文化具有深远的历史意义和现实意义。

少数民族典籍的对外传译是一项艰巨的工作，涉及将少数民族语言译成汉语、少数民族语言之间的互译和少数民族语言译成外语（主要是英语）。前两类翻译历史源远流长，最早可追溯到春秋战国时代《越人歌》的翻译，即汉、壮语之间的翻译。少数民族典籍译成外语的时间则要晚一些。据考证，维吾尔族古典长诗《福乐智慧》成书于1069年或1070年，目前尚未发现完整的原稿，只存留下来三个抄本，分别为赫拉特抄本、费尔干纳抄本与埃及抄本，其中费尔干纳抄本于12~13世纪用阿拉伯文纳斯赫体抄写，1914年发现于今中亚乌孜别克斯坦纳曼干城，现存于该共和国科学院东方研究所。这是少数民族典籍译介到国外的最早纪录。少数民族典籍外译在现代有了较快发展。一些少数民族典籍，如藏族的《格萨尔王传》、蒙古族的《江格尔》和柯尔克孜族的《玛纳斯》等英雄史诗，云南彝族的《阿诗玛》、维吾尔族的《艾里甫和赛乃姆》等民间叙事长诗已先后被翻译成英语及其他外国文字，为世人所知。这对传承少数民族经典，推动中外文化交流起到了不可替代的作用。然而，还有大量的中国少数民族典籍等待我们去翻译和研究。

云南省少数民族典籍资源十分丰富。据不完全统计，云南少数民族文字文献古籍蕴藏量达10万余册（卷），口传古籍4万余种。"云南少数民族经典作品英译文库"正是依托云南省丰富的少数民族典籍资源，借助云南师范大学外国语学院强大的翻译师资队伍,在云南人民出版社的有力支持下,首次将云南少数民族经典作品成系列对外译介的大力举措。云南师范大学外国语学院对"云南少数民族经典作品英译文库"十分重视,他们首先邀请省内外少数民族语言文化研究专家对云南民族典籍和民族文化经典作品进行筛选,做到"好中选好,优中选优",同时调配最强的翻译力量承担文库的翻译任务。我粗略看了该文库的选题,发现选题面广,覆盖范围宽,收入了云南省阿昌族、白族、傣族、纳西族、德昂族、哈尼族、景颇族、拉祜族、苗族、普米族和彝族等民族的典籍作品。云南共有25个少数民族,其中11个少数民族的典籍作品都覆盖到了,不少作品还是首次译成英文。这将彻底改变云南少数民族典籍由于对外译介数量较少,不为世界了解的尴尬局面。

对于云南师范大学外国语学院而言,把少数民族典籍英译作为翻译专业的优势特色进行建设,这将对该院的学科建设起到助推作用。"云南少数民族经典作品英译文库"所产生的翻译成果和研究成果将培养出一批优秀的典籍翻译和研究团队,凸显该院在全国的学术特色和学术影响,同时还能将翻译能力和研究能力转化为教学能力,提高云南师范大学外国语学院翻译专业研究生的培养质量,为社会输送高水平的翻译人才,有力地支撑学院翻译专业学科的建设和发展。我对云南师范大学外国语学院的翻译师资队伍较为熟悉。作为云南省唯一获得省级高校优势特色学科建设项目的外国语学院,该院具有雄厚的翻译师资力量,在云南省各高校中当属第一。多年来,该院翻译与跨文化研究团队一直承担着对外交流与合作的各种口笔译项目及任务。由外国语学院精心挑选和确定的"云南少数民族经典作品英译文库"翻译人员绝大多数都是云南省翻译领域里的知名教授或专家，有国外留学经历，且具有扎实的英汉双语语言功底，曾翻译出版多部译著和翻译作品，并且主持和参与过多项翻译项目的研究。我阅读李昌银教授发来的文库翻译人员名单，发现多名我所熟悉的知名教授、博士也在其中，感到格外放心。

"云南少数民族经典作品英译文库"的出版发行是云南省翻译界的一件大事，也是我国少数民族典籍翻译传来的又一佳音。想当年，我和《大中华文库》总协调人李林老师曾在参加全国典籍英译学术研讨会之余一起找到李昌银教授，敦促李教授向学校和同事呼吁，少数民族典籍翻译及研究是富矿，值得快挖、深挖，能早出成果，出大成果。今天，我们当年的心愿变成了美好的现实，心里感到特别高兴。再次热烈祝贺"云南少数民族经典作品英译文库"的顺利出版！

（王宏，中国典籍翻译研究会副会长、苏州大学博士生导师）

Foreword by Wang Hong

My friend Professor Li Changyin of Yunnan Normal University asked me to write a few words for the publication of *Classics of Yunnan Ethnic Groups in English Translation*. I am more than delighted to do it. As I have been doing research in the English translation of Chinese classics, I know how important his work is. In recent years, substantial progress has been made in translating Chinese ethnic classics into English and other foreign languages. Books published in this respect include *The Liao Songs of the Zhuang Nationality* (Nanning: Guangxi Normal University Press, 2008, English Edition), *Mongolian Series: Jianggeer* (Changchun: Jilin University Press, 2012, Bilingual Edition), *Tibetan Gnomic Verses Translated into English* (Changchun: Changchun Press, 2013), and *Geser Khan: a Hero* (Changchun: Jilin University Press, 2014). Several projects in the English translation of ethnic classics have received funding from the National Planning Office of Philosophy and Social Science and, as a result, a number of monographs and PhD dissertations have been published.

Meanwhile, it is encouraging to see that the first conferences on English translation of ethnic classics in China have been held in Guangxi Nationalities University and

Dalian Nationalities Institute respectively. Participants were both many and enthusiastic. Many papers were presented and a lot of topics discussed. The third conference will be hosted by South Central Nationalities University in 2016.

Why, then, has this field attracted so much attention from translators and scholars alike and accomplished so much in just a few years? The answer, I believe, lies in a rethinking of what constitutes Chinese classics as an indispensable part of human heritage. We used to see Chinese classics as more or less equal to the classics of the Han people, excluding works by other ethnic groups. Moreover, when we talk about Chinese classics, we focus too much on the literary works of ancient times. Yet Chinese classics actually refer to "important works and books before 1911, the year when the Qing dynasty fell, bringing an end to imperial rule." This definition requires us to pay attention not just to literary works, but also writings in other subjects, such as philosophy, science, law, medicine, economics, military affairs, astronomy, and geography, not only Han works, but writings by other ethnic groups as well.

The classical works of a nation are its archetypal symbols, the major carriers of its cultural genes. Chinese classics make up the core of Chinese tradition. The Chinese nation consists of 56 ethnic groups. Ethnic classics are an important part of not only Chinese traditional culture, but also of world civilization. The translation of these works into other languages is important in that it helps to promote cross-cultural communications between China and other countries and to protect and preserve the uniqueness and diversity of ethnic cultures by making them accessible to foreign readers.

Chinese ethnic classics cover a variety of areas, such as religion, literature, history, language, medicine, astrology, and calendar, with numerous editions, special media and unique ways of transmission from generation to generation. Take, for example, *An Anthology of Chinese Ethnic Classics*, a colossal project that includes 110 volumes, 20 of which, from 23 ethnic groups, have been published. The anthology reflects the variety and quantity of China's ethnic classics and provides valuable material and resources for studying, understanding and developing Chinese culture and history in a more comprehensive and sustainable way.

The translation of Chinese ethnic classics into foreign languages is a very demanding job, involving rendering from ethnic languages to Chinese, between ethnic languages, and from ethnic languages (often via Chinese) to foreign languages. The first two types of translation can be traced back to the Spring and Autumn Period, when *The Song of the Yue People* was translated from their mother tongue into Chinese. The earliest translation of ethnic classics into a foreign language is *Wisdom of Royal Glory*, a long poem of the Uygurs, which was rendered from the source language into Arabic and is now in the Oriental Institute of Uzbekistan at Namangan. But it was not until modern times that the translation of ethnic classics into foreign languages accelerated. Noticeably, ethnic epics, such as *The Story of Prince Geser* of the Tibetans, *The Story of Jianggeer* of the Mongolians, *Manas* of the Kyrgyz, and narrative poems such as *Ashima* of the Yi people, *Alip and Salam* of the Uygurs, etc., have been published. These translations have contributed to acquainting the world with Chinese ethnic classics, but many remain to be translated.

Yunnan is rich in ethnic classics, boasting more than 100 thousand volumes of written classics and over 40 thousand pieces of oral literature. Relying on such bountiful resources, as a collective endeavor of the translation team of the School of Foreign Languages and Literature, Yunnan Normal University and with the help of Yunnan People's Publishing House, *Classics of Yunnan Ethnic Groups in English Translation* is the first project to translate Yunnan ethnic classics into English on a large scale. The School adheres to a professional spirit and academic standard in carrying out the project by selecting the most authoritative texts in the source language (Chinese) and recruiting the best translators from its huge faculty. The selection of the works, covering eleven of the twenty-five ethnic groups of the province, indicates expertise and insight. The implementation of the project will change the embarrassing obscurity of Yunnan ethnic classics by making them known to the world, many of them for the first time.

In light of disciplinary development, the project is of

great importance, too. Participating in the translation will strengthen the academic foundation of the teachers, enrich their experience and enhance their translation skills and research ability. This in turn will help them become better teachers and thus able to educate students with higher quality. The publication of the books will add greatly to the faculty accomplishments of the School and raise the academic standing of Yunnan Normal University by taking the first step in this direction among the universities of Yunnan province.

This publication project is a great event not only for Yunnan itself, but also for China. Looking back, I remember that Professor Li Changyin, our friend Li Lin, editor of the *Library of Chinese Classics*, and I talked enthusiastically about initiating something like this in Yunnan when we attended a conference on the translation of ethnic classics in Soochow. Lin and I strongly suggested that Professor Li do it as soon as possible. Now I am very pleased to see our talk becoming reality. Again, my congratulations on the publication of *Classics of Yunnan Ethnic Groups in English Translation*!

(Wang Hong, PhD supervisor at Soochow University, Vice Chairman of Classics Translation Committee of CACSEC)

General Introduction

This publication project, Classics of *Yunnan Ethnic Groups in English Translation*, aims at introducing Yunnan ethnic classical works to the world by making them available to native speakers of English who might be interested in them. With the publication of the *Library of Chinese Classics*, which consists only of books written by Han authors in classical Chinese, attention now is being turned to the English translation and publication of ethnic classics, books produced by ethnic writers about their history and culture. Universities in provinces such as Guangxi, Guizhou, Liaoning, Xinjiang, and Xizang, have taken the initiative. We in Yunnan must do something, because Yunnan has the largest number of ethnic groups in China. 15 of the 25 ethnic groups in the province, the Bai, the Dai, the Hani, the Lisu, the Wa, the Lahu, the Naxi, the Jingpo, the Bulang, the Pumi, the Achang, the Jinuo, the Nu, the De'ang, and the Dulong, live in no other place but Yunnan. The classics of these people, either in their own languages or in Chinese translations, are a great treasure house, which should be accessible to English readers and scholars. But what works should be translated first?

All the 25 ethnic groups in Yunnan have their classics, epics, mythology, creation stories, folksongs, folk drama, mountain songs, and funeral lament lyrics, most of which exist in different versions in different places. According to one estimation, there are more than 100 thousand volumes of them, excluding those in oral form. After a thorough survey and extensive consultations with experts of ethnic studies, we concluded that priority must be given to epics and mythologies, as they reflect an ethnic people's philosophy, history and culture more than anything else by narrating the stories of where and how they think they came from. From many epics and mythologies, we selected 17 of the most authoritative and popular classics representing 11 Yunnan ethnic groups, the Yi, the Bai, the Miao, the Hani, the Lahu, the Naxi, the Jingpo, the Pumi, the Achang, the Dai, and the De'ang. These works are all in Chinese, translated from the original by bilingual scholars whose mother tongue is their own ethnic language and who are fluent and proficient in Chinese. Some were recorded from their oral form at rituals and performances. We did not choose texts written in the ethnic language, not least because it is very hard to find a translator who is skilled in both the ethnic language and English. Moreover, some of the classics in the ethnic language were circulated in various oral forms and fragments. The published Chinese versions have been carefully edited and translated, hence they are more reliable. The next question is: how to translate them?

It happens that all of the 17 works except one are in

verse form, with lines more or less the same length and loose rhymes, but no regular meter. A poem must be rendered into a poem; anything less is unacceptable. So here are the general rules we follow when doing the translation.

One. If the original is verse, the translated text must be verse, too.

Two. Reproduce the ideas and the images of the original as completely as possible.

Three. Reproduce the figures of speech of the original as much as possible.

Four. Do not change the number of lines in a stanza unless absolutely necessary.

Five. Do not use standard meters in English, because the Chinese original does not follow any regular meter. Use the natural rhythm of English instead, but most of the lines should look more or less the same length.

Six. Do not use rhyme unless it comes naturally and is faithful to the content of the original.

What we try to do is, to use Susan Bassnett's words, "transplant the seed", not the tree itself. As for the various aspects of form, particularly meter and end rhyme, we reproduce them when it is possible and abandon them when it is necessary.

Who will do the translations? As this is a collective project of the School of Foreign Languages and Literature of Yunnan Normal University, our team consists of a dozen faculty members and two students from our MA translation program who are already teachers in other universities. All the translators have been teaching translation and doing translation research for a long time. They have published not just academic articles on translation, but also translated books from English to Chinese or vice versa.

Traditionally, people translate into their mother tongue, not into a foreign language. But the situation is changing. Many translators today are translating from their mother tongue into a foreign language. The quality can be good, as Nike K. Pokorn and Stuart Campbell prove in *Challenging the Traditional Axioms*: *Translation into a non-mother tongue* (Amsterdam: John Benjamins Publishing Company, 2005) and *Translation into the Second Language* (New York: Routledge, 2013) respectively. The case of China provides further evidence for their argument. The translation of Chinese classics into English was initiated by James Legge and Herbert Allen Giles in the 19th century and carried on in the 20th century by Arthur Waley, David Hawkes, Burton Watson, John Minford, Stephen Owen and others. It is noticeable that these English and American sinologists were soon joined by Chinese scholars residing in the West, such as Hongming (Tomson) Gu and Lin Yutang, among others. They took up the job because they thought it was their obligation to give English readers more faithful translations than Western sinologists could, who, as their target language is their mother tongue, often misinterpret the original text and misrepresent Chinese culture. Since the 1950s, there has been an increasingly powerful trend for Mainland Chinese translators to render or re-render Chinese classics into foreign languages, English in particular. In our time, this work is gathering momentum, enthusiastically advocated and actively practiced by such well-known translation experts as Yang Xianyi of Beijing Foreign Language Press, Xu Yuanchong of Beijing University, Wang Rongpei of Dalian Foreign Language Institute, Wang Hongyin of Nankai University, Wang Hong of Soochow University, Li Zhengshuan of Hebei Normal University, and many more. These professors are not just translators, but also scholars in translation studies. More importantly, some of them, Xu Yuanchong, Wang Hong and Li Zhengshuan, for example, have had their translations published by Western publishers, which suggests that their English meets the international standard.

In the case of our project, we request that the translators do their best to produce good translations. When they submit them to us, they should represent the highest level that they can attain. Then the general editors appointed by the School read the translated texts and remove inaccurate renderings and grammar mistakes if there are any. On top of that, we've taken an indispensable measure to ensure that our English is readable. We asked Ms. Joan Cecile Boulerice, an American teacher who has been teaching English in our school since

2009, to read every text that we've translated and improve the English by making it more natural and idiomatic. This is the best we can do. Of course any problems that still remain in the translations are ours. They have nothing to do with our American teacher.

As the project is well under way, we would like to thank all those who have helped to make it possible. Ms Guo Muyu, director of the South and Southeast Asia Editorial Department, Yunnan People's Publishing House, has been most helpful in our cooperation. In addition, she has added importance to the project by turning it into a national publication project. Yunnan Normal University has supported us by paying the publication fees so that the translators won't have to be burdened with the financial responsibilities for this project. Professor Li Zhengshuan and Professor Wang Hong not only have always encouraged us to go on but have also written the forewords for the project, putting it in a global perspective. Ms Joan Boulerice's revision has ensured the fluency of the translated texts. Finally, special thanks must be given to Professor Wang Hong, again, and Mr Li Lin of Hunan People's Press for their suggestion that has helped us conceive the project from the very beginning.

(The General Editors, School of Foreign Languages & Literature, Yunnan Normal University, Kunming)

梅葛 // Meige

A Brief Introduction to *Meige*

Meige is not only called a masterpiece of the Yi people, containing folk songs, dances, and oral folk literature, but also the most significant creation epic of the Yi ethnic group. Honored as the prime genealogy and the encyclopedia of the Yi people, it covers a wide range of content in the creation of the world and creatures, marriage and love songs, funerals, and other parts, which reflect the long history and colorful life of the Yi people. *Meige* serves as a mirror of the simple world outlook and imaginative view of the universe, which were brought forth by the Yi people's ancestors in ancient times. It introduces the evolution and development of the Yi people's production and life, elaborates on production, love, marriage, and funerals, and expounds the countless ties between the Yi people and other ethnic groups in economy, culture and life. The creation myths documented in *Meige* enjoy the distinctive features of both the nation and the world. As an embodiment of the primitive ideology of human beings, *Meige* has earned its place of significance in history and its high position in literature.

The Translators

梅葛 | 目录

第一部 创 世 // 1

一 开天辟地 // 2

二 人类起源 // 20

第二部 造 物 // 51

一 盖房子 // 52

二 狩猎和畜牧 // 64

三 农 事 // 76

四 造工具 // 86

五 盐 // 99

六 蚕 丝 // 102

梅葛

目录

第三部　婚事和恋歌 // 107

　一　相　配 // 108

　二　说　亲 // 119

　三　请　客 // 167

　四　抢　棚 // 176

　五　撒　种 // 182

　六　芦　笙 // 186

　七　安　家 // 194

第四部　丧　葬 // 229

　一　死　亡 // 230

　二　怀　亲 // 243

Contents

Book One   Genesis // 1

　I. The Creation of the World // 2

　II. The Origin of Mankind // 20

Book Two   Creation // 51

　I. House Building // 52

　II. Hunting and Stockbreeding // 64

　III. Farming // 76

　IV. Making Farm Tools // 86

　V. Salt // 99

　VI. Silk // 102

Contents

Book Three   Marriage and Love Songs // 107

I. Matching // 108

II. Marriage Proposal // 119

III. Treating Guests // 167

IV. Celebrating the Wedding by Dancing // 176

V. Sowing // 182

VI. The Gourd Mouth Organ // 186

VII. Settling Down // 194

Book Four   Funerals // 229

I. Death // 230

II. Memory of Loved Ones // 243

第一部 创世
Book One　Genesis

梅葛 // Meige

一　开天辟地

I. The Creation of the World

远古的时候没有天，
远古的时候没有地。
要造天啦！
要造地啦！
哪个来造天？
哪个来造地？

格滋天神要造天，
他放下九个金果，
变成九个儿子，
九个儿子中，
五个来造天。
一个叫阿赌，
一个叫庶顽，
一个叫贪闹，
一个叫顽连，
一个叫朵闹，
这是造天的儿子。

In ancient times,
There was neither sky nor earth.
The sky must be created!
The earth must be created!
Who was going to create the sky?
Who was going to create the earth?

God Gezi was going to create the sky.
He dropped nine gold apples,
Which became his nine sons.
Five of these nine sons
Would create the sky.
One was Adu,
One was Shuwan,
One was Tannao,
One was Wanlian,
One was Duonao.
They were the ones to create the sky.

第一部　创世
Book One　Genesis

格滋天神要造地，	God Gezi was going to create the earth.
他放下七个银果，	He dropped seven silver apples,
变成七个姑娘，	Which became his seven daughters.
七个姑娘中，	Four of these seven daughters
四个来造地。	Would create the earth.
一个叫扎则，	One was Zhaze,
一个叫戬则，	One was Jianze,
一个叫慈则，	One was Cize,
一个叫勤则，	One was Qinze.
这是造地的姑娘。	They were the ones to create the earth.
造天的儿子有啦！	Here were the sons to create the sky!
造地的姑娘有啦！	And the daughters to create the earth!
造天的儿子没有衣裳穿，	Since the sons had no clothes to wear,
拿云彩作衣裳；	They wore clouds as their clothes;
造地的姑娘没有衣裳穿，	Since the daughters had no clothes to wear,
拿青苔作衣裳。	They wore moss as their clothes.
造天的儿子有啦！	Here were the sons to create the sky!
造地的姑娘有啦！	And the daughters to create the earth!
造天的儿子没有粮吃，	Since the sons had no food to eat,
拿露水当口粮；	They took dew instead;
造地的姑娘没有粮吃，	Since the daughters had no food to eat,

梅葛 // Meige

拿泥巴当口粮。	They took mud instead.
吃的有啦!	Now they had food to eat!
穿的有啦!	Now they had clothes to wear!

造天没有模子, There were no moulds for creating
造地没有模子; The sky and the earth;
天像一把伞, The sky should be like an umbrella,
地像一座桥; The earth should be like a bridge;
拿伞做造天的模子, Hence an umbrella was used as the mould for the sky.
拿桥做造地的模子; And a bridge was used as the mould for the earth;
蜘蛛网做天的底子, A cobweb became the bottom of the sky,
蕨菜根做地的底子。 And bracken roots that of the earth.

造天的五个儿子, The five sons responsible for creating the sky
胆子有斗大, Were all hedonistic.
个个喜欢赌钱, Every one of them indulged in gambling,
个个喜欢玩闹。 And every one of them indulged in playing.
大儿子守着赌, The eldest son gambled
大儿子守着玩; And played all day long.
二儿子躲着赌, The second son gambled
二儿子躲着玩; And played stealthily.
三儿子跳着赌, The third son liked to jump up and down
三儿子跳着玩; While gambling and playing.
四儿子把着赌, The fourth son was domineering

第一部　创世
Book One　Genesis

四儿子把着玩；	In gambling and playing.
五儿子忙着赌，	The fifth son was busy gambling
五儿子忙着玩。	And playing every day.
弟兄五个，	Thus the five sons were creating the sky
赌着来造天，	While gambling,
玩着来造天，	While playing,
睡着来造天，	While sleeping,
吃着来造天。	While eating.
他们天天吃喝玩乐，	They idled their time away in amusement.
一天一天懒过去，	Days went by in their laziness,
一天一天混过去。	Years passed in their idleness.
造地的四个姑娘，	The four daughters creating the earth
精心又细致，	Were meticulous and careful.
个个喜欢造地，	Everyone liked creating the earth
个个喜欢劳动。	And working hard.
大姑娘飞快地做，	The eldest daughter did the work at a gallop.
二姑娘甩团地做，	The second daughter did the work like a bee.
三姑娘手不停地做，	The third daughter did the work without stopping.
四姑娘顾不得吃饭地做。	The fourth daughter did the work without eating.
姊妹四个，	The four sisters created the earth
忘了吃穿来造地，	Without meals or sleep.
忘了睡觉来造地，	In sunshine or rain,
不管天晴下雨来造地，	Day and night,

梅葛 // Meige

不分白天黑夜来造地，	They continued their job
耐耐心心地造地，	In patience and diligence.
勤勤恳恳地造地。	Day by day,
一天一天过去，	Little by little,
一点一滴造成。	They were creating the earth.
过了很久很久，	After a long time,
五兄弟把天造好了，	The five brothers completed the creation of the sky,
四姊妹把地造好了。	The four sisters completed the creation of the earth.
不知道天有多大，	Nobody knew how wide the sky was,
不知道地有多大。	Nobody knew how big the earth was.
要量天啦！	The sky was going to be measured!
要量地啦！	The earth was going to be measured!
请什么来量天？	Who would be invited to measure the sky?
请什么来量地？	Who would be invited to measure the earth?
请飞蛾来量天，	The moth was invited to measure the sky,
请蜻蜓来量地，	And the dragonfly to measure the earth.
天上量一量，	They measured the sky.
地下量一量，	They measured the earth.
天有七拃①，	The sky was seven arm spans,
地有九拃，	And the earth nine arm spans.
天造小了，	The sky was too small,

---

① 拃：音排，上声。两手向侧平伸的长度为一拃。

第一部　创世
Book One　Genesis

地造大了，	And the earth too big.
天盖地呀盖不合。	The sky could not cover up the earth tightly.
弟兄五个不在意，	But the five brothers didn't care about it.
放心去玩耍；	They had their entertainment as usual.
姊妹四个心着急，	The four sisters were worried,
恐怕天神来责骂。	For fear of being scolded by God.
格滋天神知道了，	God Gezi learned of it,
告诉四姊妹：	And told the four sisters:
"不要心焦，	"Don't worry,
不要害怕，	And don't be afraid.
地做大了，	If the earth is too big,
有人会缩；	Someone will reduce it.
天做小了，	If the sky is too small,
有人会拉。	Someone will widen it.
地缩小，	If the earth is reduced
天拉大，	And the sky is widened,
天就能盖地啦！"	The sky can cover up the earth well!"
阿夫会缩地，	Afu could reduce the earth.
阿夫会拉天。	Afu could widen the sky.
请阿夫的三个儿子，	Afu's three sons were asked
抓住天边往下拉，	To pull the edge of the sky down,
把天拉得大又凹。	And to make it bigger and hollower.

梅葛 // Meige

放三对麻蛇来缩地，	Three pairs of snakes were sent to reduce the earth.
麻蛇围着地边箍拢来，	They circled the earth and pressed it hard.
地面分出了高低，	High and low parts appeared,
地边还箍得不齐；	But the edges were not neat.
放三对蚂蚁咬地边，	Three pairs of ants were sent to bite it,
把地边咬得整整齐齐。	Till it became tidy and neat.
放三对野猪来拱地，	Three pairs of boars were sent to dig the earth,
放三对大象来拱地，	Three pairs of elephants were sent to do the same.
拱了七十七昼夜，	After seventy-seven days and nights,
有了山来有了箐，	Mountains and valleys came into being,
有了平坝有了河。	Dams and rivers emerged.
天拉大了，	Now the sky was widened
地缩小了，	And the earth was reduced.
这样合适啦，	They were well matched,
天地相合啦。	They were well fit.
不知天牢不牢，	It was unknown whether the sky and the earth
不知地牢不牢。	Were firmly built or not.
要试天啦！	They would check the solidness of the sky!
要试地啦！	They would test the firmness of the earth!
打雷来试天，	The sky was checked by thunder,
地震来试地；	The earth was tested by earthquakes.
试天天开裂，	Cracks were made in the sky,

第一部　创世
Book One　Genesis

试地地通洞。	And rifts appeared in the earth.
天开裂要补起来，	The cracks in the sky should be mended.
地通洞要补起来；	The rifts in the earth should be filled up.
格滋天神叫五个儿子补天，	God Gezi asked his five sons to mend the cracks
格滋天神叫四个姑娘补地。	And his four daughters to fill up the rifts.
用松毛做针，	Pine needles were used as needles,
蜘蛛网做线，	Spider webs as thread,
云彩做补丁，	Clouds as patches
把天补起来。	To mend the sky.
用老虎草做针，	Tiger grass was used as needles,
酸绞藤做线，	Sour vine as thread,
地公叶子做补丁，	Digong leaves as patches,
把地补起来。	To fill up the earth.
天补好了，	Now the sky was well mended,
地补好了。	And the earth was well filled up.
打雷时天不会垮，	The sky would not collapse because of thunder.
地震时地不会塌；	The earth would not sink because of earthquakes.
可是补好的天还在摆，	But the mended sky was still swaying
补好的地还在摇；	And the filled earth still shaking,
因为没有撑天的柱，	For there were no pillars to support the sky,

梅葛 // Meige

没有撑地的柱；	There were no posts to hold up the earth.
要找撑天的柱，	Pillars must be found.
要找撑地的柱。	Posts must be found.

格滋天神说：　　　　　　　　God Gezi said:
"水里面有鱼，　　　　　　　　"In the water there are fish,
世间的东西要算鱼最大：　　　　The biggest things in the world.
公鱼三千斤，　　　　　　　　The males weigh three thousand pounds,
母鱼七百斤；　　　　　　　　The females weigh seven hundred pounds.
捉公鱼去！　　　　　　　　　Let's catch the male fish!
捉母鱼去！　　　　　　　　　Let's catch the female fish!
公鱼捉来撑地角，　　　　　　The male fish will support the corners of the earth,
母鱼捉来撑地边。"　　　　　　The female fish will prop up the edge of the earth."

公鱼不眨眼，　　　　　　　　If the male fish do not blink their eyes,
大地不会动，　　　　　　　　The earth will not move.
母鱼不翻身，　　　　　　　　Unless the female fish turn over,
大地不会摇，　　　　　　　　The earth will not shake.
地的四角撑起来，　　　　　　With the four corners propped up,
大地稳实了。　　　　　　　　The earth was firm and steady.

大地撑住了，　　　　　　　　The earth was well supported,
大地稳实了；　　　　　　　　The earth was firm and steady.
没有撑天柱，　　　　　　　　But without pillars,

第一部 创世
Book One Genesis

天还在摇摆。	The sky was still swaying.
格滋天神说：	God Gezi said:
"山上有老虎，	"In the mountains there are tigers,
世间的东西要算虎最猛。	The strongest animals on the earth.
引老虎去！	Let's trick them!
哄老虎去！	Let's lure them!
用虎的脊梁骨撑天心，	Tiger's spine can support the center of the sky.
用虎的脚杆骨撑四边。"	And tiger's leg bones can support the four sides."
造天五弟兄，	The five brothers who created the sky
胆子有斗大！	Were extremely bold.
他们会撵山，	They knew how to track down animals,
他们去引虎。	They set about luring tigers.
手中紧握大铁伞，	Holding tight a big iron umbrella,
伞把装上铁弯勾。	With an iron hook attached to the stick,
十二架山梁上引一引，	They lured tigers on twelve ridges.
老虎张着大嘴走出来，	With its mouth wide open,
老虎抖着身子走出来，	The tiger walked out of the cave, shaking itself.
老虎被引出来啦。	The tiger was lured out.
老虎张着血盆大口奔来，	The tiger charged, bloody mouth open wide.
老虎抖着斑斓的身子扑来，	The tiger attacked, shaking its colored body.
造天五弟兄，	The five brothers immediately

梅葛 // Meige

忙把伞撑开，	Opened the umbrella,
挡住了老虎，	Held the tiger off,
勾住了老虎。	And caught it on the hook.
老虎被哄住啦！	At last, the tiger was lured!
老虎被勾住啦！	The tiger was hooked!

山草掺上棕，   Wild grass was mixed
棕毛掺山草，   With palm fibers.
索子搓出来，   A rope was made of that.
不能多一拿，   No more,
不能少一拿，   No less,
索子搓成十二拿，   It was twelve arm spans.
牵着老虎走回来。   The tiger was led back.

猛虎杀死了，   They killed the fierce tiger,
大家来分虎。   And shared its body parts among them,
四根大骨莫要分，   But they didn't give out the four leg bones,
四根大骨作撑天的柱子；Which were used as pillars to support the sky.
肩膀莫要分，   They didn't give out its shoulders,
肩膀作东南西北方向。 Which were used for the four directions.
把天撑起来了，   The sky was propped up,
天也稳实了。   Firm and steady.

天上没有太阳，   In the sky, there was no sun,

第一部 创世
Book One　Genesis

天上没有月亮，	There was no moon,
天上没有星星，	There were no stars,
天上没有白云彩，	There were no white clouds,
天上没有红云彩，	There were no red clouds,
天上没有虹，	There was no rainbow.
天上什么也没有。	There was nothing in the sky.
地上没有树木，	On the earth, there were no trees,
地上没有树根，	There were no tree roots,
地上没有大江，	There were no rivers,
地上没有大海，	There were no seas,
地上没有飞禽，	There were no birds,
地上没有走兽，	There were no beasts.
地上什么也没有。	There was nothing on the earth.
虎头莫要分，	They didn't give out the tiger's head,
虎头作天头。	Which was used as the head of the sky.
虎尾莫要分，	They didn't give out its tail,
虎尾作地尾。	Which was used as the tail of the earth.
虎鼻莫要分，	They didn't give out its nose,
虎鼻作天鼻。	Which was used as the nose of the sky.
虎耳莫要分，	They didn't give out its ears,
虎耳作天耳。	Which were used as the ears of the sky.

梅葛 // Meige

虎眼莫要分，	They didn't give out its eyes,
左眼作太阳，	The left one was used as the sun,
右眼作月亮。	And the right one as the moon.
虎须莫要分，	They didn't give out its whiskers,
虎须作阳光。	Which were used as the sunbeams.
虎牙莫要分，	They didn't give out its teeth,
虎牙作星星。	Which were used as the stars.
虎油莫要分，	They didn't give out its fat,
虎油作云彩。	Which was used as the clouds.
虎气莫要分，	They didn't give out its breath,
虎气作雾气。	Which was used as the mist.
虎心莫要分，	They didn't give out its heart, which was used
虎心作天心地胆。	As the heart of the sky and the gallbladder of the earth.
虎肚莫要分，	They didn't give out its belly,
虎肚作大海。	Which was used as the sea.
虎血莫要分，	They didn't give out its blood,
虎血作海水。	Which was used as the sea water.
大肠莫要分，	They didn't give out its large intestine,
大肠变大江。	Which was used as the rivers.
小肠莫要分，	They didn't give out its small intestine,
小肠变成河。	Which was used as the brooks.
排骨莫要分，	They didn't give out its ribs,
排骨作道路。	Which were used as the roads.

第一部　创世
Book One　Genesis

虎皮莫要分，	They didn't give out its skin,
虎皮作地皮。	Which was used to cover up the ground.
硬毛莫要分，	They didn't give out its bristles,
硬毛变树林。	Which were turned into the forests.
软毛莫要分，	They didn't give out its fur,
软毛变成草。	Which was turned into the grass.
细毛莫要分，	They didn't give out its tiny hairs,
细毛作秧苗。	Which were used as the seedlings.
骨髓莫要分，	They didn't give out its bone marrow,
骨髓变金子。	Which became gold.
小骨头莫要分，	They didn't give out its small bones,
小骨头变银子。	Which became silver.
虎肺莫要分，	They didn't give out its lung,
虎肺变成铜。	Which became copper.
虎肝莫要分，	They didn't give out its liver,
虎肝变成铁。	Which became iron.
脺贴莫要分，	They didn't give out its spleen,
脺贴变成锡。	Which became tin.
腰子莫要分，	They didn't give out its kidneys,
腰子作磨石。	Which became grindstones.
大虱子变成老水牛，	The big lice became old buffalos,

梅葛 // Meige

小虱子变成黑猪黑羊，	And the small ones became black pigs and goats.
虱子蛋变成绵羊，	The eggs of the lice became sheep.
头发变成雀鸟。	And their hairs became sparrows.

最后分虎肉，
虎肉分成十二份，
一份也不多，
一份也不少。

At last, they gave out the tiger's meat,
Which was divided into twelve portions,
No more,
No less.

给老鸦一份，
老鸦吃了喜欢。
"呱！呱！呱！"
遍山遍野叫。

The crow got one portion
And enjoyed it a lot.
"Caw! Caw! Caw!" it cried
All over the mountains and fields.

给喜鹊一份，
喜鹊吃了也喜欢。
"啾！啾！啾！"
飞去踩秧田。

The magpie got one portion,
And loved it too.
"Chatter! Chatter! Chatter!" it happily
Flew to the rice seeding beds.

竹鸡分一份，
竹鸡吃了也喜欢。
"好着着！好着着！"
叫着飞了过去。

The bamboo partridge got one portion,
And liked it very much.
"Haozhezhe! Haozhezhe!"
It cried and flew away.

第一部 创世
Book One Genesis

野鸡分一份，	The pheasant got one portion,
野鸡吃了也喜欢。	And felt happy.
"嗉呼呼！嗉呼呼！"	"Souhuhu! Souhuhu!"
叫着飞了过去。	It shouted and flew away.
老豺狗分一份，	The jackal got one portion, ate it,
吃了去拖猪，	Went to prey on pigs
吃了去拖羊，	And hunt for goats,
叫着跑上山去。	Up in the mountains.
画眉分一份，	The song thrush got one portion,
画眉吃了心喜欢。	Ate it and felt happy.
"叽哩哩！叽哩哩！"	"Jilili! Jilili!" it cried
叫着飞了过去。	And flew away.
黄蚊子分一份，	The yellow mosquito got one portion,
黄蚊子吃了喜欢。	Ate it and felt happy too.
"天黄！地黄！"	"The sky is yellow; the earth is yellow!"
叫着飞了过去。	It cried and flew away.
黄蜂分一份，	The wasp got one portion,
黄蜂分着了心喜欢。	And felt very happy.
葫芦蜂分一份，	The cucurbit bee got one portion,

梅葛 // Meige

葫芦蜂分着了心喜欢。	And was joyful.
老土蜂分一份，	The humble bee got one portion,
老土蜂分着了心喜欢。	And felt delighted.
大蚊子分一份，	The big mosquito got one portion
大蚊子分着了心喜欢。	And was pleased.
绿头苍蝇分一份，	The blowfly got one portion
绿头苍蝇吃了心喜欢。	And was cheerful.
饿老鹰没有分着，	The hungry eagle got none
饿老鹰呀心不甘。	And was very angry.
一飞飞上天，	It flew into the Sky,
伸开了翅膀，	Spreading its wings,
遮住了太阳。	And covered up the sun.
天变成黑乌乌一团，	Then the sky became a pitch-dark mass,
地变成黑乌乌一团，	The earth became a pitch-dark mass too.
再也分不出白天，	One didn't know when it was day,
再也分不出夜晚。	One didn't know when it was night.
哪个能治饿老鹰？	Who could punish the hungry eagle?
绿头苍蝇能治饿老鹰。	The blowfly could.

第一部　创世
Book One　Genesis

绿头苍蝇飞上天，	It flew to the sky, lighted upon
落在老鹰翅膀上，	The wings of the eagle,
密密麻麻下了子。	And laid many eggs there.

过了三天，	Three days passed by,
过了三夜，	And three nights passed by.
老鹰翅膀生了蛆，	Maggots grew in the wings,
翅膀生蛆跌下来。	And caused the eagle to fall.
太阳发亮啦！	The sun shone again!
有了白天啦！	Day was here again!

老鹰掉在地上，	The eagle dropped to the ground,
把地遮了一半，	And covered up half of the earth.
还是只有黑夜，	Still the earth was shrouded in darkness,
还是没有白天。	Day was gone.

请谁抬老鹰？	Who could move the eagle?
蚂蚁抬老鹰。	The ants could.
老鹰抬开了，	The eagle was moved away,
昼夜分出来。	Again there came out night and day.

有白天啦！	Here was day!
有黑夜啦！	Here was night!
天亮太阳出来啦！	At dawn, the sun came out!

梅葛 // Meige

天黑月亮出来啦!	At dusk, the moon came out!

二 人类起源   II. The Origin of Mankind

天造成了,	The sky was created.
地造成了,	The earth was created.
万物有了,	There was everything in the world.
昼夜分开了,	Day and night were separated.
就是没有人,	But there were no human beings.
格滋天神来造人。	God Gezi set about creating them.

天上撒下三把雪,	Three handfuls of snow fell from the sky,
落地变成三代人。	And became three generations of people on earth.
撒下第一把是第一代,	The first handful was the first generation,
撒下第二把是第二代,	The second handful was the second generation,
撒下第三把是第三代。	The third handful was the third generation.

头把撒下独脚人,	The first generation was the men with one leg,
只有一尺二寸长;	Just twelve inches tall.
独自一人不会走,	They could not walk alone,
两人手搂脖子快如飞;	But move fast in pairs.
吃的饭是泥土,	Soil was their rice,

第一部 创世
Book One　Genesis

下饭菜是沙子。	And sand was their vegetables.
月亮照着活得下去，	They could live in the moonlight,
太阳晒着活不下去，	But not in the sun.
这代人无法生存，	This generation could not survive,
这代人被晒死了。	They were burned to death by the suns.
撒下第二把，	The second generation
人有一丈三尺长，	Was over ten feet tall.
没有衣裳，	They had no clothes to wear,
没有裤子，	They had no pants to put on.
拿树叶作衣裳，	Leaves were their clothes,
拿树叶作裤子，	Leaves were their pants.
这才有了衣裳，	Thus they had clothes,
这才有了裤子。	Thus they had pants.
没有水，	There was no water,
没有火，	There was no fire,
没有吃的，	There was no food,
没有住的，	There was no shelter.
吃的山林果，	They ate wild fruit,
住的老山洞。	They lived in caves.
没有春夏秋冬，	There was no spring, summer, fall, or winter,
不分四季四时，	And neither seasons nor time.

梅葛 // Meige

天上有九个太阳，	Nine suns were hanging in the sky,
天上有九个月亮，	Nine moons were hanging in the sky.
白天太阳晒，	During the day, the suns scorched the earth.
晚上月亮照，	At night, the moons shone brightly.
晚上过得去，	Night was all right,
白天过不去，	Daytime was unbearable.
牛骨头晒焦了，	Cattle bones were sun-baked,
斑鸠毛晒掉了。	The feathers of turtledoves were burnt off.
做着活计瞌睡来。	The men fell asleep while working.
一睡睡了几百年，	They slept for hundreds of years,
身上长青苔，	With moss all over their bodies.
这代人活不下去，	This generation could not survive.
这代人也晒死了。	They were burnt to death by the suns.
格滋天神，	God Gezi,
左手拿鋆，	An axe in his left hand,
右手拿锤，	A hammer in his right hand,
来鋆太阳，	Chopped off the suns,
来鋆月亮，	And cut off the moons.
留一个太阳在天上，	He left one sun in the sky
留一个月亮在天上，	He left one moon in the sky.
太阳落在阿娃西山，	The sun set on Awa West Hill.
月亮落在菠萝西山，	The moon set on Pineapple West Hill.
四季分出来，	Now that there were four seasons,

Book One Genesis

草皮树根长起来。	The turf and roots started to grow up.
撒下第三把，	The third generation was men
人的两只眼睛朝上生。	With their eyes turned upward.
格滋天神，	God Gezi
撒三把苦荞，	Scattered three handfuls of buckwheat
撒在米拉山；	On Mila Hill.
撒三把谷子，	He then scattered three handfuls of grain
撒在石山岭；	On Stone Ridge.
撒三把麦子，	He also scattered three handfuls of wheat
撒在寿延山。	On Longevity Hill.
麦子出穗了，	Then wheat ears came out,
谷子出穗了，	Grain ears opened,
荞子长出来了。	The buckwheat sprouted.
没有火，	There was no fire.
天上老龙想办法，	King Dragon in the sky made it
三串小火镰，	With three strings of flint,
一打两头着，	Lit on both ends.
从此人类有了火。	Since then, mankind has had fire.
什么都有了，	They had everything
日子好过了。	And lived a good life.
这代人的心不好，	But this generation wasn't kind.

梅葛 // Meige

他们不耕田不种地，	They didn't plough or till the land,
他们不薅草不拔草。	Nor did they pull the weeds.
看见田里没有牙齿草，	Seeing no crabgrass in the fields,
铲铲地皮就放水，	They loosened the soil and watered it.
白天睡在田边，	Napping on the banks in the daytime,
夜晚睡在地角，	And sleeping on the paths at night.
一天到晚，	All day long,
吃饭睡觉，	They ate and slept,
睡觉吃饭。	They slept and ate.
天神问他们：	God asked them:
"为何不耕不种？	"Why not plough the land?
为何不薅不拔？"	Why not pull the weeds?"
"田里不长牙齿草，	"No grass grows here,
没有活计做。"	So we have no work to do."
格滋天神手一撒，	With a wave of his hand,
甘香树叶落地下，	God Gezi scattered fragrant leaves around,
田里长了牙齿草。	And grass sprouted in the fields.
直眼睛的人，	Now the men with upturned eyes
从此要栽种，	Had to plough the fields
从此要薅草。	And pull the weeds.

第一部　创世
Book One　Genesis

这代人的心不好，	This generation wasn't kind.
糟蹋五谷粮食，	They wasted the grain and corn.
谷子拿去打埂子，	They built earth banks with grain,
麦粑粑拿去堵水口，	Blocked water outlets with wheat,
用苦荞面、甜荞面糊墙。	And pasted walls with buckwheat flour.
格滋天神看不过：	God Gezi could not tolerate it:
"不该这样来糟蹋！	"The waste cannot go on like this!
这代人的心不好，	This generation is not kind,
这代人要换一换。"	They must be replaced.
格滋天神派武姆勒娃下凡来，	God Gezi sent Wumulewa down to the earth,
派他把第三代人换一换，	To replace the third generation.
武姆勒娃变只大老熊，	Wumulewa turned into a big bear.
堵水漫金山。	He blocked the rivers, deluging the earth.
寻找好人种，	He searched for and saved worthy people
留下传人烟。	To reproduce the new generation of the human race.
直眼人学博若，	Xueboruo, one of the men with upturned eyes,
有五个儿子，	Had five sons and a daughter.
有一个姑娘，	The five brothers
弟兄五个人，	Ploughed the barren land on the hill,
山上犁生地，	And opened up paddy fields in the valley.
箐底开水田。	Today the fields were plowed well.

梅葛 // Meige

今天犁好的，	But what they did today
明天被老熊翻回来，	Would be undone by the bear tomorrow.
明天犁好的，	What they did tomorrow
后天被老熊翻回来。	Would be undone by the bear the day after.
整整犁了三天地，	They ploughed for three long days,
三天都被老熊翻回来。	But the bear undid their effort every time.
五弟兄来商议，	The five brothers thought and thought
五弟兄想办法：	And hit upon a good idea:
到地头下一个扣，	They laid a trap at one end of the field,
到地中下一个扣，	Another in the middle,
到地尾下一个扣。	A third at the other end.
锄头作踩板，	Using the hoe head as the staying board,
锄把作夹弓，	The hoe bar as the clamping bow,
犁头作横担，	The plowshare as the cross arm,
耕索作扣绳，	The plough rope as the trap cord,
犁杆作扣杆，	The plough beam as the sear,
犁耳作扣梢，	The plough ear as the trap tip,
犁头作扣环。	And the ploughshare as the loop.
老熊到地里，	The bear wandered into the field
踩到扣子上，	And stepped into one of the traps.
老熊被套住了，	It got caught
老熊被拴住了。	And snared tightly.

第一部　创世
Book One　Genesis

学博若的大儿子来串地，	Xueboruo's eldest came by,
看见捉住大老熊，	And was excited to see
心里很高兴。	That the bear was firmly trapped.

"学博若的大儿子，　　　"Eldest son of Xueboruo,
你来替我解一解。"　　　Please untie the loop for me."

大儿子不愿解：　　　　The young man refused:
"我白天犁好的地，　　　"In the daytime, I ploughed the field,
你夜里来翻平，　　　　 But at night, you made it even.
你的心不好，　　　　　You are so wicked.
就是要捉你，　　　　　It is you that we want to catch.
我不替你解，　　　　　I will not untie you.
我要去撑山。"　　　　 I'm going hunting."

学博若的二儿子来串地，　Xueboruo's second son came by,
看见捉住大老熊，　　　　And was happy to see
心里很高兴。　　　　　　That the bear was trapped.

"学博若的二儿子，　　　"Second son of Xueboruo,
你来替我解一解。"　　　Could you please untie the loop for me?"

二儿子不愿解：　　　　The second son refused:

梅葛 // Meige

"你的心不好, "You are evil in your heart,
就是要捉你, And deserved to be caught.
我不得闲解, I am too busy to help you,
我要去放羊。" For it is time for me to herd the goats."

学博若的三儿子来串地, Xueboruo's third son came by.
看见捉住大老熊, He was delighted to see that
心里很高兴。 The bear was caught.

"学博若的三儿子, "Third son of Xueboruo,
你来替我解一解。" Could you please untie the loop for me?"

三儿子不愿解: The third son refused:
"你的心不好, "You are evil in your heart.
就是要捉你, It is you that we want to catch.
我不替你解, I won't help you,
我要去放牛。" I'm going to graze the cattle."

学博若的四儿子来串地, Xueboruo's fourth son came by.
看见捉住大老熊, He also felt happy to find that
心里很高兴。 The big bear was caught in the trap.

"学博若的四儿子, "Fourth son of Xueboruo,
你来替我解一解。" Could you please free me?"

第一部　创世
Book One　Genesis

四儿子不愿解： The fourth son refused:
"你的心不好， "You are so unkind to us,
就是要捉你， We must catch you.
我不得闲解， I have no time to free you,
我要去犁生地。" I'm going to plow the field."

四弟兄都喊打， The four brothers wanted
四弟兄都喊杀。 To beat and kill the bear.

学博若的小儿子， Xueboruo's youngest son came,
背着小妹跑过来： With their little sister on his back.
"看它的头像祖父， "Its head looks like Grandpa's.
看它的身子像祖母， Its body looks like Grandma's.
千万不能打， We cannot beat the bear.
千万不能杀。" We cannot kill the bear."

"学博若的小儿子， "Youngest son of Xueboruo,
你来替我解一解。" Could you please free me?"

小儿子想去解， The youngest wanted to help it,
心里怪害怕。 But he was very scared.

"心里别害怕， "Don't be afraid.

梅葛 // Meige

若是救了我，
我要给你一句话。"

If you help me,
I will tell you something."

学博若的小儿子，
解开绳索，
搭下木梯，
救了武姆勒娃。

The youngest boy
Untied the loop,
Made a wooden ladder
And saved Wumulewa.

武姆勒娃说：
"人心很不好，
要换人种了，
水要漫金山，
大水快发了。
大哥打金柜，
二哥打银柜，
三哥打铜柜，
四哥打铁柜，
你们四弟兄，
赶快躲进柜。

Wumulewa said:
"This generation is unkind,
It must be replaced.
The earth will be flooded
And mountains will be submerged.
Eldest brother, make a golden cupboard;
Second brother, make a silver cupboard;
Third brother, make a copper cupboard;
Fourth brother, make an iron cupboard.
The four of you, hide yourselves
In the cupboards you make."

"小弟弟你良心好，
给你三颗葫芦籽，
赶快回去栽葫芦。

"Youngest brother, you are very kind,
I will give you three gourd seeds.
Go home quickly and plant them."

第一部　创世
Book One　Genesis

"正月初一那一天，
最好这天栽葫芦；
正月栽下葫芦籽，
三天要浇一次水；
栽下三天会出芽，
过了三天藤就爬；
又过三天开白花，
再过三天结葫芦，
最后三天会长大。

"葫芦藤有牛担粗，
葫芦叶有簸箕大，
结了一个独葫芦，
葫芦结得像囤子。

"你不要干着急，
你不要瞎猜想，
不是有妖精，
不是有妖怪，
葫芦结饱了，
摘得葫芦了。

"You should plant the gourd seeds
On New Year's Day[①].
Once they are planted,
They should be watered every three days.
On the third day, sprouts will come out.
On the sixth day, vines will begin to climb up.
On the ninth day, white flowers will blossom.
On the twelfth day, gourds will be born.
On the fifteenth day, the gourds will be ripe."

"The gourd vines are as thick as cattle poles,
The leaves are as big as dustpans.
Then only one gourd is born,
And it looks like a grain bin."

"Don't worry about it,
Don't make wild guesses.
There are no goblins,
Nor are there any monsters.
The gourd is now ripe,
Ready for the picking."

---

① The seasonal festivals and months in this epic refer to those in the lunar calendar.—Translator's note

梅葛 // Meige

"大理出小刀，	"Dali is famous for knives
是开葫芦的刀。	Good for cleaning the inside of gourds.
用高山的松香封住葫芦口，	Your sister and you will move into the gourd,
箐底的黄蜡糊住葫芦口；	Seal the opening with mountain rosin,
你兄妹搬进葫芦里，	Paste it with wild yellow wax.
饿了就吃葫芦籽。"	You can eat the gourd seeds when hungry."

四弟兄听了武姆勒娃的话，　　Following Wumulewa's words,
大哥打好了金柜；　　　　　　The eldest brother made a golden cupboard;
二哥打好了银柜；　　　　　　The second brother made a silver cupboard;
三哥打好了铜柜；　　　　　　The third brother made a copper cupboard;
四哥打好了铁柜。　　　　　　The fourth brother made an iron cupboard.
弟兄四人找住处，　　　　　　The four brothers looked for shelter.
找好住处杀老熊。　　　　　　They killed the bear when they found it.

老熊的鲜血淌成河，　　　　　The bear's blood became a river,
尸体漂河中，　　　　　　　　Where its body was floating.
脑袋顺水淌，　　　　　　　　Its head floated downstream
淌入东洋海，　　　　　　　　Into the East Sea,
塞住出水洞，　　　　　　　　Blocking the drainage tunnel,
水就涨起来。　　　　　　　　And causing a deluge.

狂风和暴雨，　　　　　　　　With gales and thunderstorms,
越淹越厉害，　　　　　　　　The flood was getting more ferocious.

第一部　创世
Book One　Genesis

水声隆隆波浪翻，	Water roaring and waves rolling,
普天之下都淹完。	The flood drowned the whole world.
学博若的四个儿子，	Xueboruo's four sons
先闸一道围，	First built a fence,
水涨到山腰。	But the water rose to the mountainside.
再筑一道围，	Then they set up another fence.
水淹过了金山。	The flood submerged the Golden Mountain.
学博若的四个儿子，	Xueboruo's four sons
躲进柜子里，	Hid in the cupboards.
金柜银柜沉下水，	The gold and silver cupboards sank,
铜柜铁柜沉下水。	The copper and iron cupboards also sank.
洪水滚滚接着天，	The roaring water rose to the sky.
海鱼吃了天上的星星，	The sea fish ate the stars,
螃蟹也在天上跑，	And the crabs roamed in the sky.
白天黑夜分不清，	Day and night were indistinguishable,
只有水声风浪声。	Only the sounds of wind and waves were heard.
洪水淹了七十七昼夜，	The flood lasted seventy-seven days and nights.
天神着了慌，	God began to worry.
下凡来车水。	He came down to deal with the flood.
东方指一指，	He pointed to the East,

梅葛 // Meige

山头现出来；	The tops of the mountains appeared.
南方指一指，	He pointed to the South,
树木草根看见了；	The trees and grass emerged.
西方指一指，	He pointed to the West,
水退到河边；	The water retreated to the river banks.
北方指一指，	He pointed to the North,
水退到河底；	The river water returned to its normal level.
中间指一指，	He pointed to the middle,
水全干了。	All the flood waters disappeared.

人种没有了，	No human beings were left,
人种死光了。	They were all dead.
天神站在山头上，	God stood on the mountain top.
看不见一只飞鸟，	He saw no birds,
听不到一点声音，	Heard no sound.
格滋天神找人种，	God Gezi went everywhere
四面八方走。	Looking for survivors.

找到岔路口，	At a crossroad,
遇到葫芦蜂：	He met a gourd bee.
"葫芦蜂，葫芦蜂！	"Gourd bee, gourd bee,
你是好蜂子，	You are so nice.
你若有好心，	If you are really kind,
请你告诉我，	Please tell me

第一部　创世
Book One　Genesis

你看见人种没有？"	Whether you've seen any human beings."
"人种我没见，	"I haven't met any.
要是遇着了，	If I met one,
我要叮死他。"	I would sting him to death."
天神发了怒，	God was enraged,
打它一鞭子，	He beat it with a whip,
蜂腰打断了，	Breaking the bee's waist.
蜂子大声叫：	The bee cried,
"接好我的腰，	"Fix my lower back,
我就告诉你。"	And I will tell you."
扯根马尾接蜂腰，	God fixed the bee's waist
蜂腰一接好，	With a hair from the horse's tail,
蜂子飞跑了。	But the bee flew away.
格滋天神骂道：	God Gezi cursed,
"七月葫芦八月包，	"Gourds mature in July and August.
你养娃娃吊着养，	Your babies grow up in a hanging hive,
九月十月放火烧。"	Which will be burnt in September and October."
天神找人种，	God ran over hills and vales
山山箐箐跑，	Looking for human beings.
遇着小松树：	He met a small pine,

梅葛 // Meige

"小松树，小松树！	"Small pine, small pine,
你是好树子，	You are so nice.
你若有好心，	If you are really so kind,
请你告诉我，	Could you tell me
你看见人种没有？"	Whether you have met any human beings?"
"人种我没见，	"I haven't met any.
要是遇着了，	If I met one,
我的叶子硬，	I will pierce him to death
戳也戳死他。"	With my sharp needles."
天神发怒了，	God was enraged.
一鞭打下去，	He whipped the pine tree
松树成三岔。	Into three pieces.
格滋天神骂道：	God Gezi cursed,
"等到人种找着了，	"When human beings are found,
人烟旺起来，	They will thrive,
砍你一棵绝一棵。"	And cut you down one by one."
天神找人种，	God ran over the ridges,
跑到山梁上，	Looking for human beings.
遇着罗汉松：	He met the fern pine:
"罗汉松，罗汉松！	"Fern pine, fern pine,
你是好树子，	You are so nice.

第一部　创世
Book One　Genesis

你若有好心，	If you are really kind,
请你告诉我，	Could you tell me
你看见人种没有？"	Whether you've met any human beings?"
"刮了三次春风，	"Three spring breezes have brought
下了三场春雨，	Three spring showers.
人种没看见，	I haven't met any human beings.
要是见了人，	If I met one,
我的叶子密，	My thick leaves would shelter him
给他来避风，	From the wind,
替他来遮雨。"	From the rain."
天神好喜欢，	God was very pleased
封赠罗汉松：	And rewarded the fern pine:
"罗汉松，是好树，	"Fern pine, you are nice.
等到人种找到了，	When human beings are found,
人烟旺起来，	They will prosper,
砍你一棵发百棵。"	You will multiply.
天神找人种，	God climbed cliffs,
找到山岩上，	Looking for human beings.
遇着小蜜蜂：	He met the little bee:
"小蜜蜂，小蜜蜂！	"Little bee, little bee,"
你看见人种没有？"	Have you seen any human beings?"

梅葛 // Meige

"人种没看见,   "I haven't seen any human beings,
葫芦见着了。   But I've seen the gourd.
我去采花粉,   I saw it floating in the river
看见葫芦漂在河里面。   When I was gathering pollen.
要是见了人,   If I met a man,
我要请他吃蜜糖。"   I would ask him to taste my honey."

天神好喜欢,   God was satisfied
封赠小蜜蜂: And rewarded the little bee:
"小蜜蜂,是好蜂,   "Little bee, you are nice.
等到人种找着了,   When human beings are found,
人烟旺起来,   They will thrive,
让你挨着人住家。"   And you will live near them.

天神找人种,   God went to riverbanks,
河边河岸找,   Looking for human beings.
遇着小柳树: He met a small willow:
"小柳树,小柳树!   "Small willow, small willow,
你看见人种没有?"   Have you seen any human beings?"

"人种没看见,   I've seen none of them,
人声听见了。   But I heard their voices.
我见一个大葫芦,   I saw a big gourd

第一部　创世
Book One　Genesis

漂在水里面，	Afloat in the river.
葫芦里面有人声。	The voices came from it.
用左手围也围不住，	I tried to get hold of the gourd
用右手围也围不住，	With my hands but failed.
葫芦淌走啦！"	It floated away!"

天神好喜欢，　　　　　　God was very glad to hear it,
封赠小柳树：　　　　　　And rewarded the small willow:
"小柳树，是好树，　　　"Small willow, you are so nice.
等到人种找到了，　　　　When human beings are found,
人烟旺起来，　　　　　　They will grow in number.
倒栽你倒活，　　　　　　You will grow well whether you are planted
顺栽你顺活。"　　　　　Normally or upside down."

天神找人种，　　　　　　God went upstream and downstream,
河头河尾找，　　　　　　Looking for human beings.
遇着老乌龟：　　　　　　He met an old turtle:
"老乌龟，老乌龟！　　　"Old turtle, old turtle,
你看见人种没有？"　　　Have you met any human beings?"

"大海中间葫芦里，　　　"In the middle of the sea floats a gourd.
人的声音听得见，　　　　I heard human voice coming from it.
你去叫叫看！"　　　　　You may go and call!"

梅葛 // Meige

天神好喜欢，	God was very happy
封赠老乌龟：	And rewarded the old turtle:
"老乌龟，心肠好，	"Old turtle, you are kind.
敲下马蹄壳，	I'll break off a piece of a hoof
给你做房子，	And give it to you as a house.
房子随身带，	You can carry it with you.
顺河有吃的。"	You can find food along the river."
天神找人种，	God went to the seaside,
来到大海边，	Looking for human beings.
海边有个乌烟雀，	There was a sparrow there,
嗟嗟地叫着飞过来，	Flying back and forth,
嗟嗟地叫着飞过去。	Chirping all the while.
天神好生气：	God was enraged:
"我找人种找不着，	"I can't find any human beings,
心里好着急；	So I'm very worried.
你这个乌烟雀，	But you, sparrow,
还有什么喜欢的？"	Why are you so happy?"
拉弓来射乌烟雀，	He pulled a bow to shoot at it.
一箭射去射不着，	But the arrow missed the target
射中海边葫芦壳，	And hit the gourd on the shore instead.
葫芦里头叫起来：	A voice came from within:
"已经五天没有人来打墙，	"It has been five days or ten days
已经十天没有人来打墙，	Since someone knocked on the wall.

第一部　创世
Book One　Genesis

今天哪个乱打我的墙？"	Now, who the hell is knocking?"

人种找到了，　　　　　God was extremely pleased
天神好喜欢，　　　　　To have found human survivors.
吩咐兄妹俩：　　　　　He told the brother and sister,
"世上人种子，　　　　　"You two are the only people
只剩你两个，　　　　　That survived on the earth.
兄妹成亲传人烟。"　　　You should marry to reproduce mankind."

兄妹两个忙回答：　　　The two siblings answered in haste:
"我们两兄妹，　　　　　"We are brother and sister,
同胞父母生，　　　　　Born of the same parents.
不能结成亲。"　　　　　So we cannot marry."

说了很多，　　　　　　More explanations were given,
比了很多：　　　　　　More comparisons were made.
兄妹在高山顶上滚石磨，They were asked to roll a millstone from mountain tops.
哥在这山滚上扇，　　　The brother rolled the upper part of the millstone from one side,
妹在那山滚下扇，　　　The sister rolled the lower part from the opposite side.
滚到山箐底，　　　　　The two stones rolled down
上扇下扇合拢来。　　　And were reunited at the bottom of the valley.

"你们两兄妹，　　　　　"You two will be a couple

学磨成一家。" Just like the millstones."

"人是人， "Men are men,
磨是磨， Stones are stones.
我们兄妹俩， We are brother and sister,
同胞父母生， Born of the same parents.
怎能学磨成一家。" How can we be a couple like the millstones?"

说了很多， More explanations were given,
比了很多： More comparisons were made.
兄妹高山顶上滚筛子， They were asked to roll
兄妹高山顶上滚簸箕。 A sieve and a dustpan this time.
哥在山阳滚筛子， The brother rolled a sieve from the southern slope,
妹在山阴滚簸箕， The sister rolled a dustpan from the northern slope.
滚到山箐底， Rolling down to the bottom of the valley,
筛子垒在簸箕上。 The sieve lay on top of the dustpan.

"你们两兄妹， "You two will be a couple
学筛子簸箕成一家。" Just like the sieve and the dustpan."

"筛子是筛子， "The sieve and the dustpan
簸箕是簸箕， Are two different things.
我们兄妹俩， But we are brother and sister,
同胞父母生， Born of the same parents.

	第一部　创世
	Book One　Genesis

怎能学它成一家。"　　　　　　How can we be a couple like them?"

说了很多，　　　　　　　　　More explanations were given,
比了很多。　　　　　　　　　More comparisons were made.
天神指着说：　　　　　　　　Pointing at the bottom of the valley, God said:
"箐底两只鸟，　　　　　　　"There are two birds down there.
一只是雄鸟，　　　　　　　　One is male,
一只是雌鸟，　　　　　　　　The other is female.
雄的飞过来，　　　　　　　　They fly towards each other,
雌的飞过去，　　　　　　　　Meet in the middle,
雌鸟雄鸟在一起，　　　　　　And become a couple.
兄妹学鸟成一家。"　　　　　You two should be a couple like them."

"人是人，　　　　　　　　　"Men are men,
鸟是鸟，　　　　　　　　　　Birds are birds.
不能学它成一家。"　　　　　We should not be a couple like them."

说了很多，　　　　　　　　　More explanations were given,
比了很多。　　　　　　　　　More comparisons were made.
天神指着说：　　　　　　　　God said, pointing at two trees,
"这边一棵树，　　　　　　　"Here is a tree,
那边一棵树，　　　　　　　　There is a tree.
一棵是公树，　　　　　　　　One is male,
一棵是母树，　　　　　　　　The other is female.

- 43 -

梅葛 // Meige

东风吹来公树摇，　　　　　　The male sways in the east wind,
西风吹来母树摇，　　　　　　The female sways in the west wind.
摇着摇着挨拢来，　　　　　　The two trees gradually get close,
挨拢成一家，　　　　　　　　And become a couple.
兄妹学树成一家。"　　　　　You should be a couple like them."

"人是人，　　　　　　　　　　"Men are men,
树是树，　　　　　　　　　　Trees are trees.
不能学它成一家。"　　　　　We cannot be a couple like them."

说了很多，　　　　　　　　　More explanations were given,
比了很多。　　　　　　　　　More comparisons were made.
兄妹二人来吆鸭，　　　　　　The brother and sister were asked
兄妹二人来吆鹅；　　　　　　To gather ducks and geese.
哥在河这边，　　　　　　　　The brother was on one side of the river,
妹在河那边，　　　　　　　　The sister was on the other side.
哥哥吆公鸭，　　　　　　　　The brother gathered the drake,
妹妹吆母鸭；　　　　　　　　The sister gathered the female duck.
哥哥吆公鹅，　　　　　　　　The brother gathered the gander,
妹妹吆母鹅；　　　　　　　　The sister gathered the female goose.
公鸭母鸭成一家，　　　　　　The drake and the female duck became a couple,
公鹅母鹅成一家。　　　　　　The gander and the female goose became a couple."

"你们兄妹俩，　　　　　　　　"You two should be a couple,

第一部　创世
Book One　Genesis

要学它们成一家。"	Just like them."
"人是人，	"Men are men,
鸭是鸭，	Ducks are ducks,
鹅是鹅，	Geese are geese.
不能学它们成一家。"	We cannot be a couple like them."
"兄妹不愿结成亲，	"If brother and sister are unwilling to marry,
世上怎能传人烟？"	How can mankind survive?"
"我们两兄妹，	"We are brother and sister,
同胞父母生，	Born of the same parents.
成亲太害羞。	It is embarrassing for us to be married.
要传人烟有办法，	There is a way for mankind to survive.
属猪那一天，	On the Day of the Pig,
哥哥河头洗身子，	My brother has a bath upstream.
属狗那一天，	On the Day of the Dog,
妹妹河尾捧水吃，	I drink river water dow[nstream]
吃水来怀孕。"	In this way, I will be p[regnant].
一月吃一次，	The sister drank the wa[ter]
吃了九个月，	For nine months.
妹妹怀孕了，	Then she was pregnant.
怀了九个月，	After a nine-month pregnancy,

梅葛 // Meige

生下一个怪葫芦。	She gave birth to a weird gourd.
哥哥不在家,	Since the brother was not at home,
妹妹好害怕,	The sister was scared
把葫芦丢在河里边。	And dropped it in the river.

天神知道了,	God knew it,
急忙顺着河水找,	And immediately looked for it along the river.
找到东洋大海边,	When he reached the shore of the East Ocean,
葫芦漂在水里面。	He saw the gourd floating in the water.

天神请来三对野猪,	God asked three pairs of boars
拱开了海埂;	To dig ditches through the sea dam.
天神请来一对獭猫,	God then asked a pair of otters
打了三个洞。	To burrow three holes in the dam.
海埂拱开了,	Ditches were dug,
洞子打开了,	Holes were burrowed.
海水还不落。	But the sea level didn't fall.
再请三对黄鳝,	Then three pairs of rice field eels were asked
请来钻海底。	To drill the bottom of the sea.
海底钻通了,	The sea bottom was drilled through
水倒淌干了,	And the sea was drained.
葫芦陷在泥浆里,	But the gourd was stuck in the mud
还是出不来。	And could not be pulled out.

Book One　Genesis

天神请来三对兔鹰，	God asked three pairs of hawks
天神请来三对虾子，	And three pairs of shrimp to help.
兔鹰抓着葫芦飞，	The hawks seized the gourd and tried to move it,
虾子顶着葫芦走，	While the shrimp held it up with their heads.
葫芦放在沙滩上，	They put the gourd on the beach,
金索银索拴葫芦，	And tying it with golden and silver cords,
金杆银杆抬葫芦，	Carried it with golden and silver poles
抬到南京应天府①，	To Yingtianfu (Nanjing) ①,
大坝柳树弯，	And put it beneath the bending trees
弯腰树下面。	By the Willow Bend of the Great Dam.
葫芦找到了，	The gourd was found and safely placed.
葫芦放好了，	God opened it
天神用金锥开葫芦，	First with a golden awl,
天神用银锥开葫芦。	Then with a silver awl.
戳开第一道，	Out of the first crack,
出来是汉族，	Came the Han people,
汉族是老大，	Who became the majority group,
住在坝子里，	Living in the plain,
盘田种庄稼，	Growing crops in the fields.
读书学写字，	Learning to read and write,

---

① 云南汉族都说祖先是由应天府迁来。这是后来的事渗入诗中。

① The Han people of Yunnan say that their ancestors came from Yingtianfu (Nanjing). The Yi chanters of *Meige* insert it in their story.

-47-

梅葛 // Meige

聪明本事大。   They are clever and capable.

戳开第二道，   Out of the second crack,
出来是傣族，   Came the Dai people,
傣族办法好，   Who are expert at
种出白棉花。   Producing cotton.

戳开第三道，   Out of the third crack,
出来是彝家，   Came the Yi people,
彝家住山里，   Who live in the mountains,
开地种庄稼。   Reclaiming barren land and planting crops.

戳开第四道，   Out of the fourth crack,
出来是傈僳，   Came the Lisu people,
傈僳力气大，   Who make a living by carrying salt
出力背盐巴。   Because they have great strength.

戳开第五道，   Out of the fifth crack,
出来是苗家，   Came the Miao people,
苗家人强壮，   Who are of sturdy build
住在高山上。   And live high up in the mountains.

戳开第六道，   Out of the sixth crack,
出来是藏族，   Came the Tibetan people,

第一部　创世
Book One　Genesis

藏族很勇敢，	Who are very brave
背弓打野兽。	And go hunting with bows.

戳开第七道，	Out of the seventh crack,
出来是白族，	Came the Bai people,
白族人很巧，	Who are skillful.
羊毛赶毡子，	They make carpets with wool,
纺线弹棉花。	Spin thread and fluff cotton.

戳开第八道，	Out of the eighth crack,
出来是回族，	Came the Hui people,
回族忌猪肉，	Who raise cattle as their meat,
养牛吃牛肉。	As eating pork is taboo for them.

戳开第九道，	Out of the ninth crack,
出来是傣族，	Came the Dai people,
傣族盖寺庙，	Who build temples.
念经信佛教。	As Buddhists, they chant sutras.

出来九种族，	Here were the people of nine nationalities.
人烟兴旺了。	Mankind has flourished ever since.

第二部 造物
Book Two　Creation

梅葛 // Meige

一　盖房子

Ⅰ. House Building

哪个来盖房？
帕颇来盖房。
盖房没有树，
哪个撒树种？
帕颇撒树种。

Who would build houses?
Papo would build houses.
There were no trees.
Who would sow the tree seeds?
Papo would sow the tree seeds.

东方山坡小姑娘，
树种草种是她撒；
帕颇向她要种子，
树种草种要来了。

It was the little girl on the East Slope
That scattered the seeds for trees and grass.
Papo asked her for some,
And she granted his request.

什么是树王？
白菀树是树王，
先撒什么树？
先撒白菀树。

Which tree was the king of trees?
The baiwan tree.
What seeds should be planted first?
The baiwan trees.

高山顶顶上，
撒了白菀树；
高山梁子上，

On the top of the mountains,
Were sowed the seeds of the baiwan trees.
On the ridges,

第二部　造物
Book Two　Creation

撒了青松和赤松；	Were sowed the seeds of the green pines and the red pines.
高山箐沟里，	In the valleys,
撒上青香树。	Were sowed the seeds of the fragrant trees.
坝区山腰上，	On the hillside of the flatland were sowed
撒了罗汉松，	The yellowwood trees,
撒了桂皮树，	The cassiabark trees,
撒了梧桐树，	The phoenix trees,
撒了梨树桃树，	Pear trees, peach trees,
撒了花红树，	The button trees,
撒了核桃树，	The walnut trees,
撒了樱桃树。	The cherry trees.
坝区山坡上，	On the hill slopes of the flatland,
撒了橄榄树；	Were planted the olive trees.
坝区岩顶上，	On the top of the rocks,
撒下鸡嗉子树。	Were planted the dogwoods.
河头两岸上，	On the banks of the upper reach,
撒了水冬瓜树；	Were planted Chinese birch;
河边两岸上，	On the banks of the lower reach,
撒了杨柳树，	Were planted the willow trees,
撒了麻栗树，	The teak trees and
撒了锥栗树。	The chestnut trees.

梅葛 // Meige

野香樟木撒了三岭，	On three ridges were planted
马缨花树撒了三岭，	The wild camphor wood trees
白皮松树撒了三凹，	And the lantana trees.
橡树栗树撒了三坡，	On three saddles were planted the white bark pines.
橡树栗树撒了三箐。	On three slopes,
树种撒下了，	In three vales were planted the oaks and the chestnut trees.
河边两岸都撒遍，	The tree seeds were scattered on both banks,
山山箐箐都撒到。	Over every mountain and in every valley.

什么是草王，	Which grass was the king of the grass?
芦苇是草王。	The reeds were.
先撒什么草籽？	What grass seeds should be planted first?
先撒芦苇草籽。	The reed seeds.

高山梁子上，	On the mountain ridges
撒下芦苇草，	Were scattered the reed seeds
撒下野芭籽；	And the wild banana seeds.
高山箐底下，	On the bottom of the valleys
撒下鸡菜籽，	Were scattered the seeds of the chicken grass,
撒下菱角草，	The water chestnut grass,
撒下蕨菜籽，	The bracken grass
撒下兔子草。	And the rabbit grass.

坝区山坡上，	On the hill slopes of the flatland

第二部 造物
Book Two   Creation

撒了山头草；	Were scattered the hill-top grass seeds.
坝区岩子上，	On the rocks of the flatland
撒了甘草籽，	Were scattered the seeds of the Liquorice plant,
撒了山草籽；	And the hill grass.
坝区地边上，	On the edges of the flatland
撒了酸草籽；	Were scattered the sour grass seeds.
坝区河边上，	On the riverside of the flatland
撒了红白厚皮草，	Were scattered the seeds of the rock grass
撒了岩草籽。	And the white and red thick-leaf grass.
河边两岸上，	On both banks of the river
撒了山野菜；	Were scattered the seeds of the wild herbs.
沟边两岸上，	On both banks of the ditch
撒了喂猪草；	Were scattered the seeds of the pig grass.
房前屋后头，	In front and at the back of the house
撒了黄麻籽。	Were scattered the seeds of the jute plant.
草种撒下了，	The seeds were planted
平坝地区上，	In the flatland,
山岩河边上，	On the rocks and riverside,
高山箐底下，	On the mountains and in the valleys.
处处都撒遍，	Every kind of seed was planted
样样都撒了。	Everywhere.

梅葛 // Meige

帕颇有九个儿子，	Papo had nine sons,
九个儿子来养树；	Who took care of the trees.
帕颇有七个姑娘，	Papo had seven daughters,
七姊妹来养草。	Who took care of the grass.
过了三十七天后，	After thirty-seven days,
树芽迎风摆，	The tree buds were fluttering in the wind
草芽迎风摇。	While the grass buds were dancing in the breeze.
三轮三十七，	After three periods of thirty-seven days,
四轮四十九，	Four periods of forty-nine days,
五轮六十一，	Five periods of sixty-one days,
六轮七十三，	Six periods of seventy-three days,
七轮八十四，	Seven periods of eighty-four days
八轮九十五；	And eight periods of ninety-five days,
树长大了，	The trees grew up,
草长大了。	The grass grew up,
长满三山岭，	Covering up three ridges,
长满偏坡地。	And all the slopes.

帕颇的九个儿子，	Papo's nine sons
把树养大了；	Tended to the trees;
帕颇的七个姑娘，	Papo's seven daughters
把草养大了。	Tended to the grass.
天上九兄弟，	The nine brothers in the sky
想盖九间房；	Wanted to build nine houses.

第二部　造物
Book Two　Creation

什么地方盖房子？	Where did they build them?
树林当中盖了九间房。	They built them in the woods.

白樱桃树盖了三间房，　　　Three houses were made of white cherry trees.
人间九种族，　　　　　　　Among the nine ethnic peoples on the earth,
傣族来住房。　　　　　　　The Dai people chose to live in them.

坝区山腰上，　　　　　　　On the hillside of the flatland,
罗汉松树盖了三间房，　　　Three houses were made of yew podcarpus trees.
哪个来住房？　　　　　　　Who would live here?
回族来住房。　　　　　　　The Hui people would.

高山梁子上，　　　　　　　On the ridges of the high mountains,
青松赤松盖了三间房，　　　Three houses were made of green and red pines.
哪个来住房？　　　　　　　Who would move in?
彝族来住房。　　　　　　　The Yi people would.

坝区平坝上，　　　　　　　In the fields of the flatland,
香树盖了三间房，　　　　　Three houses were built from fragrant trees.
哪个来住房？　　　　　　　Who would live there?
汉族来住房。　　　　　　　The Han people would.

高山梁子上，　　　　　　　On the ridges of the high mountains,
洋皮松树盖了三间房，　　　Three houses were built from douglas firs.

梅葛 // Meige

哪个来住房？	Who would move in?
打柴打猪的人来住房。	The woodcutters and wild hog-hunters would.

野白松树来盖房， The wild white pines were used to build houses.
哪个来住房？ Who would live there?
赶毡子的人来住房。 The felt makers would.

野香樟木盖了三间房， The wild camphor trees were used to build three houses.
哪个来住房？ Who would move in?
放羊的人来住房。 The shepherds would.

河边两岸盖了三间房， Three houses were built along the banks of the river.
哪个来住房？ Who would live there?
放牛的人来住房。 The cowherds would.

盖也盖好了， The houses were built,
住的住好了。 And all the people were housed.
天王地王都喜欢。 Both the sky king and the earth king were glad.

什么是兽王？ Who was the king of the animals?
兔子是兽王。 The rabbit was.
刺树盖起三间房， Three houses were built from spiny trees
兔子来住房。 And the rabbit would move in.

第二部　造物
Book Two　Creation

高山梁子上，	On the ridges of the high mountains
盖起三间石头房，	Were built three stone houses.
什么来住房？	Who would live there?
老虎来住房。	The tiger would.
坝区山腰上，	On the hillsides of the flatland
盖起三间土平房，	Were built three clay houses.
什么来住房？	Who would move in?
豹子来住房。	The leopard would.
高山梁子上，	On the ridges of the high mountains
橡树盖起三间房，	Were built three houses from oak trees.
什么来住房？	Who would live there?
老熊来住房。	The bear would.
高山顶顶上，	On the top of the mountains
刺杆盖起三间房，	Were built three houses from spiny poles.
什么来住房？	Who would move in?
豺狼来住房。	The wolf would.
坝区河边上，	Along the riverside of the flatland
樱桃树木来盖房，	Were built houses from cherry trees.
什么来住房？	Who would live there?
麂子来住房。	The muntjac would.

梅葛 // Meige

石岩下面盖起三间房，	Beneath the cliffs were built three houses.
什么来住房？	Who would live there?
马鹿来住房。	The deer would.

山中石岩下，　　　　　　Beneath the cliffs in the mountains
香樟树木盖起三间房，　　Were built three houses from camphor trees.
什么来住房？　　　　　　Who would move in?
岩羊来住房。　　　　　　The blue sheep would.

不够又盖三间房，　　　　The houses were not enough, three more
盖在岩洞里，　　　　　　Were built in the caves.
什么来住房？　　　　　　Who would stay there?
野牛来住房。　　　　　　The bison would.

坝区河岸上，　　　　　　On the riverside of the flatland
盖起三间房，　　　　　　Were built three houses.
什么来住房？　　　　　　Who would move in?
豪猪来住房。　　　　　　The porcupine would.

高山梁子上，　　　　　　On the ridges of the high mountains
盖起三间土洞房，　　　　Were built three mud holes.
什么来住房？　　　　　　Who would live there?
穿山甲来住房。　　　　　The pangolin would.

第二部　造物
Book Two　Creation

河里石头盖起三间房，	Three houses were built out of river stones.
什么来住房？	Who would live there?
水獭来住房。	The otter would.
兽类的房子盖好了，	The houses for the animals were all built
兽类有了房子住。	And the animals could live there.
什么是鸟王？	Who was the king of the birds?
凤凰是鸟王。	The phoenix was.
坝区山腰上，	On the hillsides of the flatland
梧桐树盖起三间房，	Were built three houses from plane trees,
凤凰来住房。	And the phoenix would live there.
坝区岩子上，	On the cliffs of the flatland
盖起三间房，	Were built three houses.
什么来住房？	Who would move in?
大雁来住房。	The wild geese would.
林中落叶盖起三间房，	In the forests were built three houses from fallen leaves.
什么来住房？	Who would live there?
岩鸡来住房。	The cliff pheasant would.
半山橡子林中间，	In the oak woods on the hillsides

梅葛 // Meige

刺枝盖起三间房，	Were built three houses from spiny branches.
什么来住房？	Who would live there?
老鹰来住房。	The eagle would.

高山箐沟里，　　　　　　　In the valleys
橡子树叶盖起三间房，　　　Were built three houses from oak leaves.
什么来住房？　　　　　　　Who would move in?
箐鸡野鸡来住房。　　　　　The valley pheasant would.

坝区山腰上，　　　　　　　On the hillsides of the flatland
樱桃树枝来盖房，　　　　　Houses were built from cherry branches.
什么来住房？　　　　　　　Who would come and stay there?
斑鸠来住房。　　　　　　　The turtledove would.

河边两岸上，　　　　　　　On the banks of the river
核桃树盖起三间房，　　　　Were built three houses from walnut trees.
什么来住房？　　　　　　　Who would move in?
老鸹喜鹊来住房。　　　　　The crow and the magpie would.

林中落叶盖起三间房，　　　In the forests were built three houses from the fallen leaves.
什么来住房？　　　　　　　Who would live there?
杂鸟来住房。　　　　　　　The unnamed birds would.

高山梁子上，　　　　　　　On the ridges of the high mountains

第二部　造物

Book Two　Creation

青松盖起三间房，	Were built three houses from green pines.
什么来住房？	Who would live there?
猫头鹰来住房。	The owl would.
坝区山腰上，	On the hillsides of the mountains
用土舂起三间房，	Three clay houses were built.
什么来住房？	Who would stay there?
鹦虎雀子来住房。	The sparrow would.
再用落叶盖起三间房，	Three more houses were built from the fallen leaves.
什么来住房？	Who would move in?
鹦哥来住房。	The parrot would.
山中岩子上，	On the cliffs of the mountains
花红树木盖起三间房，	Were built three houses from conocarpus erectus trees.
什么来住房？	Who would live there?
小燕子来住房。	The swallow would.
不够再来盖，	The houses were not enough,
拿草盖起三间房，	Three thatched cottages were built.
什么来住房？	Who would live there?
蚂蚱来住房。	The grasshopper would.
河里盖了三间石头房，	In the river, three stone houses were built.

- 63 -

什么来住房？
石蚌来住房。

江底盖了三间石头房，
什么来住房？
鲤鱼来住房。

各样房子都盖齐，
各样房子都盖好，
鸟兽虫鱼有房住。
盖也盖好了，
住的住好了，
天王地王都喜欢。

Who would move in?
The oyster would.

On the bottom of the river were built three stone houses.
Who would live there?
The carp would.

All kinds of houses were constructed.
All kinds of houses were well built.
All the birds, animals, worms and fish had houses to dwell in.
The construction project was completed.
All the creatures were comfortably housed.
The king of the sky and the king of the earth were both pleased.

二 狩猎和畜牧

II. Hunting and Stockbreeding

上山打猎去，
上山撵麂子去；
撵麂子要有猎狗，
撵麂子要有麻索，

They went hunting in the mountains,
Hunting the muntjacs.
But they needed a hound,
They needed hempen ropes,

第二部 造物
Book Two　Creation

撵麂子要用猎网。	They needed a hunting net.
哪里有猎狗？	Where could a hound be found?
哪里出麻索？	Where could hempen ropes be bought?
哪里出猎网？	Where could a hunting net be made?

大理苍山黄石头，　　　　The yellow stone on Cangshan Mountain
黄石头变黄狗，　　　　　Turned into a yellow dog.
它就是猎狗。　　　　　　That was the hound.

傈僳族会撒麻，　　　　　The Lisu people could scatter the seeds of the hemp plant.
傈僳族会种麻，　　　　　They could take care of it
傈僳族会剥麻，　　　　　And separate the fibers when the harvest time came.
找傈僳族去，　　　　　　They went to look for the Lisu people.
找到山腰上，　　　　　　They found them on the hillsides,
到了傈僳族住的地方。　　Where they lived.

撒麻的人有了，　　　　　Now there were people to scatter seeds,
种麻的人有了，　　　　　There were those who could grow hemp,
剥麻的人有了，　　　　　And those who could separate the fibers.
还没有人搓麻索，　　　　But nobody could make hempen ropes,
还没有人结猎网。　　　　Neither could they weave a hunting net.

格滋天神说：　　　　　　God Gezi said,
"没有搓麻索的人不要着急，　"Don't worry about the ropes.

梅葛 // Meige

没有结网的人不要心焦； Don't be anxious about the hunting net.
去找特勒么的女人， Go and find Teleme's woman.
她会搓麻索， She can make the ropes.
她会结猎网。" She can weave the net."

特勒么的女人， Teleme's woman could make a rope
一天能搓三丈， As long as ten meters in a day,
三天能搓九丈； And thirty meters in three days.
一天能结三丈， She could weave the net as long as ten meters in a day,
三天能结九丈。 And thirty meters in three days.
越搓越喜欢， The more ropes she made, the happier she became.
越结越高兴； The more nets she wove, the more pleased she was.
麻索越搓越长， She made longer and longer ropes.
猎网越结越好。 She wove better and better nets.

猎狗找到了， Now the hound had been found;
麻索搓成了， The hempen ropes had been made;
猎网也结好了。 The hunting net had been woven.
吆着猎狗， They could go into the mountain,
拿着麻索， The hound in front,
拿着猎网， Rope in one hand, net in the other,
上山撵麂子。 To hunt the muntjacs.

公麂子出在茶山， The male muntjacs lived on the Tea Hill,

第二部　造物
Book Two　Creation

母麂子出在东洋大海石岩边；	The females lived on the cliffs of the East Sea.
有麂子的地方知道了，	They knew where to find them,
还没有撵麂子的人。	But there was no muntjac hunter.
天神的儿子，	Among the sons of God,
开天的那五兄弟，	The five brothers who made the sky,
大儿子阿赌会撵山，	Adu, the eldest son, was a good hunter.
叫他撵麂子去。	They asked him to hunt the muntjacs.
阿赌领着猎狗，	Taking the hound with him,
拿着麻索，	The hempen rope in one hand,
拿着猎网，	And the hunting net in another,
到茶山去撵公麂子，	Adu went to the Tea Hill to hunt the male muntjacs,
到东洋大海去撵母麂子。	To the East Sea to hunt the females.
大儿子阿赌，	Adu, the eldest son,
到了茶山上，	Got to the Tea Hill,
走进大树林，	Walking into the woods,
放出恶猎狗，	Sending out the fierce hound,
一只麂子也没有。	But found no muntjacs.
大儿子阿赌，	Adu, the eldest son,
到了东洋大海边，	Came to the East Sea,
走进小树林，	Walking into the woods,
放出恶猎狗，	And sending out the ferocious hound.
撵出来三四只麂子。	Three or four muntjacs ran out.

梅葛 // Meige

麂子跑出来，	When the muntjacs ran out,
阿赌拼命追，	Ahdu pursued them as fast as he could,
从山头到山脚，	From the top to the bottom of the hill,
从河头到河尾，	From one end of the river to the other,
追过一山又一山，	From one mountain to another,
追过一林又一林，	From one wood to another,
追到大河边。	Till he arrived at the big river.
河水弯又弯，	The river was winding.
河水清又清，	The river was clean.
河水深，	The river was deep.
波浪滚，	Waves were rolling.
麂子顺着小路跑，	The muntjacs fled along the path.
麂子顺着小路逃。	On both sides of the river,
河边小路旁，	Where so many vines grew,
长满了藤窝，	Intertwining with one another,
藤子牵藤子，	Like a bird's nest.
绊住麂子脚，	One muntjac stumbled.
绊是绊住了，	It was entangled,
杀是杀不着，	But could not be killed.
捞起海里的大石头，	Adu picked up a big stone in the sea,
甩进藤窝打麂子，	And threw it at the muntjac.
麂子打死了，	The muntjac was killed.

第二部　造物

Book Two　Creation

麂子皮拿来做衣裳，	The chamois was made into clothes;
麂子肉分给大家吃。	The meat was shared.
打的野物不够吃，	They couldn't live by hunting alone.
要去盘田种地收五谷。	They had to plow the fields and grow grain.
盘田没有牛，	Without farm cattle, the fields could not be plowed,
种地没有牛，	And the seeds could not be planted.
要去找牛啦。	They must go and find farm cattle.
牛从哪里来？	Where could the cattle be found?
大理苍山上，	On Cangshan Mountain in Dali,
露水下下来，	The dew drops fell,
红露水变成红牛，	The red ones became red cattle;
黄露水变成黄牛，	The yellow ones became yellow cattle;
黑露水变成黑牛。	The black ones became black cattle.
哪个先看见？	Who was the first to see the cattle?
葫芦包爱露水，	The gourd saw them first,
它去采露水，	Because it liked the dew
它先看见牛。	And went to collect it.
哪个把牛找回来？	Who would pull the cattle back?
特勒么的女人，	Teleme's woman,
左手拿盐巴，	With salt in her left hand
右手拿春草，	And the spring grass in her right hand,

梅葛 // Meige

把牛哄住了,	Lured the cattle,
树藤来拴牛,	Tied them up with vines,
把牛牵回来。	And pulled them back.

牛拴回来啦, Now they had the cattle,
牛已经有啦! They were cattle owners!
没有放牛的地方, But there was no pasture for the cattle.
什么地方好放牛? Where could they graze the cattle?
高山箐沟里, The pasture on both sides of the river
河边两岸青草地, And in the valleys of the high mountain
那是放牛的好地方。 Was a good place to graze them.

有了牛, Now they had the cattle
还没有猪, But they had no pigs.
什么地方有猪? Where could pigs be found?
南京应天府, The Willow Bend of the Great Dam
大坝柳树湾, In Yingtianfu (Nanjing)
是出猪的地方。 Was well-known for its pigs.

猪从哪里来? How did the pigs come into being?
白云彩变白露, The white clouds became white dew;
黑云彩变黑露, The black clouds became black dew.
天上下白露, The white dew dropped from the sky,
天上下黑露, The black dew dropped from the sky.

第二部　造物
Book Two　Creation

露水会扎地，	When the dew hit the ground,
白露扎出白石头，	White stones emerged,
黑露扎出黑石头。	Black stones appeared.
天神下凡来，	God came down to the earth.
打烂白石头，	He broke the white stones,
白猪钻出来，	Then white pigs came out.
打烂黑石头，	He broke the black stones,
黑猪钻出来。	Then black pigs came out.
有了白猪，	Now they had white pigs,
有了黑猪，	And black pigs as well.
还没有羊。	But they had no sheep or goats.
什么地方有羊？	Where could they be found?
南京应天府，	The Willow Bend of the Great Dam
大坝柳树湾，	In Yingtianfu (Nanjing)
是出羊的地方。	Was well-known for its sheep and goats.
羊从哪里来？	How did sheep and goats come into being?
大理苍山有三个松树桩，	On Cangshan Mountain in Dali,
松树桩里有三条白虫，	Three white worms lived in three pine stumps.
白虫变成白绵羊；	The white worms became white sheep.
大理苍山有三个铁栗木树桩，	On Cangshan Mountain in Dali,
铁栗木树桩里有三条黑虫，	Three black worms lived in three chestnut stumps.
黑虫变成黑山羊。	The black worms became black goats.

梅葛 // Meige

有了猪，	Now they had pigs,
有了羊，	Sheep and goats.
还没有放猪的人，	But there was nobody to pasture the pigs.
还没有放羊的人。	There was nobody to herd the sheep and goats.
什么人会放猪？	Who could pasture the pigs?
什么人会放羊？	Who could herd the sheep and goats?
汉族会放猪，	The Han people could pasture pigs.
彝族会放羊。	The Yi people could herd sheep.

放猪的人有了， Swineherds were found.
放羊的人有了， Shepherds were found.
还没有吆猪棍， But there were no pig whips.
还没有赶羊鞭。 There were no sheep whips.
拿什么做吆猪棍？ What could be made into pig whips,
拿什么做赶羊鞭？ What could be made into sheep whips?
没有吆猪棍不要怕， They needn't worry about pig whips.
没有赶羊鞭不要怕。 They needn't worry about sheep whips.
山上有黄竹， The whangee grew on the hills.
砍节黄竹能吆猪， They could be made into pig whips.
砍节黄竹能赶羊。 They could be made into sheep whips.

放猪的女人， The women who pastured pigs
放羊的男人， And the men who herded sheep

第二部　造物
Book Two　Creation

下雨天气冷,	Had no coir raincoats or bamboo hats to wear
没有蓑衣和笠帽。	On cold rainy days.
没有蓑衣不要怕,	They needn't worry about coir raincoats.
没有笠帽不要怕。	They needn't worry about bamboo hats.
山上有茅草,	The couch grass grew on the hills.
割回茅草连蓑衣;	It could be cut to sew coir raincoats.
山上有篾子,	The bamboo strips grew on the hills.
编好篾子,	They could be woven together
铺上棕叶子,	And covered with palm leaves
篾帽做好了。	To make rain hats.
身上穿蓑衣,	Wearing the coir raincoats
风吹不进,	Could prevent the wind and rain
雨淋不湿。	From getting in.
头上戴笠帽,	Wearing the bamboo hats
风吹不着,	Could shelter them
雨淋不着。	From the wind and rain.
放猪的女人,	The women who pastured pigs
放羊的男人,	And the men who herded sheep
没有鞋子穿,	Had no shoes to wear.
爬山脚要疼。	Their feet hurt when climbing the mountains.
山上有茅草,	There was couch grass on the mountains.
割来打草鞋,	They could be made into shoes.
穿上新草鞋,	Putting on the new shoes,

梅葛 // Meige

爬山脚不疼。	They felt no pain in their feet.

什么都有了， Everything was prepared.
还没有放猪的地方， But there was no place to graze pigs.
还没有放羊的地方， There was no pasture to herd sheep.
什么地方好放猪？ Where could they graze pigs?
什么地方好放羊？ Where could they herd sheep?
河岸长满爬根草， The riversides full of grass
池边尽是烂泥塘， And the muddy ponds around
那是放猪的好地方， Were the best places to graze pigs.
有三条大箐沟， Three big ditches
长满了藤窝， Filled with vine nests
有三匹山岭， And three valleys
长满了水马松， Full of water-horse pines
那是放羊的好地方。 Were the best places to herd sheep.

放猪的地方有了， Now they knew where to graze pigs
放羊的地方有了， And where to herd sheep.
在河边放猪， They drove their pigs to the riverside.
在山上放羊， They led their sheep to the hills.
放猪放得好， The pigs ate well.
放羊放得好， The sheep grazed well.
猪长得肥， The pigs grew fat.
羊长得壮。 The sheep grew sturdy.

第二部　造物
Book Two　Creation

山野放猪没有伴，	The swineherds were alone in the mountains.
山野放羊没有伴；	The shepherds were solitary in the fields.
放猪没有伴不要怕，	They needn't worry about loneliness.
放羊没有伴不要怕。	They needn't worry about solitude.
四川人的三个儿子会砍竹竿，	A man from Sichuan had three sons
四川人的三个儿子会做篾活，	Who could cut bamboo and make bamboo tools.
竹头拿来做葫芦笙，	The bamboo end was made into a gourd mouth organ,
竹中间拿来做笛子，	The middle part was shaped into a flute,
竹根拿来做响篾。	And the bamboo root was turned into a jaw harp.
放猪放羊，	The gourd mouth organ was a companion
葫芦笙做伴，	For the swineherds and shepherds.
放猪放羊，	The flute was another companion
笛子做伴，	For the swineherds and shepherds.
放猪放羊，	The jaw harp was a third companion
响篾做伴。	For the swineherds and shepherds.
放猪的女人有芦笙，	The female swineherds had the gourd mouth organ.
放羊的男人有芦笙；	The shepherds had the gourd mouth organ.
放猪的女人有笛子，	The female swineherds had the flute.
放羊的男人有笛子；	The shepherds had the flute.
放猪的女人有响篾，	The female swineherds had the jaw harp.
放羊的男人有响篾。	The shepherds had the jaw harp.

梅葛 // Meige

吹着芦笙，	They tooted the gourd mouth organ,
吹着笛子，	Blew the flute,
弹起响篾。	Played the jaw harp
山头吹一调，	From the hilltop
山尾弹一曲，	To the valley.
欢乐得起来，	They made merry.
唱得起来，	They sang.
放猪的女人喜欢，	The female swineherds were happy,
放羊的男人喜欢，	The shepherds felt pleased.

三　农　事　　　　　Ⅲ. Farming

坎上种苞谷，	Above the banks they planted corn.
坎下种荞子，	Below the banks they planted buckwheat.
水冬瓜树下的荞子好，	The buckwheat under Chinese birches was good.
锥栗树下的荞子好，	The buckwheat under chestnut trees was good, too.
有松树的坡地，	On the pine slopes
甜荞长得好。	Sweet buckwheat grew well.

山坡杂树多，	Various trees grew on the hillside.
根多不好盘庄稼，	Too many roots made it hard to plant the crops.
人类拿刀子，	Men wanted to cut them all

第二部　造物

Book Two　Creation

要把树砍完。	With their field choppers.
兔子争了先，	The rabbit acted first.
先去砍树枝，	It tried to cut off the branches,
砍也砍不倒。	But failed.
豺狼去砍枝，	The wolf tried to cut them off,
还是砍不倒。	But failed.
老虎去砍枝，	The tiger tried to cut them off,
还是砍不倒。	But failed.
麂子去砍枝，	The muntjac tried to cut them off,
还是砍不倒。	But failed.
麻雀去砍枝，	The sparrow tried to cut them off,
还是砍不倒。	But failed.
大雁又来砍，	The wild goose tried to cut them off,
还是砍不倒。	But failed.
老鸹又来砍，	The crow tried to cut them off,
还是砍不倒。	But failed.
野鸡也来砍，	The pheasant tried to cut them off,
还是砍不倒。	But failed.
竹鸡也来砍，	The bamboo partridge tried to cut them off,
还是砍不倒。	But failed.
鹦哥也来砍，	The parrot tried to cut them off,
还是砍不倒。	But failed.
乌鸦也来砍，	The raven tried to cut them off,
还是砍不倒。	But failed.

梅葛 // Meige

百兽都砍了，	All the animals tried,
百兽砍不倒。	But failed.
百鸟都砍了，	All the birds tried,
百鸟砍不倒。	But failed.

人来砍杂树，	Human beings came to do it.
先把刀磨好，	They sharpened their choppers
拿刀来砍枝，	Before doing the cutting.
几刀便砍倒！	They cut off the branches in a few strokes!
地王就决定：	Then the king of the earth decided:
人类盘庄稼。	Human beings should plant the crops.

五月砍到六月来，	From May to June,
六月砍到七月来，	From June to July,
七月砍到八月来，	From July to August,
八月砍到九月来；	From August to September,
山山箐箐，	They cut down all the trees
河头河尾，	On the hills, in the valleys,
杂树全都砍光了。	On the banks of the river.

十月晒一月，	They let the cut trees dry
冬月接着晒，	From October to November,
冬月晒一月，	From November to December,
晒到腊月尾。	To the end of December.

第二部　造物
Book Two　Creation

过了旧历年，	After New Year's Eve,
正月初一那一天，	On New Year's Day,
房前屋后雀鸟叫，	Birds sang around the house.
梁下雀鸟来做窝，	The swallows made nests under the eave.
节令分出来了，	It was now time
要忙庄稼活路了。	To be busy with farm work.

二月二十七，	On the twenty-seventh day of February,
布谷鸟叫起来，	The cuckoo sang,
石蚌叫起来，	The white blotched snappers cried.
要放火烧荞地了。	It was time to burn the buckwheat fields.
野兽来烧火，	The animals came to light the fire,
还是烧不着。	But failed.
鸟类来烧火，	The birds came to light the fire,
还是烧不着。	But failed too.
最后来决定：	Finally, it was decided that
还是人来烧。	Human beings would do the job.

属牛日来烧，	Burning the fields on the Day of the Ox
恐怕烧着牛。	Would probably harm the ox.
属虎日来烧，	Burning the fields on the Day of the Tiger
恐怕烧着虎。	Would probably harm the tiger.
属兔日来烧，	Burning the fields on the Day of the Rabbit
恐怕烧着兔。	Would probably harm the rabbit.

梅葛 // Meige

属龙日来烧，	Burning the fields on the Day of the Dragon
恐怕烧着龙。	Would probably harm the dragon.
属蛇日来烧，	Burning the fields on the Day of the Snake
恐怕烧着蛇。	Would probably harm the snake.
属马日来烧，	Burning the fields on the Day of the Horse
恐怕烧着马。	Would probably harm the horse.
属羊日来烧，	Burning the fields on the Day of the Goat
恐怕烧着羊。	Would probably harm the goat.
属猴日来烧，	Burning the fields on the Day of the Monkey
恐怕烧着猴。	Would probably harm the monkey.
属鸡日来烧，	Burning the fields on the Day of the Rooster
恐怕烧着鸡。	Would probably harm the rooster.
属狗日来烧，	Burning the fields on the Day of the Dog
恐怕烧着狗。	Would probably harm the dog.
属猪日来烧，	Burning the fields on the Day of the Pig
恐怕烧着猪。	Would probably harm the pig.
最后商量好，	Finally they decided to do the burning
选在属鼠日，	On the Day of the Rat,
老鼠会打洞，	As the rat could burrow a hole
不会被火烧。	And would not be harmed by the fire.
从此火着了，	With the fire lighted,
荞地烧起来。	The buckwheat fields were burnt.
火烟冲上天，	The smoke shot up to the sky
火烟冲过江，	And across the river.

第二部　造物
Book Two　Creation

火焰挡不住，	The flames could not be stopped.
仓房烧毁了，	The storehouse was reduced to ashes
籽种烧光了，	While the seeds were all burnt up.
荞种没有了。	No buckwheat seeds were left.
亏得天上小麻雀，	Thanks to the sparrows in the sky,
四面八方拣荞种，	Who picked up seeds from far and near.
荞种拣来了，	Now the seeds were collected.
三月二十日，	On the twentieth of March,
开地撒荞子。	It was time to scatter the seeds in the fields.
属龙日来撒，	If the seeds were scattered on the Day of the Dragon,
庄稼像龙一样旺；	The crops would grow as prosperous as a dragon.
属虎日来撒，	If the seeds were scattered on the Day of the Tiger,
庄稼像虎一样好。	The crops would be as strong as a tiger.
哪个来犁地？	Who would plow the fields?
男人来犁地。	The men would.
哪个来撒种？	Who would scatter the seeds?
妇女来撒种。	The women would.
撒好八十八座梁，	The seeds were scattered over eighty-eight ridges
撒好七十七匹坡。	And seventy-seven slopes.
过了十三天，	Thirteen days passed,
庄稼长得肥又旺，	The crops grew well.

梅葛 // Meige

三十七天后，　　　　　　　　Thirty-seven days passed,
庄稼长得更好了。　　　　　　The crops grew better.

薅草节令到，　　　　　　　　The weeding season was coming,
铲草节令到，　　　　　　　　It was time to dig up the weeds.
这回七姊妹，　　　　　　　　The seven sisters
一人薅一天。　　　　　　　　Took turns to do it.
到了九月土黄天，　　　　　　In September,
庄稼盘好了。　　　　　　　　The crops were ready for harvesting.

箐底到山顶，　　　　　　　　From the valley bottom to the hilltop,
山凹到平坝，　　　　　　　　From the hollow to the flatland,
没有不种庄稼的地方，　　　　Crops were everywhere.
到处的庄稼都盘好了。　　　　Everywhere they were ripe.
庄稼长得好，　　　　　　　　The crops grew very well.
玉米长得像马尾，　　　　　　The corn silk was like horse tails.
荞子长得像葡萄。　　　　　　The buckwheat ears were like grapes.
兽类去看，　　　　　　　　　The animals went to the fields,
看了很佩服；　　　　　　　　Admiring what they saw.
鸟类也去看，　　　　　　　　The birds went there
看了很佩服；　　　　　　　　And felt amazed.
从此就是人类盘庄稼。　　　　Since that time, mankind has planted the crops.

人来盘庄稼，　　　　　　　　Men planted crops

第二部 造物
Book Two Creation

要按节令盘。	According to seasons.
把年月日分出来，	Years, months and days should be decided
把四季分出来，	And the four seasons should be divided,
才好盘庄稼。	So that the crops could be planted on time.
哪个来分年月日？	Who would decide the years, the months and the days?
天神来分年月日。	God would.
一年十个月，	There would be ten months[①] in a year
一月四十天[①]。	And forty days in a month.
分了年月日，	After this, people started to plant crops
盘田种地收五谷，	And tried to get a good harvest.
年月分错了，	But as the devision was wrong,
五谷不成熟。	The crops would never be mature.
怎样来算年？	How could the years be calculated?
怎样来算月？	How could the months be counted?
怎样来算日？	How could the days be figured out?
房后有棵大松树，	There was a big pine behind the house.
一年长一台，	It grew one knot every year,
松树就是记年的。	Thus was for a calculator of years.
房前有棵棕榈树，	There was a palm in front of the house
一月发一匹，	And every month a new leaf would sprout.

① 传说最早的时候，人类是这样错分年月日的。

① It is said that early human beings divided the year and the months in this way.

- 83 -

梅葛 // Meige

棕树就是记月的。	So the palm could be used to count the months.
地边有窝爬根草，	Near the field there was a nest of grass
一天发一匹，	From which a new leaf came out every day.
爬根草就是记日的。	So the grass could be used to mark the days.
年月日有了，	Now they had the years, months and days.
还没有四季。	But there were no seasons yet.
怎样分四季？	How could the seasons be divided?
河边杨柳发芽了，	The willows on the riverside were in bud,
大山梁子松树上，	On the pines on the mountain ridges,
布谷鸟儿声声叫，	The cuckoo was singing.
大山大箐里，	In the valleys,
李桂秧① 叫起来了，	The liguiyang bird was chirping.
春季就到了。	That meant spring was coming.
河边水田里，	In the paddy fields by the river,
蛤蟆叫三声，	The toads cried three times.
大山水箐里，	In the valleys and on the mountains,
青蛙叫三声，	The frogs croaked three times.
夏季就到了。	Then one knew that Summer came.
山上山下知了叫，	When the cicadas sang uphill and downhill,
秋季就到了。	Autumn arrived.
天心雁鹅飞，	The wild geese flew in the sky,
飞飞地上歇，	Descended to the ground for a rest,

---

① 李桂秧：一种鸟的俗名。

第二部 造物
Book Two　Creation

雁鹅叫三声，	And let out three cries.
冬季就到了。	That was the beginning of winter.

算年月日的有了，　　Now they knew how to calculate
四季也分出来了，　　The years, months and days,
从此大地上，　　　　And the four seasons were divided,
好盘庄稼了。　　　　It was easy to grow crops on the earth.

一年十二个月[①]，　　Now there were twelve months in a year[①].
月月要生产。　　　　In every month there was farm work to do.
正月去背粪，　　　　In the first month, the manure must be carried to the
二月砍荞把，　　　　　　field.
三月撒荞子，　　　　In the second month, the buckwheat ends must be cut.
四月割大麦，　　　　In the third month, they scattered the buckwheat seeds.
五月忙栽秧，　　　　In the fourth month, they reaped the barley.
六月去薅秧，　　　　In the fifth month, they transplanted the seedlings.
七月割苦荞，　　　　In the sixth month, they weeded the fields.
八月割了谷子掰苞谷，　In the seventh month, they cut the bitter buckwheat.
九月割了甜荞撒大麦，　In the eighth month, they reaped the rice and the corn.
十月粮食装进仓，　　In the ninth month, they harvested the sweet buckwheat and
冬月撒小麦，　　　　　　scattered the barley.

---

① 通过长期的生产实践，人类掌握了自然规律，于是正确的年、月、日就分出来了。

① Later, men finally learnt to divide the year into twelve months.

— 85 —

梅葛 // Meige

腊月砍柴忙过年。	In the tenth month, all the grains were put in the storehouse. In the eleventh month, the wheat seeds were scattered. In the twelfth month, people chopped firewood and celebrated the New Year.

四　造工具

IV. Making Farm Tools

天神来吩咐，
盘田种庄稼。
庄稼哪个种？
庄稼哪个盘？
天王生的九个儿子，
地王生的七个姑娘。

God came to give his command
That the fields be tilled and the crops be planted.
Who would till the fields?
Who would plant the crops?
The king of the sky's nine sons would.
The king of the earth's seven daughters would.

没有造农具用的铁，
没有造农具用的铜，
到处去找铁，
到处去找铜。

There was no iron to make the tools with.
There was no copper to make the tools with.
They searched for iron everywhere.
They looked for copper everywhere.

哪个见铜花？
哪个见铁花？

Who had ever seen copper flowers?
Who had ever seen iron flowers?

第二部　造物
Book Two　Creation

山上的花鸟见铜花，	The flower birds on the hill had seen copper flowers.
地上的岩蜂见铁花。	The rock bees on the ground had seen iron flowers.

早晨岩蜂去采花，	In the morning the rock bees went to gather flowers
花鸟飞到石岩上，	And the flower birds flew to the rocks.
岩蜂见到铁花了，	The rock bees saw the iron flowers
花鸟见到铜花了。	And the flower birds saw the copper flowers.

石岩下面铜水流，	Under the rocks molten copper flowed.
石岩对面铁水淌，	On the opposite side, molten iron flowed.
拿也拿不起，	You could not take it.
挨也挨不得。	You could not touch it.

哪个采铜花？	Who would pick up the copper flowers?
哪个采铁花？	Who would pick up the iron flowers?
阿查阿告颇①，	Acha'agaopo would.
拿起竹帚扫铜花，	He collected the copper flowers
拿起竹帚扫铁花；	And the iron flowers with a broom.
铜花烫得很，	The copper flowers were too hot.
铁花烫得很，	The iron flowers were too hot.
挨也挨不得，	They could not be touched.
扫也扫不起。	They could not be collected.

---

① 阿查阿告颇：人名。

梅葛 // Meige

古时杀老虎，	In ancient times, when a tiger was killed,
剩下虎骨四小节，	Four pieces of its bone were left.
拿来当扫帚，	They could be used as brooms
扫下铜花来，	To sweep the copper flowers
扫下铁花来。	And the iron flowers.
哪个先拣铜？	Who would be the first to pick up
哪个先拣铁？	The copper and the iron?
啄木鸟先拣铜，	The woodpecker would.
啄木鸟先拣铁。	The copper and the iron were so hot
烫又烫得很，	That the woodpecker couldn't shake them off
甩又甩不掉。	Because they stuck to its beak.
人来拣铜，	Men decided to pick up
人来拣铁，	The copper and the iron.
剪下羊毛皮，	They covered their fingers
套在手指上，	With sheepskin and
脚上穿草鞋，	Put on straw sandals
来拣铜和铁。	And picked up the copper and the iron.
没有装铜的篮子，	There were no baskets
没有装铁的篮子，	To carry the copper and the iron.
哪个找竹种？	Who would look for the bamboo seeds?
哪个撒竹种？	Who would plant them?

第二部　造物
Book Two　Creation

门世地培阿①地方，	In the place named Menshidipei'a
住着阿省莫若②，	Lived Ashengmoruo.
阿省莫若有竹种，	He had bamboo seeds.
阿底莫若③去要竹种。	Adimoruo went to Ashengmoruo for help.
阿底莫若找回竹种来，	He came back with some bamboo seeds
撒到河边沙滩上。	And scattered them along the river.
二月二十日，	On the twentieth day of February,
竹种撒下了，	The bamboo seeds were scattered.
地头转一回，	In thirteen days
地尾转一回，	They inspected the field for the first time.
已满十三日。	In twenty-five days,
二轮二十五，	They made a second inspection.
三轮三十七，	When in thirty-seven days they came again,
竹芽长得像鼠耳。	The bamboo sprouts had grown like mouse ears.
二月二十撒竹种，	The bamboo seeds were scattered on the twentieth day of February.
三月二十日，	By the twentieth day of March,
已满一个月；	They had grown for one month.
四月二十日，	By the twentieth of April,
已满两个月；	They had grown for two months
竹子长成节。	

---

① 门世地培阿：地名。
② 阿省莫若：人名。
③ 阿底莫若：人名。

梅葛 // Meige

| | And the bamboo rings appeared. |

栽竹子的季节到了， It was time
栽竹子的日子到了， To transplant the bamboo.
哪个栽竹子？ Who would do it?
阿底莫若栽竹子。 Adimoruo would.
正是五月端阳节， May fifth, the Day of the Pig, the Dragon Boat Festival,
又是属猪栽竹日。 Was also the day of bamboo transplanting.
五月初五栽竹子， So, on May fifth, the bamboos were transplanted.
六月初五满一月， By June fifth, they had grown for one month.
七月初五满两月， By July fifth, they had grown for two months
栽下的竹子发了芽， And taken root in the soil
竹子长得绿莹莹。 And had become glittering green.
哪个来壅土？ Who would cover the roots with soil?
凤凰来壅土。 The phoenix would.
竹根壅上土， With the roots covered with the soil,
竹子长得旺。 The bamboos were flourishing.

长到八月二十日， The bamboos grew till the twentieth of August,
长到九月二十日， Till the twentieth of September,
长到十月二十日， Till the twentieth of October,
长到冬月二十日， Till the twentieth of November,
长到腊月二十日， Till the twentieth of December,
长到正月二十日， Till the twentieth of January of the next year,

第二部　造物
Book Two　Creation

长到二月二十日；	Till the twentieth of February.
栽下的竹子长成林，	At last, the bamboos became a forest,
栽下的竹子长得绿莹莹。	Glittering green.
哪个来破竹？	Who would split the bamboo?
胡高①来破竹。	Hugao would.
破竹编篮子，	He split the bamboo into strips
编成圆篮子，	To weave round baskets
拿来给马驮。	For horses to carry things with.
胡高又破竹，	Hugao split more bamboos
破竹声音沙沙响，	With the rustling sound.
编成长篮子，	He wove long baskets
拿来给人背。	For people to carry things with.
哪个来称铜？	Who would weigh the copper?
告颇②来称铜。	Gaopo would.
哪个来称铁？	Who would weigh the iron?
告颇来称铁。	Gaopo would.
称好的铜铁装在篮子里。	He weighed them and put them in the baskets.
铜铁称好了，	The copper and the iron were all weighed,
没有马来驮。	But there was no horse to carry them.
哪个来养马？	Who would raise horses?

---

① 胡高：人名。
② 告颇：人名。

梅葛 // Meige

阿巴①来养马。	Aba would.
青草地上去放马，	If he grazed horses in the pasture,
草地放马马不壮；	They wouldn't grow strong.
河边去放马，	If he grazed them on the river banks,
马吃河边象鼻草，	Where they could eat the elephant-trunk grass,
马就长膘壮起来。	They would grow stout and strong.
正月二十日，	On the twentieth day of January,
放马放到石坎上，	The horse was grazing above the stone bank.
石坎下面有野牛，	There was a wild ox below.
马往石坎下面跑，	The horse was running down,
牛往石坎上面跑，	The wild ox was running up.
野牛哞哞叫，	The horse whinnied,
老马嘶嘶叫，	The ox lowed.
野牛配老马，	The ox mated with the horse.
老马起驹了，	The horse was pregnant
下了一匹小叫马，	And gave birth to a baby horse.
准备来驮铜，	The baby horse should carry
准备来驮铁，	The copper and the iron when it grew up.
驮铜驮铁驮不成，	But it didn't. Instead,
成了皇帝状元骑的马。	It served the Emperor and the Zhuangyuan①.
布谷鸟儿叫了，	When the cuckoo sang,

---

① 阿巴：人名。

① Zhuangyuan was the title conferred on the person withe the best score in the highest imperial examination. – Translator's note

第二部　造物
Book Two　Creation

又过一年了。	Another year passed.
正月二十日，	On the twentieth day of January,
母马起驹了，	The horse was pregnant again
生下一匹小骡子，	And gave birth to a baby mule,
四脚镰刀花，	With sickle-shaped feet.
这回有骡子驮铜了，	The mule could carry
这回有骡子驮铁了。	The copper and the iron.
鸡树板做鞍头，	Chicken tree wood was used as the pommel,
青菜皮树做鞍板，	The wood of green bark tree as the saddle plate,
橡子做架子，	The wood of rubber tree as the saddle,
树皮做架绳，	The wood of tree bark as the rope,
枫树做楸珠，	The wood of maple tree as the beads
枫树做楸网，	And the net,
棕皮做硬褡，	Palm bark as the hard lining,
獐子皮做软褡，	And roebuck skin as the soft lining.
配好鞍架驮铜铁。	The saddle was ready to carry the copper and the iron.
哪个来赶马？	Who would drive the horse?
俄考来赶马。	Ekao would.
俄考力气大，	With his great strength,
端起驮子不费劲。	He could easily lift the pack.
驮着铜铁下坡坡，	The horse was carrying copper and iron downhill,

梅葛 // Meige

石头挡在路当中，	But stones blocked the road.
哪个来开路？	Who would remove them?
七月下大雨，	It rained hard in July.
到处淌山水，	Torrents rushed down
山水滚滚流，	And swept away
路当中的石头都冲走。	The stones in the road.

驮着铜铁过横路，　　　The horse was about to cross a road,
大树挡在路当中，　　　But a big tree stood in the middle of the road.
哪个来开路？　　　　　Who would remove the tree?
啄木鸟来开路。　　　　The woodpecker would.

驮着铜铁坡上走，　　　The horse was going uphill.
石坎挡在坡当中，　　　A stone bank blocked the way.
哪个来开路？　　　　　Who would smooth the way?
穿山甲来开路。　　　　The pangolin would.

道路开通了，　　　　　The road was cleared and smooth.
驮着铜铁到处找，　　　Ekao and his horse went on,
四面八方走遍了，　　　But nowhere could they find
没有打铜的人，　　　　A coppersmith
没有打铁的人。　　　　Or a blacksmith.

驮到四川峨眉山，　　　They went to Emei Mountain in Sichuan

第二部　造物
Book Two　Creation

驮到云南滇池边，	And to the bank of Dianchi Lake in Yunnan.
没有会打刀的人，	But they found no one able
没有会打农具的人。	To make a knife or other farm tools.
驮到永仁去，	Finally, they went to Yongren County
走过仁和街，	And, passing Renhe Street,
只听叮当打铁声，	Heard the sound of striking iron,
不见铁匠是哪个。	But saw no blacksmith in sight.
驮到中和、直苴去，	They then went to Zhonghe and Zhiju,
没有会打锄头的人，	But found no one able
没有会打镰刀的人。	To make hoes and sickles.
驮到大村去，	They went to Dacun,
驮到茨拉去，	They went to Cila,
没有打铜打铁的人。	But found no coppersmith or blacksmith.
驮到白草岭，	They went to the Baicao Ridge,
驮到宾川城，	They went to the city of Binchuan,
没有打铜打铁的人。	But found no coppersmith or blacksmith.
驮到盐丰去，	They went to Yanfeng,
驮到姚安去，	They went to Yao'an,
没有打铜打铁的人。	But found no coppersmith or blacksmith.

梅葛 // Meige

驮回六苴来，	Then they went back to Liuju,
还是找不到。	But in vain.

驮到大理苍山顶，　　They went to the top of Cangshan Mountain
驮到永昌城。　　　　And to Yongchang City.

蒙化出铁，　　　　　Menghua produced iron,
东川出铜，　　　　　Dongchuan produced copper,
沙拉出好铅，　　　　Shala produced lead.
就是没有打铜打铁的人。But there was no coppersmith or blacksmith.

驮着铜铁到牟定，　　On the way to Mouding,
路上听见马鹿叫；　　They heard the sound of deer.
走过牟定岔路口，　　Passing the crossroad,
看见打死很多鹿；　　They saw many dead deer.
牟定城外有条河，　　Outside Mouding there was a river,
有个姑娘在河边洗衣服；Where a girl was washing clothes.
马鹿被打得哞哞叫，　A deer was beaten so hard that it bleated loudly
跳进水里到处游；　　And jumped into the river and swam around.
进了牟定城，　　　　In the city of Mouding,
有了打铜的人，　　　They found coppersmiths
有了打铁的人，　　　And blacksmiths and people
有了铸锅的人。　　　Who made pans.

第二部　造物

Book Two　Creation

马鹿头拿来做砧，	The head of a deer was used as the anvil,
马鹿角拿来做锥，	Its horns were used as the awls,
马鹿脚拿来做钳子，	Its feet were used as the pincers,
马鹿身子做风箱，	Its body was used as the bellows.
开始打铜打铁了。	In this way they made tools of copper and iron.
铜的用处多得很，	Copper was very useful.
铁的用处多得很；	Iron was very useful.
打出铁来一团团，	A mass of hot iron
铁团丢进冷水里，	Was thrown into cold water.
再从水里拿出来，	When taken out,
拿出就能做工具。	It was ready for making tools.
先打犁头三大把，	Three plowshares were made first
用来开田种庄稼；	To plow the fields for the crops.
后打镰刀三大把，	Three scythes were then made
用来割谷子；	To reap the millet.
再打一把锯，	Then a saw was made
拿来锯木板。	To saw boards.
打了锯子打剪刀，	After that, scissors were made, too,
剪布裁衣有工具。	To cut cloth for making clothes.
工具都打好了，	When all the tools were made,
九个儿子拿着农具种庄稼，	The nine sons started to plant crops with the tools,
七个姑娘背着刀子放牛羊。	The seven girls herded the cattle and sheep with the

梅葛 // Meige

                    scythes.

正月过新年，	In January, people celebrated the New Year,
二月三月过去了，	Then February and March passed.
五月端午来，	In May, when the Dragon Boat Festival came,
九个儿子看见橡子林，	The nine sons saw the oak woods
看见赤松青松林。	And the woods of red and green pines.
到了五月天，	In the days of May,
一天三次雨；	It rained three times a day.
橡子树砍来做犁架，	The oak trees were cut and turned into the wooden part of the plow,
安上铁犁头；	Fitted with the iron plowshare.
水牛黄牛架起来，	The water buffalo and the ox were harnessed,
脖子架弯担，	With a bent pole on the neck,
拴上皮索子。	Tied with a leather rope.
六月二十属龙日，	The twentieth day of June was the Day of the Dragon.
开始犁生地：	It was time to plough virgin land.
水冬瓜树下犁荞地，	Under the alnus trees, the land was burnt
砍下水冬瓜树枝烧荞地；	And ploughed to grow buckwheat.
松树底下撒甜荞，	Under the pine trees, the land was burnt
松树砍来烧荞地；	For sweet buckwheat to grow.
荞子长得好，	The buckwheat grew

第二部　造物
Book Two　Creation

颗颗像葡萄。　　　　　　As big as grapes.

五　盐

V. Salt

男人服侍树，	Men took care of the trees.
女人服侍草；	Women looked after the grass.
树叶不残缺，	The tree leaves were luxuriant,
青草长得旺；	And the grass lush green.
野兽不会来，	Wild animals dared not come near
雀鸟不离窝；	And birds did not leave their nests.
高山好放羊，	The mountains were a good place for grazing sheep,
白羊遍山冈。	Which looked like white dots here and there.

山坡去放羊，	One day,
一只大绵羊不见了！	A big sheep was missing from the slope.
山山箐箐都找遍，	They searched every vale and hill,
找来找去找不到。	But it could not be found anywhere.
三十三天后，	Thirty-three days later,
绵羊回来了。	The big sheep came back.
绵羊回羊群，	Once it returned to the flock,
羊群围拢来；	Other sheep gathered around.
羊群围着大绵羊，	They gathered around

- 99 -

梅葛 // Meige

去它身上舔。　　　　　　　And licked its body.
放羊老人起疑心，　　　　　The old shepherd became suspicious.
手摸羊毛嘴里尝，　　　　　He touched its wool and tasted it,
心里自思量：　　　　　　　Thinking to himself:
"大绵羊身上有咸味，　　　 "Since the wool of the big sheep tastes salty,
大绵羊一定吃了盐巴水，　　It must have drunk salt water.
看看盐水在哪方。"　　　　 Let me see where it came from."
老人拿来铁链子，　　　　　The old man found an iron chain
小心拴在羊脚上，　　　　　And tied it to one foot of the sheep,
看看绵羊去哪方。　　　　　And followed the sheep.

大绵羊沿着山下走，　　　　The big sheep walked down the hill
一走走到安丰井；　　　　　To Anfeng Well.
继续往上走，　　　　　　　Then it went uphill
走到白盐井。　　　　　　　To White Salt Well.
一片大森林，　　　　　　　A thick forest appeared
林密草又深，　　　　　　　With tall trees, thick grass,
林中淌盐水，　　　　　　　Salt water flowing through.
兽类围水边，　　　　　　　The animals came to the river,
舔水吃盐巴。　　　　　　　And licked the salt water.
老人跟着绵羊走，　　　　　Led by the big sheep,
看见盐水笑眯眯。　　　　　The old man was glad to find out salt source.

河头写字贴上，　　　　　　A sign was posted where the river started,

第二部　造物
Book Two　Creation

河尾插上木牌；	And a board was put up where it ended.
各族人一齐跑来看，	People of all ethnic groups came
都说真是好盐水。	And spoke highly of the salt water.
傈僳族来煮盐，	The Lisu people boiled the water
没有煮成功。	But failed to extract the salt.
汉族来煮盐，	The Han people tried
头回煮不成，	But failed, too.
后来仔细想，	But they thought about it
二回煮成了。	And succeeded in getting salt.
大家听说煮出盐，	Hearing the good news about the salt,
纷纷搬到石羊来。	People moved to Shiyang one after another.
山坡有荞子，	On the hillsides
山上有大麻，	There was buckwheat and hemp.
平坝有谷子，	In the flatland
平坝有小麦，	There was rice and wheat.
人户增多了，	Since the population increased quickly,
变成石羊镇。	Shiyang became a town.
牧羊老人看见了，	The old shepherd was happy to see it,
望着四山眯眯笑。	Smiling at the mountains around.

梅葛 // Meige

六 蚕 丝　　　　VI. Silk

东洋大海石岩边，　　　　Near the cliffs of the East Sea,
柞桑树有三林，　　　　There were three groves of mulberry oaks,
甜桑树有三林，　　　　Three groves of sweet mulberries,
马桑树有三林；　　　　And three groves of mulberry trees.
天神撒下蚕种来，　　　　As God dropped the silkworm eggs,
一撒撒在树丫上，　　　　They fell on the tree limbs.
桑树底下三堆屎，　　　　Under the trees
江西挑担人，　　　　Were three little heaps of silkworm droppings.
来到桑树下，　　　　The load carrier from Jiangxi
看见了蚕屎，　　　　Came and saw them.
找到了蚕种。　　　　He discovered the silkworm eggs.

蚕种找着了，　　　　Now the silkworm eggs were found,
哪个抱①蚕子？　　　　But who would hatch the eggs?
汉家姑娘抱蚕子。　　　　The girl of the Han nationality.
三年润一月，　　　　There is an extra month every three years
一年打两春，　　　　And the third year has two springs.
打春后三天，　　　　Three days after the beginning of the first spring,

---

① 抱：孵化的意思。

第二部　造物
Book Two　Creation

桑树发出来，	Mulberry trees shot up
蚕儿钻出来。	And the silkworms came out.

蚕有了，	Now they had the silkworms
桑叶也有了，	And the mulberry leaves,
没有簸箕和筛子，	But there were no dustpans and sieves.
怎么来养蚕？	How could the silkworms be raised?
去找竹子来，	They found bamboo
去请篾匠来，	And sent for the craftsman,
把簸箕编出来，	Who made the dustpans
把筛子编出来。	And made the sieves,
蚕养在簸箕筛子里。	In which the silkworms were raised.

要扫蚕了，	It was time to clean the dustpans and sieves.
一天扫三回，	This was done three times a day
三天扫九回。	And nine times in three days.
怎样喂蚕？	How could the silkworms be fed?
先喂什么？	What should be given first?
后喂什么？	What should be given second?
先喂柞桑叶，	The mulberry leaves should be given first,
再喂甜桑叶，	Then the sweet mulberry leaves,
后喂马桑叶，	And last the Coriaria leaves.
蚕就养大了。	In this way, the silkworms grew.

梅葛 // Meige

哪个来拣蚕？	Who would separate the silkworms?
汉家姑娘来拣蚕。	The girl of the Han nationality would.
一天拣三回，	She did it three times a day,
三天拣九回；	And nine times in three days.
小的拣一堆，	Small ones were separated
大的拣一堆；	From big ones.
小的拣在簸箕里，	Small ones were put in the dustpans
大的拣在筛垫上；	And big ones in the sieves.
小的一天喂一次，	The small ones were fed once a day
大的一天喂三次。	And the big ones three times a day.

蚕养老了，	The silkworms grew older and older,
没有吐丝的地方。	But there was no place to spin the silk.
汉家田埂上，	The fennel grass grew
长着茴香草；	On the ridges of the Han people.
割来茴香草，	They cut some and brought it home,
把蚕放草上。	And put the silkworms on it.
属羊日吐丝，	The silkworms began to spin on the Day of the Sheep
蚕茧结成了。	And cocoons came into being.

大理铁锣锅，	The steel pans in Dali
昆明大铁锅，	And the big iron pans in Kunming
用来煮蚕茧。	Were used to boil the cocoons.
哪个来挑丝线？	Who would select the silk?

第二部　造物
Book Two　Creation

哪个来纺丝线？	Who would spin the silk threads?
剑川人用黄竹筷子挑蚕丝，	Jianchuan people reeled in the silk with chopsticks.
剑川人纺丝线。	And they also spun the silk threads.
蚕丝挑出来，	The silk was reeled in
丝线纺出来，	And silk thread was spun.
白茧纺出白丝线，	White cocoons made white thread.
红茧纺出红丝线，	Red cocoons made red thread.
黄茧纺出黄丝线，	Yellow cocoons made yellow thread.
各色丝线都纺好，	With the silk thread of all colors spun,
用它来绣花衣裳。	Splendid clothes were embroidered.

第三部 婚事和恋歌
Book Three   Marriage and Love Songs

梅葛 // Meige

一　相　配

Ⅰ. Matching

八月十五，
天王降下历书来，
汉族写字在书上，
四面八方都传到，
传遍各地方。

On the fifteenth day of August,
The king of the sky issued the almanac,
On which the Han people made the records of the life.
The almanac spread in all directions
To every corner of the world.

到了正月二十日，
汉家姑娘去背土，
男人拿土做春牛，
做出春牛是黄嘴，
做出春牛脚也黄，
做出春牛手也黄。

On the twentieth day of January,
The girls of the Han people fetched clay,
The men turned it into an ox,
With a yellow mouth,
Yellow back feet
And yellow forefeet.

正月二十五，
春牛做成了，
人人迎春牛，
抬着春牛闹哄哄，
芦笙吹一对，
唢呐吹一对，

On the twenty-fifth day,
The clay ox was completed.
Everybody was happy to see it.
They carried it through the street.
Two musicians played the gourd mouth organ.
Another two played the suona.

第三部　婚事和恋歌
Book Three　Marriage and Love Songs

笛子吹一对,	Still another two played the flute.
跳神匠来一对,	Two sorcerers danced around.
街头到街尾,	People welcomed the ox
吹吹唱唱迎春牛,	By singing and chanting.
春牛赶下河,	They drove it into the river.
从此春风吹起来。	The spring breeze began to blow from that time.
春风吹到河两岸,	When the spring breeze blows over the river,
河边柳树先发芽。	The willows germinate first.
吹到白樱桃树上,	When it touches the white cherry trees,
白樱桃树就发芽。	They start to sprout.
吹到松林里,	When it rushes through the pine woods,
松树就发芽。	They begin to bud.
吹到桃李梨树上,	When it passes by the peach, pear and plum trees,
桃李梨树就发芽。	They all begin to sprout.
吹到高山柏树上,	When it kisses the cypress trees,
柏树就发芽。	They show their tender buds.
吹到罗汉松树上,	When it rests on the yellowwood trees,
罗汉松树就发芽。	They start to germinate.
吹到草丛里,	When it blow over the grass,
百草就发芽。	All of them are budding.
没有不发芽的树,	All the trees germinate.
没有不发芽的草。	All the grass sprouts.
世间万物都发芽,	Everything in the world buds.

梅葛 // Meige

发芽要开花。	After that, they bloom.
八月十五到，	On the fifteenth day of August,
日月就开花。	The sun and the moon become full.
十冬腊月到，	When winter comes,
星星就开花。	The stars twinkle brighter.
六月七月到，	In June and July,
白云黑云朵朵开。	White clouds and black clouds get together.
正二三月到，	In January, February and March,
风吹百花开。	All flowers bloom in the spring breeze.
天花开来落地上，	When the flowers in the sky drop to the earth,
大山小山鲜花开，	The mountains are covered with flowers
河边坝子鲜花开，	The flatland near the river is full of flowers.
四面八方鲜花开。	There are flowers everywhere.

什么是树王？	Which tree is the king of trees?
白樱桃树是树王。	The white cherry tree.
白樱桃树开了花，	When its petals are blown
花瓣吹落刺树上，	Onto the thorn trees,
大小刺树鲜花开。	All of them start to bloom.
花蕊落在青松赤松上，	When their pistils fly onto the pines,
青松赤松开了花。	All the pines blossom.
落在柏枝梢梢上，	When they fall on the top of cypress branches,
柏枝梢梢也开花。	The branches are dotted with flowers.
落在香橄木树根根上，	When they fall onto the roots of olive trees,

第三部　婚事和恋歌
Book Three　Marriage and Love Songs

香橄木树也开花。	The olive trees blossom.
落在芭蕉上,	They fall on the banana trees,
芭蕉也开花。	Which blossom at once.
落在箐中水沟里,	They fall in the ditches in the valley,
水沟边上树开花。	The trees there bloom.
落在马缨花树上,	They fall on the lantana trees,
马缨花树也开花。	The lantana trees bloom.
落到坝区山腰里,	They fall on the hillside by the flatland,
花红梨树也开花。	The crab apple trees and the pear trees bloom.
吹到梧桐树上,	They fall on the plane trees,
梧桐树也开花。	These trees are in blossoms.
吹到河边两岸上,	When they fall on both banks of the river,
柳树也开花。	Flowers appear on the willows.
树木开完花。	Seeing all the trees in blossom,
草也想开花。	Grass also wants to bloom with flowers.
什么是草王?	Which one is the king of grass?
芦苇是草王。	It is the reeds.
芦苇先开花,	The reeds are the first to blossom.
花瓣吹到山中毒草根根上,	When their petals drift onto the roots
毒草就开花。	Of the poisonous herbs, they begin to bloom.
吹到山竹根根上,	When they drift onto the roots of the mangosteens,
大小山竹都开花。	All the mangosteens are in full bloom.
吹到河边艾草根,	When they drift onto the roots of the wormwood,

— 111 —

梅葛 // Meige

艾草也开花。	They are covered with flowers.
吹到黄麻上，	When they drift onto the ephedras,
黄麻也开花。	They blossom too.
没有不开花的树，	All the trees blossom.
没有不开花的草。	All the grass blooms.

一轮一十三，　　　　　One round includes thirteen days,
二轮二十六，　　　　　Two rounds, twenty-six days.
一个月开花，　　　　　The trees and grass bloom
一个月不开花。　　　　Every other month.
树开完了花，　　　　　The blossoming period of the trees
草开完了花；　　　　　And grass is over.
树木开的花落了，　　　The flowers of the trees wither away.
草儿开的花落了。　　　The flowers of the grass fall.

什么是兽王？　　　　　Which animal is the king of the animals?
兔子是兽王。　　　　　The rabbit.
兔子先开花，　　　　　Rabbits thrive first in spring.
吹到老虎老熊脊背上，　When their flowers drift onto the backs
老虎老熊也开花。　　　Of the tigers and the bears, they thrive, too.
吹到狐狸黄鼠狼头上，　When the flowers drift onto the heads
狐狸黄鼠狼也开花。　　Of the foxes and the weasels, they thrive.
吹到马鹿岩羊头顶上，　When the flowers drift onto the heads
马鹿岩羊也开花。　　　Of the red deer and the blue sheep, they thrive, too.

第三部　婚事和恋歌

Book Three　Marriage and Love Songs

吹到獐子麂子头顶上，	When the flowers drift onto the heads
獐子麂子也开花。	Of the river deer and the muntjacs, they thrive, too.
吹到松鼠头顶上，	When the flowers drift onto the heads
松鼠也开花。	Of the squirrels, they thrive, too.
吹到河头鱼窝里，	When the flowers fall into the fish nest in the river,
鱼也开了花。	The fish also thrive.
吹到石蚌头顶上，	When the flowers drop on the heads
石蚌也开花。	Of the star snappers, they also thrive.
没有不开花的兽，	All the animals thrive.
没有不开花的鸟。	All the birds thrive.
什么是鸟王？	Which bird is the king of the birds?
凤凰是鸟王。	The phoenix.
凤凰先开花，	The phoenix that grow up first.
吹到大雁头顶上，	When the spring breeze blows over the heads
大雁就开花。	Of the wild geese, they grow up soon.
吹到岩鸡头顶上，	When the spring breeze blows over the heads
岩鸡也开花。	Of the rock chickens, they grow up, too.
吹到老鸹喜鹊头顶上，	When the spring breeze blows over the heads
老鸹喜鹊也开花。	Of the crows and the magpies, they grow up.
吹到斑鸠头顶上，	When the spring breeze blows over the heads
斑鸠也开花。	Of the turtle doves, they begin to grow up.
吹到啄木鸟头上，	When the spring breeze blows over the heads
啄木鸟也开花。	Of the woodpeckers, they begin to grow up, too.

— 113 —

梅葛 // Meige

吹到布谷鸟头上,	When the spring breeze blows over the heads
布谷鸟也开花。	Of the cuckoos, they begin to grow up, too.
吹李桂秧到头上,	When the spring breeze blows over the heads
李桂秧也开花。	Of the liguiyang birds, they begin to grow up, too.
没有不开花的鸟。	All the birds grow up.
家禽耕畜要开花。	The poultry and the farm animals also want the growth.
春风吹到骡马头顶上,	When the spring breeze blows over the heads
骡子和马都开花。	Of the mules and the horses, they grow stronger.
吹到水牛头顶上,	When the spring breeze blows over the heads
水牛也开花。	Of the water buffalos, they grow stronger soon.
吹到绵羊山羊头顶上,	When the spring breeze blows over the heads
绵羊山羊也开花。	Of the sheep and the goats, they grow bigger, too.
吹到公鸡母鸡头顶上,	When the spring breeze blows over the heads
公鸡母鸡也开花。	Of the roosters and the hens, they grow bigger.
吹到鹅鸭头顶上,	When the spring breeze blows over the heads
鹅鸭也开花。	Of the geese and the ducks, they grow bigger, too.
吹到门外狗头上,	When the spring breeze blows over the heads
狗也开了花。	Of the dogs outside the door, they grow up quickly.
吹到屋里猫头上,	When the spring breeze blows over the heads
猫也开了花。	Of the cats inside the house, they begin to grow up.
没有不开花的耕畜,	All the farm animals grow stronger.
没有不开花的家禽。	All the poultry grows bigger.

第三部　婚事和恋歌
Book Three　Marriage and Love Songs

树开花了，	The trees blossom.
草也开花了，	The grass blossoms.
百兽开花了，	The animals thrive.
百鸟也开花了，	The birds grow up.
家禽开花了，	The poultry grows bigger,
耕畜也开花了，	The farm animals grow stronger.
没有不开花的草木，	There are no trees or grass that does not blossom.
没有不开花的鸟兽。	There are no birds or animals that do not thrive.
草木鸟兽开完花，	When their growing period is over,
人类忙着把花开。	Mankind hurries to develop.
春风吹到傣族头顶上，	When the spring breeze touches the heads
傣族也开花。	Of the Dai people, they begin to develop.
吹到高山彝族头顶上，	When it touches the heads of the Yi people
彝族也开花。	On the high mountains, they develop.
吹到坝子里的汉族头顶上，	When it touches the heads of the Han people
汉族也开花。	In the flatlands, they begin to develop.
吹到回族头顶上，	When it touches the heads of the Hui people,
回族也开花。	They develop, too.
吹到赶毡匠头上，	When it touches the heads of the felt makers,
赶毡的人也开花。	They develop, too.
吹到高山庙里和尚头顶上，	When it touches the heads of the monks
和尚也开花。	In the temples, they all develop.

梅葛 // Meige

百草百木都开花，	All the trees and grass bloom.
百鸟百兽都开花，	All the birds and animals thrive.
世人都开花，	All the people in the world develop.
开花结果要相配。	After growing mature, matching is needed to bear fruits.
八月十五到，	On the fifteenth day of August,
日月就相配；	The sun and the moon become a couple.
吃了什么来相配？	What do they eat before that?
吃了金玉珠宝来相配。	Gold, jade and pearls.
十冬腊月到，	When winter months come,
大星小星配；	Big stars marry little stars.
吃了什么东西来相配？	What do they eat before that?
吃了寒霜露水来相配。	Frost and dew.
六月七月天，	In June and July,
白云黑云来相配。	White clouds marry black ones.
正二三月到，	In January, February and March,
春风空气来相配。	The spring breeze marries the air.
天要地来配，	The sky marries the earth,
地要树来配。	And the earth marries trees.
天上吹来一阵风，	A gust of wind blows from the sky
吹到河当中，	To the surface of the river.
风和水波配。	Then the wind and the waves get married.
河配岩来岩配石，	Rivers marry cliffs and cliffs marry rocks.
岩石又和树相配。	Rocks are married to trees.

第三部　婚事和恋歌
Book Three　Marriage and Love Songs

柿树梨树两相配，	The persimmon trees marry the pear trees,
罗汉松和大风配。	And the yellowwood trees marry the gale.
什么是兽王？	Which animal is the king of animals?
兔子是兽王。	The rabbit.
兔子吃了什么来相配？	What do rabbits eat before they marry?
吃了小麦来相配，	Wheat.
什么兽力气最大？	Which animal is the strongest?
老虎力气最大。	The tiger.
老虎吃了什么来相配？	What do tigers eat before they marry?
吃了小兽来相配。	Small animals.
豺狼吃了什么来相配？	What do jackals eat before they marry?
吃了羊子来相配。	Sheep.
黄鼠狼吃了什么来相配？	What do weasels eat before they marry?
吃了蜂子来相配。	Bees.
岩羊吃了什么来相配？	What do blue sheep eat before they marry?
吃了岩草来相配。	Rock grass.
野猪要相配，	The wild boars will get married
拱地吃树根来相配。	After digging and eating tree roots.
大熊小熊来相配，	The big bears marry the small ones
吃了苦葛根来相配。	After eating the roots of the bitter kudzu vines.
没有不相配的兽，	There are no animals that do not marry.
就连地上的蚂蚁都相配。	Even the ants on the ground get married.

梅葛 // Meige

什么是鸟王？	Which bird is the king of the birds?
凤凰是鸟王。	The phoenix.
凤凰要相配，	The phoenixes will get married.
吃了什么来相配？	What do they eat before that?
吃了小虫来相配。	Little worms.
大雁吃了什么便相配？	What do the wild geese eat before they marry?
吃了坝子里的黄谷便相配。	The yellow corn in the flatland.
老鹰吃了什么便相配？	What do eagles eat before they marry?
吃了蚂蚁竹鸡便相配。	Ants and bamboo partridges.
斑鸠吃了什么就相配？	What do turtledoves eat before they marry?
吃了樱桃果子就相配。	Cherries and fruits.
麻雀要相配，	The sparrows will be married
吃了谷子来相配。	After eating corn.
没有不相配的鸟。	There are no birds that do not get married.
虫虫也相配，	The worms get married, too.
先是蚂蚁配；	The ants are the first to marry.
蚂蚁吃了什么来相配？	What do they eat before they get married?
吃了粮食来相配。	Grain.
蚯蚓来相配，	The earthworms get married.
吃了什么来相配？	What do they eat before that?
吃了泥土来相配。	Mud.
大蛇来相配，	The snakes get married.
吃了什么来相配？	What do they eat before that?

第三部　婚事和恋歌
Book Three　Marriage and Love Songs

吃了蚯蚓来相配。	Earthworms.
蜜蜂吃了什么配？	What do the bees eat before they marry?
吃了花蕊来相配。	Pistils.
没有不相配的树木花草，	There are no plants that do not marry.
没有不相配的鸟兽鱼虫，	There are no animals that do not get married.
没有不相配的人；	There are no people that do not get married.
样样东西都相配，	All the things in the world marry
地上的东西才不绝。	So that they will not go extinct.
天有天的规：	There are rules in the sky:
白云嫁黑云；	White clouds marry black ones,
月亮嫁太阳；	The moon is married to the sun.
天嫁给地；	The sky is married to the earth.
男女相配，	Men and women should get married
人间才成对。	So that people become couples in the world.

二　说　亲

II. Marriage Proposal

男：
我家里没有女，
我家里没有花；
我的心里急，
我的心里慌；

Man:
No girl in my home,
No flower in my home,
I feel anxious,
I feel flustered.

梅葛 // Meige

要向你家讨个女，
要向你家要朵花，
请你答应给我家。

女：
你家没有女，
你家没有花；
要向我家讨，
要女又要花；
请你别处找，
请你别家讨；
我家没有女，
我家没有花。

男：
你一定说没有女，
你一定说没有花，
这么说起来，
我的心里慌。
怎么没有女？
怎么没有花？
我家小花猫，
去你家偷肉吃，
小花猫看见了，

Could you marry your daughter to me?
Could you give your flower to me?
Please promise me.

Woman:
No girl in your home,
No flower in your home,
You ask me
For my daughter and flower.
Please go somewhere else,
Please ask someone else.
I don't have a daughter,
I don't have a flower.

Man:
You insist that you do not have a daughter,
You insist that you do not have a flower.
Hearing what you said,
I feel flustered.
How could you have no daughter?
How could you have no flower?
My little spotted cat
Went to your house to steal meat,
He saw that

第三部　婚事和恋歌
Book Three　Marriage and Love Songs

你家有个女，	There is a girl in your house,
你家有朵花。	There is a flower in your house.
我家小黑狗，	My little black dog
舔你家姑娘的围裙，	Licked your girl's apron,
小黑狗也看见了，	He saw that
你家有个女，	There is a girl in your house,
你家有朵花。	There is a flower in your house.
你家小姑娘，	Your little girl
一定给我家。	Must be married to me.

女： **Woman:**

你一定要向我家讨女，	You insist on asking me for a girl.
你一定要向我家要花；	You insist on asking me for a flower.
我家没有女，	No girl in my home.
我家没有花。	No flower in my home.
你家小花猫，	Your little spotted cat
只会偷肉吃，	Can only steal meat.
它不会说话，	He cannot speak,
它没有看见女，	He did not see any girl.
它没有看见花。	He did not see any flower.
你家小黑狗，	Your little black dog,
只会舔围裙，	Can only lick an apron.
它也不会说话，	He cannot speak, either.
它没有看见女，	He did not see any girl.

- 121 -

梅葛 // Meige

它没有看见花。
我家没有女，
我家没有花，
请你别村去讨女，
请你别村去要花。

男：
你说你家没有女，
你说你家没有花？
三个葫芦蜂，
来到你家采露水，
看见你家有朵花。
三窝小蜜蜂，
飞到你家来采花，
看见你家有个小姑娘。
你家有女又有花，
请你答应给我家。

女：
你说三窝小蜜蜂，
看见我家有个小姑娘？
你说三个葫芦蜂，
见着我家有朵花？

He did not see any flower.
No girl in my home,
No flower in my home.
Please go to other villages to look for a girl,
Please go to other villages to ask for a flower.

Man:
You said you didn't have a daughter in your home,
You said you didn't have a flower in your home?
Three wasps
Came to your home to drink dew.
They saw a flower in your home.
Three swarms of bees
Flew to your house to gather honey.
They saw a girl in your home.
You have a daughter and a flower.
Please let me marry your daughter and give me your flower.

Woman:
You said three swarms of bees
Saw a girl in my home?
You said three wasps
Saw a flower in my home?

Book Three　Marriage and Love Songs

它们是来采露水，	They came to drink dew.
它们是来采花，	They came to gather honey.
它们说的不是实话。	What they told you is not true.
我家没有小姑娘，	I do not have a girl in my home.
我家没有花。	I do not have a flower in my home.
处处是村子，	There are so many villages.
请你别家去找花。	Please find your flower elsewhere.

男：　　**Man:**

你家躲着女，	You hide your daughter.
你家藏着花。	You conceal your flower.
江西货郎哥，	The Jiangxi street vendor
卖针卖线到你家，	Sold you needles and thread,
你家小姑娘，	Your little daughter,
爱针又爱线。	Loves needles and thread.
货郎看见了，	The street vendor saw her.
货郎跟我说，	The street vendor told me,
货郎跟我讲，	The street vendor informed me,
你家有个小姑娘。	You have a girl in your home.
躲也躲不住，	It's useless to hide her.
藏也藏不住，	It's useless to conceal her.
你家小姑娘，	Your little daughter
一定给我家。	Must be married to me.

梅葛 // Meige

女：
你说得我心欢，
你说得我心乐。
我家有个女，
我家有朵花。
货郎来我家，
我家小姑娘，
爱针又爱线，
实在买了针，
实在买了线。
躲也躲不住，
藏也藏不住。
不给不好说，
我就答应给你家。

天上有云才下雨，
地下有媒才成亲，
要请媒人来，
上门来说亲。

男：
姑娘给我家，
你家奶奶答应了，
你家老爹答应了，

Woman:
What you said gives me joy,
What you said makes me happy.
I have a daughter in my home.
I have a flower in my home.
The street vendor came to my house.
My little daughter
Loves needles and thread.
She did buy some needles,
She did buy some thread.
It's useless to hide her.
It's useless to conceal her.
It's hard to say no.
I promise you.

There is no rain without clouds.
There is no marriage without a matchmaker.
You have to send a matchmaker here,
To request my daughter's hand.

Man:
If marrying your daughter to me
Is agreed to by your grandma,
And by your grandpa,

第三部　婚事和恋歌
Book Three　Marriage and Love Songs

明天就去找媒人，
请媒来说亲。

I will send a matchmaker here tomorrow
To make the request.

女：
古时哪个先成亲？
哪个最先做媒人？
哪个跟着学媒人？

Woman:
Who was the first to get married in ancient times?
Who was the first to make a match?
Who learned from the first matchmaker?

男：
张仕、白花先成亲，
梅树李树先做媒，
媒人向它学，
学它做媒人。

Man:
Zhang Shi and Bai Hua were the first to get married.
Plum trees were the first to make a match.
Matchmakers learned from them,
Learned to be a matchmaker.

女：
哪个月来说亲？
哪一天来说亲？
什么时候媒人到我家？

Woman:
In which month are you going to propose?
On which day are you going to propose?
When will the matchmaker come to my home?

男：
正月是头月，
初二日子好，
我请媒人来，
正月初三到你家。

Man:
January is the first month of the year.
The second day of January is a good day.
I will send a matchmaker then,
Who will arrive on the third day.

梅葛 // Meige

女：
说亲日子订好了，
哪月吃定酒？
哪日讨红庚？

Woman:
The day to propose is set,
When shall we hold the engagement feast?
When will you send the matchmaker to ask for my girl's birth date?

男：
二月初八日，
双月双日日子好，
讨红庚就在那一天。

Man:
February eighth is a good day,
With two even numbers.
I'll send the matchmaker on that day.

女：
拿什么来讨红庚？
你要说给我。

Woman:
What will you bring on that day?
You have to tell me.

男：
背着草烟来讨红庚，
背着猪膀来讨红庚，
背着定酒来讨红庚。

Man:
I will bring tobacco shreds,
I will bring pork trotters,
I will bring engagement wine.

女：
定酒背来了，

Woman:
When you come with the wine,

第三部　婚事和恋歌
Book Three   Marriage and Love Songs

要请哪些人？	Who shall we invite?

男：
外公请来，
外婆请来，
舅舅请来，
舅妈请来，
姨妈请来，
姑爹请来，
奶奶请来，
老爹请来，
族中老小都请来。

Man:
We shall invite maternal grandpa,
We shall invite maternal grandma,
We shall invite uncles,
We shall invite their wives,
We shall invite mother's sisters,
We shall invite aunts' husbands,
We shall invite paternal grandma,
We shall invite paternal grandpa,
We shall invite both the old and the young.

客人请来了，
定酒吃过了，
我家一时讨不起，
说不定要等三年，
说不定要等五年。

Guests are invited.
The engagement feast is held.
But we cannot afford a wedding right now.
We have to wait for three years,
Maybe even five.

女：
我家小姑娘，
一天一天长大了，
心也大起来了，
你家不讨不行了，

Woman:
My little girl
Grows up day by day.
Her ambition is growing too.
You have to marry her now,

梅葛 // Meige

我家不嫁不行了。
择个好日子，
你家快快讨。

男：
大年初二日子好，
讨亲就在那天讨。

女：
大年初二日子好，
是走亲戚的日子，
不是讨亲的日子。

男：
二月初九日子好，
讨亲就在那天讨。

女：
二月初九日子好，
是平民百姓串会的日子，
不是讨亲的日子。

男：
三月二十八，

She has to marry you now.
Choose a good day,
Get married as soon as you can.

Man:
The second day of the New Year is good.
The wedding will be on that day.

Woman:
The second day of the New Year is good
For visiting relatives,
Not for getting married.

Man:
The ninth day of February is good.
The wedding will be on that day.

Woman:
The ninth day of February is good
For folks to get together,
Not for getting married.

Man:
The twenty-eighth day of March

第三部　婚事和恋歌

Book Three   Marriage and Love Songs

讨亲就是那天好。 | Is a good day to get married.

女：
三月二十八，
是牟定城里赶街日，
不是讨亲的日子。

Woman:
The twenty-eighth day of March
Is the market-day in Mouding town,
Not good for getting married.

男：
好不过四月初八那一天，
讨亲就在那天讨。

Man:
The eighth day of April is
The best day to get married.

女：
四月初八那一天，
是大官小吏科考日，
不是讨亲的日子。

Woman:
The eighth day of April is
The day for the imperial examinations,
Not good for getting married.

男：
五月初五日子好，
讨亲就在那天讨。

Man:
The fifth day of May is a good day,
A good day to get married.

女：
五月初五日子好，
是药王菩萨的生日，
不是讨亲的日子。

Woman:
The fifth day of May is a good day.
It's the birthday of Medicine King Bodhisattva,
Not good for getting married.

- 129 -

梅葛 // Meige

男：
好不过六月二十四，
讨亲就在那天讨。

女：
六月二十四虽然好，
是给田公地母烧香的日子，
不是讨亲的日子。

男：
七月十四日子好，
讨亲就在那天讨。

女：
七月十四日子好，
那天晚上要送祖，
不是讨亲的日子。

男：
好不过八月十五那一天，
讨亲就是那天好。

Man:
The twenty-fourth day of June is
The best day to get married.

Woman:
The twenty-fourth day of June is good
For burning incense to the Earth God and Goddess,
Not good for getting married.

Man:
The fourteenth day of July is a good day,
A good day to get married.

Woman:
The fourteenth day of July is good
For sacrificial practices,
Not for getting married.

Man:
The fifteenth day of August is the best day,
The best day to get married.

第三部　婚事和恋歌

Book Three　Marriage and Love Songs

女：
八月十五好倒好，
是月亮和太阳相遇的日子，
不是讨亲的日子。

Woman:
The fifteenth day of August is good
For the moon and the sun to meet,
But not good for getting married.

男：
九月初九日子好，
讨亲就在那天讨。

Man:
The ninth day of September is a good day,
A good day to get married.

女：
九月初九日子好，
是九星大会日，
不是讨亲的日子。

Woman:
The ninth day of September is good
For the nine stars to assemble,
But not good for getting married.

男：
冬月头十天，
冬至那天好。

Man:
Of the first ten days of November,
The winter solstice is a good day to get married.

女：
冬至日子好倒好，
那是皇帝老倌过年日，
大官小吏过节日，
不是讨亲的日子。

Woman:
The winter solstice is good.
It is the emperor's New Year's Day,
And the holiday for court officials,
Not good for getting married.

- 131 -

梅葛 // Meige

男：
一年十二月，
腊月那月好。
一月三十天，
初八那天好。
腊月腊八日子到，
我家就来讨。

女：
腊月腊八日子好，
我家喜欢了，
我家答应了。

男：
日子择定了，
高山砍树枝，
搭起棚子来，
杀猪又宰羊，
酒席办起来。
四方客人都请到，
花衣花裙穿出来。
芦笙吹得响，
唢呐吹得响，
吹吹打打讨媳妇。

Man:
There are twelve months in a year.
The twelfth is the best.
There are thirty days in a month.
The eighth is the best.
On the eighth day of December
We will hold the wedding ceremony.

Woman:
The eighth day of December is good.
My family like that day.
Let's make it a deal.

Man:
The date is selected.
Trees will be cut down.
A shed will be put up.
Pigs and sheep will be butchered.
A feast will be prepared.
Guests from far and wide will be invited,
All will be dressed up.
Some will blow loud the gourd mouth organ,
Others will blow loud the suona,
I am getting married to the sound of music.

第三部　婚事和恋歌
Book Three　Marriage and Love Songs

女：
我家没吃的，
我家没穿的，
没吃没穿怎么嫁？

男：
我家喂的三年大肥猪，
养的七年老绵羊；
肥猪宰一个，
绵羊拉一双，
好酒挑两罐，
新布拿三件，
环子打一双，
再挑一个小盒子。
挑进你家门，
亲亲热热送你家。

女：
酒罐哪里歇？
小盒哪里放？
羊子哪里拴？

Woman:
We have nothing to eat.
We have nothing to wear.
How can our girl get married like this?

Man:
There's a three-year-old fat hog in my home.
There's a seven-year-old sheep in my home.
I will slaughter the pig.
I will select two sheep,
Pick two jars of good wine
And three pieces of new cloth,
Make a pair of earrings,
Choose a small box,
Carry them all to your house,
As betrothal gifts.

Woman:
Where to put the jars?
Where to put the box?
Where to tie the sheep?

梅葛 // Meige

男：
你家厦子下，
四方桌子摆起来，
小盒放中间，
两个酒罐摆两边，
你家厦子下，
绵羊拴在柱子上。

女：
摆也摆好了，
拴也拴好了，
我要问问你，
小盒哪个做？
酒罐哪里来？

男：
剑川木匠做小盒，
用楸木板做，
做得真是好；
直山直台人做酒罐，
用黄泥白泥做，
做得实在好。

Man:
Under your roof,
Square tables will be set up,
The small box put in the middle,
The two jars placed on both sides.
Under your roof,
The sheep will be tied to the pillar.

Woman:
That's a good idea,
I must say.
But I have to ask you,
Who will make the box?
Where will you get the jars?

Man:
Jianchuan carpenters
Make fine small boxes
With catalpa wood.
The Zhitai people of Zhishan
Make very good jars
With yellow and white mud.

第三部　婚事和恋歌
Book Three　Marriage and Love Songs

女：

小盒里头装什么？

酒罐里头装什么？

什么绳子拴小盒？

什么绳子拴酒罐？

男：

小盒里头装着老肥肉，

酒罐里头装着好烧酒；

红色丝线拴小盒，

红色丝线拴酒罐。

女：

小盒拴好了，

酒罐拴好了，

拴得又稳当，

拴得又好看。

哪个开小盒？

哪个开酒罐？

男：

舅舅开小盒，

开出肥肉来待客。

外公外婆开酒罐，

Woman:

What is in the box?

What is in the jars?

What rope is used to tie the box?

What rope is used to tie the jars?

Man:

The box is filled with fat meat,

The jars are filled with good wine.

Red silk ribbon is used to bundle the box,

Red silk ribbon is used to bundle the jars.

Woman:

The box is bundled up,

The jars are bundled up.

They are safe and secure,

They are nice and pretty.

Who will open the box?

Who will open the jars?

Man:

Uncle will open the box and

Take out the meat to treat our guests.

Grandparents will open the jars,

梅葛 // Meige

外公开左边，
外婆开右边，
开出烧酒来待客。

女：
肉已开出来，
酒已开出来，
待客怎样待？
请你说给我。

男：
桌子摆起来，
碗筷拿出来，
酒酒肉肉摆出来，
小菜端出来。
待客这样待，
恭恭敬敬地待。
客已待好了，
姑娘走得了。

女：
我家新姑娘，
头上没包的，
身上没穿的，

Grandpa from the left,
Grandma from the right,
Pouring out the wine to treat our guests.

Woman:
The meat box is opened,
The wine jars are uncapped,
How do we treat our guests?
Please tell me.

Man:
Tables will be set up,
Tableware will be placed,
Wine and meat are laid out,
Accompanied by other dishes.
This is the way to treat our guests,
With sincerity and respect.
After the guests are treated,
It's time for your girl to go with us.

Woman:
My daughter the bride,
She has no headscarf,
She has no clothes,

第三部　婚事和恋歌
Book Three　Marriage and Love Songs

脚上没穿的，	She has no shoes,
手上没戴的，	She has no jewelry,
没穿没戴怎出嫁？	How can our girl get married like this?

男： **Man:**

头上没包的，　　　　She has no headscarf.
给她青色包头布。　　I'll give her a blue one.
身上没穿的，　　　　She has no clothes.
给她新衣裳。　　　　I'll give her new clothes.
脚上没穿的，　　　　She has no shoes.
给她新花鞋。　　　　I'll give her new shoes.
手上没戴的，　　　　She has no jewelry.
金银手镯给她戴。　　I'll give her gold and silver bracelets.

女： **Woman:**

青色包头布，　　　　With the blue headscarf,
包得真好看。　　　　She looks pretty.
脚上新花鞋，　　　　With the new shoes,
穿起也好看。　　　　She looks lovely.
还要问问你：　　　　I have to ask you:
新衣哪里来？　　　　Where do the clothes come from?

男： **Man:**

剑川人抽蚕丝，　　　Jianchuan people unravel raw silk from cocoons.

- 137 -

梅葛 // Meige

剑川人纺丝线, Jianchuan people spin the silk into thread.
丝线织绸缎, Threads are woven into silk fabric.
新衣做出来。 Clothes are made of silk fabric.

女： **Woman:**
蚕丝抽好了, Silk is unraveled.
丝线纺好了, Threads are spun up.
什么马来驮？ What horse will carry the threads?
驮到哪里歇？ Where will the horse stop for a break?

男： **Man:**
枣骝花马驮丝线, A skewbald horse will carry the threads.
花脚骡子驮丝线 A variegated-feet mule will carry the threads.
驮到昆明城, When they arrive in Kunming city,
城里歇两驮, They take two breaks inside the city,
城外歇两驮, Two more outside the city,
城正中间歇两驮。 And still another two in the middle of the city.

女： **Woman:**
丝线驮来了, Now that the silk is here,
驮来可要织？ Shall we weave it into cloth?
要织又在哪里织？ Where shall we do the weaving?

第三部　婚事和恋歌
Book Three　Marriage and Love Songs

男：
昆明城里街子上，
三层楼上头，
红栗、麻栗做机床，
牛角做梭子，
黄竹做扣子，
织布就在那里织。

女：
织去又织来，
织成什么布？

男：
织去织来织成龙布，
织去织来织成蛇布；
织去织来织成绸子，
织去织来织成缎子；
织成绸缎做新衣，
新衣送给新娘穿。

女：
你说织成龙布，
你说织成蛇布；
那是九皇大会上，

Man:
In the street of Kunming city,
On the third floor of a building,
Red chestnut and teakwood are used as the frame,
Ox horns are used as the shuttle,
Whangee is used to make buttons.
That is where we do the weaving.

Woman:
Knitting and weaving,
What cloth shall we expect?

Man:
The thread is woven into dragon-patterned cloth.
The thread is woven into snake-patterned cloth.
The thread is woven into silk fabric.
The thread is woven into satin.
The silk fabric and satin are made into
New clothes for the bride to wear.

Woman:
You said weaving dragon-patterned cloth.
You said weaving snake-patterned cloth.
But they are what the god of fire wears

梅葛 // Meige

火神大将穿的衣，On the Nine Chieftains' conference,
不是新娘穿的衣。Not what bride wears at the wedding.
你说织成绸子，You said weaving silk fabric.
你说织成缎子，You said weaving satin.
那是大官小吏穿的衣，But they are for court officials,
不是新娘穿的衣。Not for the bride.
实实说给你：Let me tell you:
新娘穿的棉布衣。The bride wears cotton clothes.
棉籽出在哪一点？Where do the cottonseeds come from?
请你说给我。Please tell me.

男： **Man:**
耿马制定山，On Zhiding Mountain in Gengma,
有三个竹筒，There are three bamboo tubes.
竹筒里面装棉籽，In the tubes are cottonseeds,
棉籽就从那里来。That is where cottonseeds come from.

女： **Woman:**
花籽找着了，The seeds are found,
拿来哪里撒？But where will you sow them?

男： **Man:**
耿马制定山，On Zhiding Mountain in Gengma,
有三丘板田，There are three mud fields,

第三部　婚事和恋歌
Book Three　Marriage and Love Songs

有三丘蒿子地，
那就是撒花的田，
那就是种花的地。

And three sargassum fields.
That is where we will sow the seeds.
That is where we plant cotton.

女：
撒花田有了，
种花地有了，
没有撒花人，
没有种花人。

Woman:
Now there is the field to sow the seeds
And the field to plant cotton.
But there is nobody to sow the seeds.
There is nobody to plant cotton.

男：
傣族人三个，
阿卡人三个，
就是撒花人，
就是种花人。

Man:
Three Dai people and
Three Aka people.
They will sow the seeds,
They will plant cotton.

女：
撒花人有了，
种花人有了，
什么节令撒花？
什么节令种花？

Woman:
Now we have seeds sowers
And cotton planters.
When to sow the seeds?
When to plant cotton?

男：
惊蛰撒头花，

Man:
Awakening of Insects is the day to sow the first batch of

梅葛 // Meige

清明撒二花，
立夏撒尾花。

seeds,
Tomb-Sweeping Day is the day to sow the second batch of seeds,
Beginning of Summer is the day to sow the last batch of seeds.

女：
春雨下三阵，
花籽出齐了。
什么人薅花？
什么人铲花？

Woman:
After three spring rains,
All seeds will sprout.
Who will weed the fields?
Who will loosen the soil?

男：
傣族小姑娘，
拿着锄头来薅花，
拿着锄头来铲花。
薅也薅得好，
铲也铲得好。
秋雨下三阵，
花就长大了。

Man:
Dai girls are the ones
To weed the fields with hoes,
To loosen the soil with hoes.
They are good at weeding the fields,
They are good at loosening the soil.
After three autumn rains,
Cotton will be grown up.

女：
哪月来采花？
哪日来采花？

Woman:
In which month will the cotton be picked?
On which day will the cotton be picked?

第三部　婚事和恋歌
Book Three　Marriage and Love Songs

哪个来采花？
用什么东西来装花？

Who will pick the cotton?
What container will be used to hold the cotton?

男：
九月霜降后，
就可采棉花；
傣族小姑娘，
采花就是她。
手里捏不下，
围腰里面兜，
围腰里面兜不下，
装在麻布口袋里头。

Man:
After Frost's Descent in September,
Cotton is ready to be picked.
Dai girls are the ones
To pick cotton.
When their hands are full,
They put the cotton into their aprons.
When their aprons are full,
They put it into gunnysacks.

女：
棉花拿到家，
什么地点来晒花？

Woman:
When the cotton is brought home,
Where shall we dry it?

男：
房前屋后稻场上，
就是晒花的好地方。

Man:
The rice fields around the house
Are good places to dry the cotton.

女：
花也晒干了，
花也晒好了，

Woman:
When the cotton is dried,
Dried completely,

- 143 -

梅葛 // Meige

花籽怎样隔? | How shall we separate the seeds?

男:
编起黄竹大揽筛,
花籽一隔就隔开。

Man:
You can weave a big sieve with whangee,
And separate the seeds easily.

女:
哪个来踩花?
哪个来称花?
哪个来装花?

Woman:
Who will tread the cotton?
Who will weigh the cotton?
Who will pack the cotton?

男:
傣族小姑娘来踩花,
傣族小伙子称花又装花。
满担一百二,
平担九十六,
棉花称好了,
麻布口袋装。

Man:
Dai girls will tread the cotton,
Dai boys will weigh and pack it.
Two full crates weigh 60 kilograms,
Two half-full crates weigh 48 kilograms.
When the cotton is weighed,
You put it into gunnysacks.

女:
装也装好了,
什么马来驮?

Woman:
When the cotton is put into gunny bags,
What horse will carry them?

第三部　婚事和恋歌
Book Three　Marriage and Love Songs

男：

枣骝滚蹄马，
紫毛玉顶马，
就是驮花马。

Man:

Skewbald horses with horseshoes and
Purple horses with beige head-hairs
Are the ones to carry cotton bags.

女：

枣骝滚蹄马，
紫毛玉顶马，
是没兴头的马，
不是驮花马。

Woman:

Skewbald horses with horseshoes and
Purple horses with beige head-hairs
Are horses with short tempers,
Not suitable for carrying cotton bags.

男：

骡马枣骝马，
就是驮花马。

Man:

Mules and skewbald horses
Are both suitable for carrying cotton bags.

女：

骡马枣骝马，
是盘田种地收五谷的马，
不是驮花马。

Woman:

Mules and skewbald horses
Are used for plowing and harvesting,
Not suitable for carrying cotton bags.

男：

小疙瘩骡子，
就是驮花马。

Man:

Small mules are
Suitable for carrying cotton bags.

梅葛 // Meige

女：
小疙瘩骡子，
是驮铜铁的马，
不是驮花马。

Woman:
Small mules are
Used to carry copper and iron,
Not cotton bags.

男：
骡子四脚白，
骡子玉尾花，
身子就像花，
就是驮花马。
过街过得去，
驮到哪里都不费力气。

Man:
Mules have white hoofs.
Mules have beige tails.
Their bodies look like cotton.
They are best for carrying cotton bags.
They can cross the street and
Easily carry the bags anywhere.

女：
驮花可过街？
驮花可过关？
过街过关怎么过？

Woman:
Can they cross the street?
Can they cross the pass?
But how?

男：
驮花要过街，
驮花要过关，
走过城里街，
骡子歇在街子上，
收税人走过来，

Man:
Carrying cotton across the street,
Carrying cotton over the pass,
They take down the mule's load
To have a rest in the street.
The tax collector comes over,

第三部　婚事和恋歌
Book Three　Marriage and Love Songs

大印盖三颗，	Printing three stamps
托子盖三颗；	Affixing three seals.
过街这样过，	This is how they cross the street,
过关这样过。	This is how they go over the pass.

女：
哪个先买花？
请你说给我。

Woman:
Who will be the first to buy the cotton?
Please tell me.

男：
三个白族小姑娘，
戥子插在腰带上，
她们先买花。

Man:
Three Bai girls, with steelyard balance
Inserted in their belts,
Will be the first to buy the cotton.

女：
买花买得了，
什么人弹花？
什么人纺花？
什么人纺线？
什么人织布？
请你说给我。

Woman:
They buy the cotton,
But who will fluff the cotton?
Who will spin the cotton?
Who will spin them into threads?
Who will weave the threads into cloth?
Please tell me.

男：
白族小伙子，

Man:
The Bai boys are

- 147 -

梅葛 // Meige

他们会弹花；
白族小姑娘，
她们会织布。

Good at fluffing cotton.
The Bai girls are
Good at weaving cloth.

女：
织布要机床，
什么材料做机床？
什么手艺做机床？

Woman:
They need a machine to weave.
What materials are used to make the machine?
What skills are needed to make the machine?

男：
织布要机床，
红栗麻栗做机床，
青冈栎树做床柱，
牛角做梭子，
黄竹做扣子。
张班鲁班做机床，
张班鲁班做纺架。

Man:
They need a machine to weave.
Red chestnut and teakwood are used to make a machine.
Oriental white oak is used as posts,
Ox horns are used to make shuttles,
Whangee is used to make buttons.
Young carpenters make a machine.
Young carpenters make spinning wheels.

女：
织去又织来，
织成什么布？

Woman:
Knitting and weaving,
What cloth will be produced?

男：
织织来织成红布蓝布，

Man:
Red and blue cloth.

第三部　婚事和恋歌
Book Three　Marriage and Love Songs

织织来织成青布黄布。　　　　Green and yellow cloth.

女：
大件有多长？
小件有多长？

Woman:
How long are the large pieces?
How long are the small pieces?

男：
大件四丈八，
小件二丈四。

Man:
The large pieces are fifty feet long.
The small pieces are twenty-five feet long.

女：
大件小件织出来，
各种颜色都齐全，
新娘穿的倒有了；
金银首饰哪里来？
金银哪里出？
请你说给我。

Woman:
Large and small pieces are woven
In various colors.
Now the bride has clothes to wear.
But where is the gold and silver jewelry?
Where will the gold and silver jewelry come from?
Please tell me.

男：
金子出在金沙江，
银子出在银沙江。

Man:
The gold is from Gold-Sand River.
The silver is from Silver-Sand River.

女：
哪个先晓得？

Woman:
Who were the first to find them?

梅葛 // Meige

请你说给我。

Please tell me.

男：
湖广三女子，
金银她们先晓得。

Man:
Three women from Huguang
Were the first to find the gold and silver.

女：
湖广三女子，
她们怎样晓得的？

Woman:
Three women from Huguang,
How did they find the gold and silver?

男：
湖广女子养鹅，
湖广女子养鸭，
鹅鸭吆到金江银江去，
鸭用黄嘴拣金子，
鹅用白嘴拣银子。

Man:
The three women raise geese.
The three women raise ducks.
They drive them into the two rivers.
Ducks pick gold with their yellow beaks,
Geese pick silver with their white beaks.

女：
什么是装金子的袋？
什么是装银子的袋？

Woman:
What bags will be used to hold the gold?
What bags will be used to contain the silver?

男：
鸭嗉子是装金袋，
鹅嗉子是装银袋，

Man:
Duck crops are bags for gold.
Goose crops are bags for silver.

第三部　婚事和恋歌
Book Three　Marriage and Love Songs

女：
什么人打金子？
什么人打银子？

男：
湖广人打金子，
湖广人打银子；
打成金手箍，
打成银手箍，
打成金环子，
打成银环子；
你家新姑娘，
戴也戴齐了，
这回也得了！

女：
我家新姑娘，
新衣新鞋穿好了，
金银首饰戴好了，
就是头上没有花，
你说怎么办？

Woman:
Who is the goldsmith?
Who is the silversmith?

Man:
People from Huguang are the goldsmiths.
People from Huguang are the silversmiths.
They make gold bracelets.
They make silver bracelets.
They make gold earrings.
They make silver earrings.
Your daughter
Has jewelry to wear.
She has nothing to complain about.

Woman:
Our daughter can now wear
New clothes and shoes,
Gold and silver jewelry.
But she doesn't have any flower on her head.
What should we do?

梅葛 // Meige

男：
正月给她戴朵门采花，
二月给她戴朵龙头花。

Man:
She can wear a door flower in January
And a sprekelia flower in February.

女：
正月门彩花，
是新年门上戴的花；
二月龙头花，
是菩萨戴的花，
不是新娘戴的花。

Woman:
Door flower in January
Is put on the doors on the New Year's Day.
Sprekelia flower in February
Is the flower the Bodhisattva wears.
They are not flowers for the bride.

男：
三月黄菜花，
四月小秧花，
就是新娘戴的花。

Man:
Yellow rape flowers in March
And little rice flowers in April
Are flowers for the bride.

女：
三月黄菜花，
是蜜蜂采的花；
四月小秧花，
是小秧戴的花，
不是新娘戴的花。

Woman:
Yellow rape flowers in March
Are for the bees to collect honey.
Little rice flowers in April
Are the flower rice seedlings wear.
They are not flowers for the bride.

第三部　婚事和恋歌

Book Three   Marriage and Love Songs

男：

五月秧穗花，

六月纸香花，

就是新娘戴的花。

Man:

Ears of grain in May

And paper flowers in June

Are flowers for the bride.

女：

五月秧穗花，

是盘田种地时戴的花；

六月纸香花，

是田公地母戴的花，

不是新娘戴的花。

Woman:

Ears of grain in May

Are what farmers wear when farming.

Paper flowers in June

Are the flowers Earth God and Goddess wear.

They are not flowers for the bride.

男：

七月苦荞花，

八月朝阳花，

就是新娘戴的花。

Man:

Buckwheat flowers in July

And sun flowers in August

Are flowers for the bride.

女：

七月苦荞花，

是五谷戴的花；

八月朝阳花，

是太阳月亮相会戴的花，

不是新娘戴的花。

Woman:

Buckwheat flowers in July

Are the flowers grain wear.

Sun flowers in August

Are what the sun and the moon wear

When they meet, not flowers for the bride.

梅葛 // Meige

男：
九月开菊花，
十月剪刀花，
是新娘戴的花。

Man:
Chrysanthemums in September
And scissor flowers in October
Are flowers for the bride.

女：
九月开菊花，
是九皇大会花；
十月剪刀花，
是饥荒年成花，
不是新娘戴的花。

Woman:
Chrysanthemums in September
Are the flower for the Nine Chieftains' conference.
Scissor flowers in October
Are the flower blooming in famine years.
They are not good for the bride.

男：
冬月硬子花，
腊月蜡梅花，
就是新娘戴的花。

Man:
Lotus in November and
Wintersweet in December
Are flowers for the bride.

女：
冬月硬子花，
腊月蜡梅花，
头花开空花，
后朵才结果，
不是新娘戴的花。

Woman:
Lotus in November,
Wintersweet in December,
The first flower is barren,
The second flower bears fruit,
Not flowers for the bride.

第三部　婚事和恋歌
Book Three　Marriage and Love Songs

男：
院子中间十盆花，
院子外边松头花，
就是新娘戴的花。

Man:
The ten potted flowers in the courtyard
And the pine flowers outside the courtyard
Are flowers for the bride.

女：
院子中间十盆花，
院子外边松头花，
是笔墨砚瓦花，
是手上拿的花，
不是新娘戴的花。

Woman:
The ten potted flowers in the courtyard
And the pine flowers outside the courtyard,
Are painted with brush and ink.
They are flowers held in the hands,
Not for the bride to wear.

男：
梁上八卦花，
是新娘戴的花。

Man:
The Eight Diagrams on the beam
Is the flower for the bride.

女：
梁上八卦花，
是房屋戴的花，
不是新娘戴的花。

Woman:
The Eight Diagrams on the beam
Is the flower the house wears,
Not the flower for the bride.

男：
永北街子上，
有些开不败的花，

Man:
On Yongbei Street,
There are flowers that will never wither.

梅葛 // Meige

就是新娘戴的花。	They are flowers for the bride.

女：
永北街子上，
开不败的花，
是大官小吏吃酒吃茶的花，
不是新娘戴的花。

Woman:
On Yongbei Street,
The flowers that never wither
Are flowers to entertain court officials,
Not flowers for the bride.

男：
硬花① 有三朵，
软花有三朵，
你家要挑哪样花？

Man:
Three hard flowers,①
Three soft flowers,
Which would you prefer?

女：
硬花有三朵，
软花有三朵，
我家新姑娘，
要的是硬花。

Woman:
There are three hard flowers
And three soft flowers.
Our daughter
Prefers the hard ones.

男：
硬花戴着头也亮，
软花戴着身也亮，
这回嫁得了！

Man:
Hard flowers make the head shine,
Soft flowers make the body shine.
Now the girl is ready to get married!

---

① 硬花：即金花、银花。

① Hard flowers: gold flowers and silver flowers.

第三部　婚事和恋歌
Book Three　Marriage and Love Songs

女：
嫁是要嫁了，
我家新姑娘，
脚还没有洗，
叫我怎样交给你？

Woman:
The girl will get married,
But our daughter the bride
Hasn't washed her feet.
How can I give her to you?

男：
赵州新瓦盆，
就是洗脚盆，
左边抹三下，
右边抹三下，
脚洗干净了，
花鞋也穿好了，
这下嫁得成了。

Man:
The new earthen pot made in Zhaozhou
Is the foot basin.
Wipe three times from the left,
Wipe three times from the right,
And her feet will be clean.
Put on a pair of embroidered shoes,
The girl is ready to get married.

女：
嫁是要嫁了，
新郎新娘的陪郎是哪个？

Woman:
The girl will get married, but
Who are the best groomsmen and who the bridesmaids?

男：
小伙小伴接新郎，
嫂嫂妹妹陪新娘，
接的陪的都来了，

Man:
Brothers and friends will be the groomsmen,
Sisters and elder brother's wife will be the bridesmaids.
All companions are ready,

梅葛 // Meige

这回嫁得成了。

The girl is ready to get married.

女：
房外有三对雀，
叽哩叽哩叫；
我家姑娘胆子小，
她不敢出来。

Woman:
There are three pairs of sparrows outside,
Twittering and chirping.
My timid girl
Is too shy to come out.

男：
房外叽哩声，
不是雀在叫，
是苴却石马三对葫芦笙。
新娘不要怕，
快快走出来。

Man:
The twittering and chirping outside
Is not from three pairs of sparrows.
It is from three pairs of gourd mouth organ.
Our little bride, don't be afraid.
Please come out.

女：
我家姑娘出嫁了，
做爹做妈的心不乐。

Woman:
My girl is getting married.
Her Mom and Dad feel sad.

男：
不怕不必怕，
不愁不要愁；
白米饭有三碗，
糯米饭有三碗，

Man:
Don't be afraid.
Don't be worried.
There are three bowls of white rice.
There are three bowls of sticky rice.

第三部　婚事和恋歌
Book Three　Marriage and Love Songs

红肉有三碗，	There are three bowls of red meat.
阿爹左边来，	Dad stands on the left.
阿妈右边来，	Mom stands on the right.
新姑娘张开嘴，	The bride opens her mouth
衔给阿爹两嘴，	And puts two mouthfuls
装在袖里头；	Into her Dad's sleeves
衔给阿妈两嘴，	And another two mouthfuls
装在围腰头。	Into her Mom's apron.
阿爹心也乐，	Dad is happy.
阿妈心也乐。	Mom is delighted.

女： **Woman:**

我家老奶年纪老，	Our grandma is so old.
孙女嫁出去，	When her granddaughter gets married,
没人来服侍，	She will be left unattended.
要根拐棍来探路。	She needs a walking stick.

我家老爹年纪老，	Our grandpa is so old.
要吃好东西，	He wants to eat something good.
猪心和猪肝，	You should give him
要送老爹吃。	Pig heart and liver.

房后有山神，	There is the mountain god behind the house.
要杀公鸡来酬谢，	You must kill a rooster to sacrifice.

梅葛 // Meige

山神答应了，	Only when the mountain god agrees,
成亲才周到。	Can the marriage be called appropriate.

房下有畜神，　　　　　　There is the livestock god under the house.
也要杀鸡谢，　　　　　　You must kill a rooster to sacrifice.
畜神答应了，　　　　　　Only when the livestock god agrees,
成亲才有儿和女。　　　　Will the new couple have kids.

家堂香火旺，　　　　　　To sustain the family's prosperity,
也要杀鸡来酬谢。　　　　You must kill a rooster to reward the gods.

这些事情办到了，　　　　When these things are done,
我家姑娘就嫁了。　　　　My girl will be yours.

男：　　　　　　　　　**Man:**
大事办得到，　　　　　　Big things can be done.
小事办得到，　　　　　　Small things can be done.
事事都办到，　　　　　　Everything can be done,
一样一样照着办，　　　　Done as you ask,
样样都办好，　　　　　　Done in a good manner.
这回嫁得了。　　　　　　Now the girl may get married.

女：　　　　　　　　　**Woman:**
嫁是要嫁了，　　　　　　The girl will get married,

第三部　婚事和恋歌
Book Three　Marriage and Love Songs

我家姑娘心不乐,
用什么来哄新姑娘?

But she is not delighted.
How can you please the bride?

男:
白米饭拿来哄新姑娘,
羊膀子拿来哄新姑娘,
喜酒拿来哄新姑娘,
哄得新娘嘻嘻笑。

Man:
White rice will be used to please the bride,
Sheep leg will be used to please the bride,
Wedding wine will be used to please the bride,
Making her laugh merrily.

女:
我家新姑娘,
到了你家坐哪里?

Woman:
When my girl arrive at your home,
Where will she be seated?

男:
自家院子头,
四方桌子上,
新娘坐那里。

Man:
In our courtyard,
There is a square table.
That's where the bride will be seated.

女:
坐倒坐下了,
哪个来喂喜酒?
哪个来背新娘?
背到哪里去?

Woman:
When she sits down,
Who will offer her wedding wine?
Who will carry her on the shoulder?
Where will they carry her?

梅葛 // Meige

男:
媒人来喂喜酒,
孃孃来背新娘,
背到喜棚头。

Man:
The matchmaker will offer the bride wedding wine.
Father's sister will carry the bride on the shoulder.
They will go right to the wedding shed.

女:
新亲[①]来到了,
没有住处怎么办?

Woman:
New relatives[①] arrive,
But can you accommodate them?

男:
房前三块玉米地,
房前三块菜籽地,
搭起棚子来,
盖起棚子来,
盖棚盖三格,
新亲住这里。

Man:
There are three corn fields in front of the house,
There are three vegetable fields in front of the house.
A shed will be put up there,
A shed will be built up there.
The shed will be divided into three rooms,
In which relatives will lodge.

女:
从前哪个先盖棚?
请你说给我。

Woman:
Who was the first to build a shed?
Please tell me.

男:
欧梭莫梭人,

Man:
The Ousuomosuo people

---

① 新亲:新娘家来的人。

① New relatives: people of the bride's family.

第三部　婚事和恋歌
Book Three　Marriage and Love Songs

他们先盖棚。

Were the first to build a shed.

女：
先进棚子来，
抬头看天天补着，
低头看地地补着，
这是什么天？
这是什么地？

Woman:
Coming into the shed
And looking up, I see a patched heaven.
Looking down, I see a patched earth.
What heaven is this?
What earth is this?

男：
抬头看天天补着，
这是天底下的天，
树叶子做的天，
是讨亲嫁娶的天。
低头看地地补着，
这是地头上的地，
松毛做的地，
是讨亲嫁娶的地。

Man:
The patched heaven you see
Is a heaven under heaven.
It is made of leaves
For wedding ceremonies.
The patched earth you see
Is an earth above the earth.
It is made of pine needles
For wedding ceremonies.

女：
新亲有三百，
吃酒吃三天，
新亲坐下了，
你家待客怎么待？

Woman:
There will be three hundred relatives,
The wedding feast will last for three days.
When the relatives sit down,
How would you treat them?

- 163 -

梅葛 // Meige

男：
三年装下好白米，
三年喂下老肥猪，
三年蒸下好烧酒；
好酒好肉待客人，
恭恭敬敬待客人。

女：
吃也吃完了，
吃也吃光了。
棚上的树叶晒干了，
棚下的松毛晒黄了。
对不起你家了，
姑娘交给你，
我们要散了。

男：
三年装下的好白米，
还没有吃完；
三年喂下的老肥猪，
还没有吃完；
七年养下的大绵羊，
还没有吃完；

Man:
Good rice reserved for three years,
Fat hog raised for three years,
Good wine aged for three years.
Guests will be treated with good wine and meat,
Guests will be treated with sincerity and respect.

Woman:
Food is finished,
Bowls and plates are empty.
Leaves on the shed are dried up,
Pine needles on the ground have turned yellow.
Sorry for causing you so much trouble.
Our girl is yours.
It's time for us to leave.

Man:
Good rice reserved for three years
Is yet to be finished.
Fat hog raised for three years
Is yet to be finished;
Large sheep raised for seven years
Is yet to be finished.

第三部　婚事和恋歌
Book Three　Marriage and Love Songs

我要留住你，	I want you to stay.
吃的不好莫嫌弃，	I hope you like the food.
昨天你交新姑娘，	Yesterday you gave your girl
新姑娘交给了媒人，	To the matchmaker,
没有交给公婆。	Not to her parents-in-law.
今天你交新姑娘，	Today you give your girl
要交给公婆。	To her parents-in-law.
姑娘找不着活计做，	The bride does not know what to do.
要你来安置。	You must tell her.

女： **Woman:**

妈的姑娘啊，	Oh my dear daughter,
三月撒荞子，	Sow buckwheat seeds in March,
五月去栽秧，	Transplant seedlings in May.
八月割谷子，	August is for harvesting millet,
冬月种小麦，	November is for growing wheat.
你要忙着做。	You have to keep yourself busy.
推的拿到磨盘上，	Put things on the millstone and turn the mill,
舂的拿到碓盘上，	Put things in the mortar and pound them,
撮箕扫帚拿着去，	Always have a dustpan and a broom in your hand,
一年四季要这样做，	And do this all year round.
别人的爹妈是你的公婆，	Your husband's parents are your parents-in-law,
公婆不准做的事，	Don't do the things
你就千万别去做。	They don't allow you to do.

梅葛 // Meige

活计安置好了，
我们要回去了。

男：
实在要回去，
我也没办法，
羊头羊蹄羊肠子猪脊膘，
搭起十二道桥，
把你送过去。

女：
十二道桥搭起来，
新亲要走了，
可有赶亲棍①？

男：
五炷喜香一壶酒，
一支羊膀一块肉，
就是赶亲棍。

亲戚做好了，
两家哈哈笑。

① 赶亲棍：新亲要走时送的礼物。

Now that I have told her what to do,
We want to go back home.

Man:
If you really want to go back,
I can do nothing to detain you,
Sheep head, sheep hoof, sheep gut and pig meat
Are used to put up twelve bridges,
Bridges to take you home.

Woman:
Twelve bridges are put up,
Your new relatives are hitting the road.
Do you have gifts for them?

Man:
Five sticks of wedding incense and a jug of wine.
A sheep leg and a piece of meat.
These are the club to drive you off.

Relatives are treated well.
The two families laugh out loud.

Book Three　Marriage and Love Songs

三　请　客[①]　　Ⅲ. Treating Guests[①]

娶亲了，	On the wedding day,
把客人请来，	The invited guests arrive.
外公外婆来了，	Grandparents are here,
舅妈姨妈来了，	Aunts are here,
姑爹来了，	Uncles are here,
小伙子小姑娘来了，	Boys and girls are here and
族中老人都来了。	Senior members in the family are all here.

主：　　　　　　　　**The host:**
哪个带信来？　　　　Who brought you the message
你才到我家。　　　　That led you to my home?

客：　　　　　　　　**The guest:**
什么是鸟王？　　　　Who is the king of birds?
凤凰是鸟王。　　　　The phoenix is the king of birds.
凤凰带信来，　　　　The phoenix brought me the message,
我才到你家。　　　　Leading me to your home.

---

① 这一节诗，是彝族人民在喜庆和节日的宴会上唱的。

① This poem is sung by the Yi people at wedding banquets and festival banquets.

梅葛 // Meige

主：
凤凰只是飞过房头上，
没有带信到你家。

The host:
The phoenix was just flying over your house.
It did not bring you the message.

客：
大雁带信来，
我才到你家。

The guest:
The wild goose brought me the message,
Leading me to your home.

主：
大雁只从天上过，
没有带信到你家。

The host:
The wild goose was just flying overhead.
It did not bring you the message.

客：
岩鸡带信来，
我才到你家。

The guest:
The chukar partridge brought me the message,
Leading me to your home.

主：
岩鸡只从林中过，
没有带信到你家。

The host:
The chukar partridge was just passing through the bush.
It did not bring you the message.

客：
老鹰带信来，
我才到你家。

The guest:
The eagle brought me the message,
Leading me to your home.

第三部　婚事和恋歌

Book Three　Marriage and Love Songs

主：

老鹰石岩上面飞，

没有带信到你家。

客：

竹鸡箐鸡带信来，

我才到你家。

主：

竹鸡箐鸡箐里走，

没有带信到你家。

客：

老鸹喜鹊带信来，

我才到你家。

主：

老鸹只从房头过，

喜鹊只在门外飞，

没有带信到你家。

The host:

The eagle was flying over the cliff.

It did not bring you the message.

The guest:

The bamboo partridge and pheasant brought me the message,

Leading me to your home.

The host:

They were walking in the bamboo grove.

They did not bring you the message.

The guest:

The raven and magpie brought me the message,

Leading me to your home.

The host:

The raven was just flying over your house.

The magpie was just flying outside.

They did not bring you the message.

梅葛 // Meige

客：
绿斑鸠带信来，
我才到你家。

The guest:
The green turtledove brought me the message,
Leading me to your home.

主：
绿斑鸠在荞地上头飞，
没有带信到你家。

The host:
The green turtledove was flying above the buckwheat field.
It did not bring you the message.

客：
画眉带信来，
我才到你家。

The guest:
The thrush brought me the message,
Leading me to your home.

主：
画眉从树下飞过去，
没有带信到你家。

The host:
The thrush was flying under the trees.
It did not bring you the message.

客：
布谷鸟带信来，
我才到你家。

The guest:
The cuckoo brought me the message,
Leading me to your home.

主：
布谷鸟分节令去了，
没有带信到你家。

The host:
The cuckoo was harbingering the coming of spring.
It did not bring you the message.

第三部　婚事和恋歌
Book Three   Marriage and Love Songs

客：
鹦哥带信来，
我才到你家。

The guest:
The parrot brought me the message,
Leading me to your home.

主：
鹦哥在树上，
没有带信到你家。

The host:
The parrot was in a tree.
It did not bring you the message.

客：
飞天鸟带信来，
我才到你家。

The guest:
The flying bird brought me the message,
Leading me to your home.

主：
飞天鸟到天王跟前缴粮去了，
到地王跟前缴粮去了，
没有带信到你家。

The host:
The flying bird was handing in grain
To the king of the sky and to the king of the earth,
It did not bring you the message.

客：
小蜜蜂带信来，
我才到你家。

The guest:
The little bee brought me the message,
Leading me to your home.

主：
小蜜蜂清早采露水去了，

The host:
The little bee was collecting morning dew.

梅葛 // Meige

没有带信到你家。

It did not bring you the message.

客：
山兔子带信来，
我才到你家。

The guest:
Wild hare brought me the message,
Leading me to your home.

主：
兔子只在山里跑，
没有带信到你家，

The host:
Wild hares were running in the mountains,
They did not bring you the message.

客：
马鹿带信来，
我才到你家，

The guest:
The red deer brought me the message,
Leading me to your home.

主：
马鹿石岩边上跑，
没有带信到你家。

The host:
The red deer was running on the edge of the cliff.
It did not bring you the message.

客：
獐子麂子带信来，
我才到你家。

The guest:
The river deer and muntjac brought me the message,
Leading me to your home.

主：
獐子被猎人捉去了，

The host:
The river deer was caught by the hunter.

第三部　婚事和恋歌
Book Three　Marriage and Love Songs

麂子被猎人网去了，
没有带信到你家。

The muntjac was trapped by the net.
They did not bring you the message.

客：
穿山甲带信来，
我才到你家。

The guest:
The pangolin brought me the message,
Leading me to your home.

主：
穿山甲进洞去了，
没有带信到你家。

The host:
The pangolin was in its hole.
It did not bring you the message.

客：
豪猪带信来，
我才到你家。

The guest:
The porcupine brought me the message,
Leading me to your home.

主：
豪猪钻洞去了，
没有带信到你家。

The host:
The porcupine was drilling holes.
It did not bring you the message.

客：
狐狸带信来，
我才到你家。

The guest:
The fox brought me the message,
Leading me to your home.

梅葛 // Meige

主：
狐狸偷吃的去了，
没有带信到你家。

The host:
The fox was stealing food.
It did not bring you the message.

客：
石蚌带信来，
我才到你家。

The guest:
The frog brought me the message,
Leading me to your home.

主：
石蚌在沟中洞里叫，
没有带信到你家。

The host:
Frog was croaking in the ditch.
It did not bring you the message.

客：
白鱼带信来，
我才到你家。

The guest:
The white fish brought me the message,
Leading me to your home.

主：
白鱼水中游，
没有带信到你家。

The host:
White fish was swimming in the water.
It did not bring you the message.

客：
地瓜根根带信来，
我才到你家。

The guest:
The sweet potato brought me the message,
Leading me to your home.

第三部　婚事和恋歌
Book Three　Marriage and Love Songs

主：
地瓜根根确实带了信，
我们两家来认亲。

团团桌边坐，
喜喜欢欢来划拳，
一样肉也没有，
一样酒也没有。
请把青菜当肉吃，
请把凉水当酒喝。

客：
七十七样菜，
桌子摆得满满的。
土锅里面有好猪肉，
坛子里面有好白酒，
吃了好肉，
喝了好酒，
吃也吃饱了，
喝也喝够了，
吃了不再道谢啦，
喝了不再道谢啦。

The host:
The sweet potato indeed brought you the message.
Let's call each other family.

Let's sit round the table
And happily play the finger-guessing game.
There is no meat.
There is no wine.
Please take vegetables as meat.
Please take cold water as liquor.

The guest:
With seventy-seven dishes,
The table has no empty space.
Good pork in the clay pot,
Good wine in the jar.
Eating good meat,
Drinking good wine.
We eat to our hearts' content,
We drink to our hearts' satisfaction,
Thank you so much for the food.
Thank you so much for the wine.

- 175 -

梅葛 // Meige

四 抢 棚①   IV. Celebrating the Wedding by Dancing

主：
抢棚的哥哥
抢棚的妹妹，
我要问问你们，
我家娶亲你们怎么知道的？

The host:
Brothers who come to celebrate the wedding,
Sisters who come to celebrate the wedding,
I have to ask you,
How came you know this wedding?

客：
春风吹三遍，
冬风刮三遍，
春风吹来我知道，
冬风刮来我知道，
我们爱玩爱跳，
有没有玩跳的地方？

The guest:
The spring breeze blows three times,
The winter breeze blows three times.
I know it when the spring breeze blows,
I know it when the winter breeze blows.
We love playing and dancing.
Is there any place for dancing and playing?

主：
玩跳的地方倒有，

The host:
Sure we have a place for dancing and playing,

---

① 在新娘即将进门时，村里的青年男女就聚集在一起打跳（跳舞），表示庆贺和欢乐。

第三部　婚事和恋歌

Book Three　Marriage and Love Songs

我要问问你们，
从前哪个先抢棚？
从前哪个先抢跳？
你们可知道？

But I must ask you,
Who was the first to celebrate a wedding by playing?
Who was the first to celebrate a wedding by dancing?
Do you have any idea?

客：
先抢棚的是李之成①，
先打跳的是李之成。

The guest:
Li Zhicheng① was the first to celebrate the wedding by playing,
Li Zhicheng was the first to celebrate the wedding by dancing.

主：
李之成在哪里打跳，
你们可知道？

The host:
Where did Li Zhicheng dance?
Do you have any idea?

客：
李之成在南京城里打跳，
在皇帝老倌花园里打跳。
今晚你家娶亲，

The guest:
In the city of Nanjing,
In the emperor's garden.
You have a wedding tonight.

---

① 李之成：是彝族民间故事"百雀农"中的男主角。皇帝夺去了他的妻子，他穿上百雀衣，吹着芦笙，装扮成一个惹人发笑的人到皇官打跳，用巧计杀死了皇帝。

① Li Zhicheng is the protagonist in "The Farmer of a Hundred Birds", a Yi folk tale. The Emperor took away his wife. So he put on the clothes of a hundred birds, dressed up as a funny clown, went to the royal palace to dance and play his gourd mouth organ, and killed the Emperor.

梅葛 // Meige

我们爱玩， We love playing,
我们爱跳， We love dancing.
玩跳的地点在哪里？ Where is the place for playing and dancing?

主： **The host:**
房前有三块玉麦地， There are three cornfields in front of the house,
有三块黄菜地， And three vegetable fields.
玩跳的地点在那里， These are the places for playing and dancing.
玩跳时怎样装扮？ How will you dress up when playing and dancing?
头上戴什么？ What hats are you going to put on?
身上穿什么？ What clothes are you going to wear?

客： **The guest:**
大理草帽头上戴， Dali straw hats on our heads,
绣球结起来， Plus a ball made of strips of silk,
雉鸡尾插起来， And some pheasant feathers.
红绿花衣身上穿， Red and green clothes wrap us up,
麻布花鞋穿起来， Colorful linen shoes are on our feet.
我们这样装扮， That's how we dress.
我们爱玩爱跳， We love playing and dancing.
你家喜欢不喜欢？ Do your family like it or not?

主： **The host:**
我家也爱玩， My family also loves playing,

第三部　婚事和恋歌
Book Three　Marriage and Love Songs

我家也爱跳，	My family also loves dancing.
怎么不喜欢。	How can we not like it!
听见一个声音，	I heard a sound,
不像人的声音，	Unlike human voice,
不像鸟的声音，	Unlike the sound of birds.
那是什么声音？	What is it?

客：　　　　　　　　　　**The guest:**

那是葫芦笙，	That is the gourd mouth organ.
芦笙吹起来，	When it is blown,
玩也玩得成，	We can play,
跳也跳得成。	We can dance.

主：　　　　　　　　　　**The host:**

葫芦笙是怎样做成的。	Do you know
你们可知道？	What the gourd mouth organ is made of?

客：　　　　　　　　　　**The guest:**

葫芦配竹子，	Gourd with bamboo.
做成葫芦笙。	That's what it is made of.

主：　　　　　　　　　　**The host:**

哪里来的葫芦种？	Where do the gourd seeds come from?
哪里来的竹子种？	Where do the bamboo seeds come from?

梅葛 // Meige

客：
从前哥哥捉野鸡，
野鸡没捉到，
捉到一只小白兔；
划开兔子头，
葫芦种在里面，
竹子种也在里面。

主：
哪个种葫芦？
哪个种竹子？

客：
阿省莫若，
阿底莫若，
他俩种葫芦，
他们种竹子。

主：
葫芦笙做成了，
用什么来做葫芦心？

The guest:
Once upon a time, a brother caught a pheasant,
But it ran away.
He caught a little bunny.
He cut open the bunny's head.
Inside were gourd seeds,
Inside were bamboo seeds too.

The host:
Who planted the gourds?
Who planted the bamboos?

The guest:
Ashengmoruo
And Adimoruo
They planted the gourds,
They planted the bamboo.

The host:
The gourd mouth organ is made,
But what is used to make its reed?

第三部　婚事和恋歌
Book Three　Marriage and Love Songs

客：
竹子削成响舌子，
就是葫芦心。

主：
响舌做成葫芦心，
为何吹起没声音？

客：
黄蜡拿一团，
糊起响舌子，
吹起有声音，
吹起响又响。

主：
你们爱玩爱跳，
左边转还是右边转，
你们可知道？

客：
左边转三转，
接着右边转，
脚要使力跳，
嘴要使劲吹，

The guest:
Bamboo is whittled into a ring tongue.
That is the reed of the pipe.

The host:
Why the reed made of ring tongue
Makes no sound?

The guest:
When a lump of yellow wax
Is pasted onto the ring tongue,
The pipe makes a sound,
Loud and clear sound.

The host:
You love playing and dancing.
You should turn left or right,
Do you have any idea?

The guest:
Turn left three times,
Then turn right three times,
Jump high,
Blow loud,

- 181 -

梅葛 // Meige

我们玩跳到天亮。	We play and dance till dawn.

五　撒　种①

V. Sowing①

女：
你我亲，
十年不办婚，
五年不办婚，
今年才办婚。
办婚可赶过年，
办婚可赶过月，
办婚可赶过日？

Woman:
We have been in love for a long time,
We've been waiting first for ten years,
And then for five gears,
Till this year when we can finally get married.
Must wedding wait for this year,
This mouth,
And this day?

男：
你我亲，
今年才办婚，
赶年赶过了，
赶月赶过了，

Man:
We have been in love for a long time,
And will finally get married this year.
We've been waiting for this year,
This month,

---

① 撒种：是在讨了媳妇的第二天清早唱的一段，用二人扮牛，在子棚里犁地撒种（男的代表新郎家，女的代表新娘家）。

① Sowing: it is sung on the morning following the wedding day. In the performance in the wedding shed, a man is plowing the field and a woman is scattering seeds. They represent the bridegroom's family and the bride's family respectively.

第三部　婚事和恋歌

Book Three　Marriage and Love Songs

赶日赶过了，	And this day.
赶年赶好年，	This year is the lucky year.
赶月赶好月，	This month is the lucky month.
赶日赶好日。	This day is the lucky day.
今天就是好日子，	Today is the lucky day.
婚事办起来。	Let's get married today.
天亮早早起，	We will get up early in the morning,
棚子下边犁地又撒种；	Plow and sow under the shed.
犁牛头上没有角，	The yak has no horns,
犁牛脚上没有蹄，	The yak has no hoofs.
这不是真犁牛，	It is not a real yak,
是办婚事的犁牛。	It is a wedding yak.

女：

Woman:

头上没有角，　　No horns on the head,
脚上没有蹄，　　No hoofs on the feet,
这种犁牛哪里出？　Where does the yak come from?

男：

Man:

南京应天府，　　The Willow Bend of the Great dam,
大坝柳树湾，　　In Yingtianfu（Nanjing）．
办婚事用的犁牛，　That's where the wedding yaks
出在那地方。　　Come from.

梅葛 // Meige

女：

牛在哪里架？

牛用什么喂？

男：

家堂面前架双牛，

点起香来烧起纸，

白米肥肉当牛草，

高粱酒当牛水。

女：

什么人吆牛？

怎样来装扮？

男：

小伙子吆牛，

锄头倒扛着，

篮子倒背着；

倒扛锄头装扮肩膀，

倒背篮子装扮身子，

头发帽子装扮头。

女：

牛也吆来了，

Woman:

Where do you harness the yak?

What is used to feed it?

Man:

We harness it in front of the house.

We burn incense and paper offerings.

We feed it with rice and meat

And give it sorghum wine to drink.

Woman:

Who will drive the yak?

How will you dress yourself?

Man:

The young man drives the yak,

With a hoe on his back,

And a basket upside down.

The hoe decorates his back.

The basket ornaments his body.

Hair and hat dress up his head.

Woman:

Now that the yak is here,

第三部　婚事和恋歌
Book Three　Marriage and Love Songs

这回撒种了；	It's time to sow the seeds.
籽种哪里来？	Where do the seeds come from?
哪个来撒种？	Who is to sow the seeds?

男：
南山雪脉山，
籽种那里来。
媒婆背籽种，
媒人撒种子。
甜荞羼大麦，
苦荞羼小麦，
黑豆羼红豆，
谷子羼豌豆，
五谷撒得满满的。

Man:
The south mountain and the snow mountain.
These are where the seeds come from.
The matchmaker will carry
And sow the seeds.
Common buckwheat mixed with barley,
Tartary buckwheat mixed with wheat,
Black beans mixed with red beans,
And millet mixed with peas,
Five cereals are all sowed.

女：
五谷撒满了，
转来要放牛，
放牛哪里放？

Woman:
Five cereals are all sowed.
It's time to graze the yak.
But where to graze it?

男：
到了家堂前，
喜香烧起来，
黄纸开起来，

Man:
In front of the house,
Where incense is burning,
Yellow paper offerings are burning,

- 185 -

梅葛 // Meige

牛在那里放。 | That's where we graze the yak.

女：
牛也放好了，
吆回哪一方？

Woman:
The yak is well fed.
Where do we take it?

男：
南京应天府，
大坝柳树湾，
吆回那一方。

Man:
To the Willow Bend of the Great Dam,
In Yingtianfu (Nanjing).
That's where we take the yak.

六　芦　笙

VI. The Gourd Mouth Organ

彝家出了两个人，
一个叫阿省莫若，
一个叫阿底莫若，
他俩有竹子种，
他俩有葫芦种。

There were two Yi people.
One was Ashengmoruo,
The other was Adimoruo.
They had bamboo seeds.
They had gourd seeds.

阿省莫若拿着竹子种，
来到东洋大海沙滩上，
正当雷公发脾气，

Ashengmoruo came to the beach of the east sea
With bamboo seeds.
Just then the thunder roared,

第三部　婚事和恋歌
Book Three　Marriage and Love Songs

雷声隆隆忙撒种。　　　　It was the time to sow the seeds.

正月二十属鼠日，　　　　The twentieth day of January, the Day of the Rat,
属鼠那天撒竹种，　　　　Was a good day for sowing bamboo seeds.
竹子出得真是好。　　　　Bamboos grew well.

四月二十日，　　　　　　The twentieth day of April,
竹种撒下三个月，　　　　Three months after the seeds were sowed,
阿省莫若走来看，　　　　Ashengmoruo came to check them.
竹子长成节。　　　　　　The young bamboos already had joints.

到了移植时，　　　　　　When it was time for transplanting,
选择一个好日子，　　　　A good day was chosen.
恰在五月端午节，　　　　It was the Dragon Boat Festival.
阿底莫若去栽竹。　　　　Adimoruo started his bamboo plantation.

石岩底下栽竹子，　　　　Planted under rocks,
长到石岩上面来，　　　　The bamboos struggled out.
竹子头被虫吃了，　　　　The bamboo tips were eaten by worms,
去到树林里，　　　　　　He went into the woods
请来啄木鸟，　　　　　　To ask woodpeckers for help.
啄木鸟医竹子，　　　　　Woodpeckers cure bamboos.
竹子医好了。　　　　　　His bamboos were healed.

-187-

梅葛 // Meige

哪个种葫芦？	Who plant gourds?
傣族种葫芦。	The Dai people.
二月二十属羊日，	The twentieth day of February is the Day of the Goat.
属羊那天种，	If you sow the seeds on that day,
葫芦长得好，	Gourds will grow up strong and healthy,
葫芦花好像棉花一个样。	And their flowers are cotton-like.

竹子长大了，	Bamboos grow up,
葫芦长好了。	And gourds grow up, too.
竹子砍成节，	Bamboos are hacked into short sticks,
葫芦挖成洞，	Holes are dug in the gourds.
竹片做舌头，	Bamboo sheets are used to make tongues,
放进竹节里，	And put into bamboo joints,
竹节安在葫芦上，	Which are mounted onto gourds.
公配母来母配子，	Reeds are put into gourds,
五个竹节各有音。	Five joints have five tones.
葫芦配竹节，	Gourd with bamboo,
做成葫芦笙。	Gourd mouth organs are made.

哪个做成的葫芦笙？	Who make gourd mouth organs?
傣族做成的葫芦笙。	The Dai people.
什么人来吹？	Who play them?
傣族人来吹。	The Dai people.

第三部　婚事和恋歌
Book Three　Marriage and Love Songs

竹节烙洞洞,	Flutes are made
笛子做出来。	By burning holes in bamboo sticks.
竹子削去皮,	Jaw harps are made
响篾做出来。	By peeling bamboos.

响篾胸前挂,　　　The jaw harp hangs against the chest,
笛子腰上插。　　　The flute hangs on the waist belt.
做时不爱人,　　　They are hard to make,
吹起爱死人。　　　But pleasant to play.
男在高山吹笛子,　Boys play flutes on high mountains,
女在箐底吹树叶。　Girls blow leaves in bamboo forests.
男在高山唱,　　　Boys sing on high mountains,
女在箐底来回音;　Girls sing back in the valleys.
女在箐底唱,　　　Girls sing in the valleys,
男在高山来回音。Boys sing back on high mountains.

刀子石上磨,　　　By grinding knife on stones,
伙伴唤拢来。　　　Friends are called together.
石头不会动,　　　Stones don't move.
调子能吹合,　　　Tones can blend.
唱得合心意,　　　Antiphonal singing is joyful.
绕着来相会。　　　Boys and girls come a long way to meet.

好吃的是猪肉,　　Pork is yummy.

-189-

梅葛 // Meige

好喝的是白酒，	Wine is tasty.
白米人人爱，	Rice is loved by all,
哪个不爱玩，	So is playing.
玩了吹了回家来。	Having had a good time, everybody goes home.

女的不好过，　　　　　　　The woman feels sick,
以为是害伤风病。　　　　　Thinking she has a cold.
不是伤风病。　　　　　　　But it's not a cold.
不是伤风病，　　　　　　　It's not a cold:
有了身孕了。　　　　　　　She is pregnant.
怀了九个月，　　　　　　　In nine months,
娃娃就要生下来。　　　　　She will have a baby.

住在哪间屋里？　　　　　　Which room will she live in?
住在堂屋里。　　　　　　　In the main room.
堂屋里面有老人，　　　　　But the elderly live there.
堂屋里面不能生娃娃。　　　It is not the place for delivery.

住在哪间房里？　　　　　　Which room will she live in?
住在灶房里。　　　　　　　In the kitchen.
灶房里面有兄妹，　　　　　But the siblings live there.
灶房里面不能生娃娃。　　　It is not the place for delivery.

住在楼上房间里，　　　　　How about the upstairs room?

第三部　婚事和恋歌
Book Three　Marriage and Love Songs

楼上是装谷米粮食的地方，	The upstairs room is for storing grain.
楼上不能生娃娃。	It's not the place for delivery.

搬到两边厢房里，　　　　How about one of the wing rooms?
叔伯大人望得见，　　　　Uncles may see me.
厢房里不能生娃娃。　　　It is not the place for delivery.
搬到内屋里面住，　　　　She will move into the back room,
才把娃娃生下来。　　　　Which is the only place for delivery.

哪个剪脐带？　　　　　　Who will cut the umbilical cord?
祖母剪脐带。　　　　　　Grandma.
脐带剪断了，　　　　　　When the umbilical cord is cut,
娃娃包在围腰里，　　　　And the baby is wrapped in an apron,
要来洗娃娃。　　　　　　It needs to be washed.

没有清水洗，　　　　　　There is no clean water.
跑到池塘边，　　　　　　People run to the pond,
池塘清水鱼游过，　　　　But fish swim in the pond,
鱼游过的水不能洗娃娃。　So the pond water cannot be used.

又往大河跑，　　　　　　People run towards the river,
跑到大河边，　　　　　　To the riverside,
只见浑水淌，　　　　　　But the water is muddy.
浑水不能洗娃娃。　　　　It cannot be used.

梅葛 // Meige

又往箐里跑，	People run to the valley,
箐里有井水，	Where there is a well.
井水牛吃过，	But cattle drink well water,
牛吃过的水不能洗娃娃。	So it cannot be used.

又往岩石下面跑，　　　People run to the rock.
岩石下面有泉水，　　　Under the rock is spring water,
泉水钢铁气味大，　　　But it has an irony taste,
这样的水不能洗娃娃。　So it cannot be used.

又往林中跑，　　　　　People run into the forest,
林中有清水，　　　　　Where there is brook water,
清水百鸟来喝过，　　　But birds come to drink it,
百鸟喝过的水不能洗娃娃。So it cannot be used.

到处跑遍了，　　　　　People have searched in all places.
只得跑回来，　　　　　They have to run back.
房后马缨花树下，　　　Under the lantana trees behind the house,
马缨花树下清水流，　　Flows a stream of clean water.
流水挑来洗娃娃，　　　Cleaned in this water,
娃娃就像马缨花。　　　The baby will look like a lantana flower.

新街买的锅，　　　　　In the pot bought from the New Street,

第三部　婚事和恋歌
Book Three　Marriage and Love Songs

冷水煨涨了，	The clean water is boiling.
好好洗娃娃，	Given a good wash,
娃娃长大逗人爱。	The baby will grow up lovely and cute.
什么做洗槽？	What is used to make the bathtub?
马樱花树做洗槽。	Azalea trees are used to make a wash tank.
什么陪伴洗？	What is used as shower foam?
马樱花儿陪伴洗。	Azalea flowers are used as shower foam.
中和的麻布做衣裳，	Linen from Zhonghe is used to make clothes,
白井的棉布做裤子。	Cloth from Baijing is used to make trousers.
生下三天后，	Three days after the birth,
就要取名字。	It is time to name the baby.
松树林中取名字，	They name it in the pine forest,
荞子花中取名字，	Among the buckwheat flowers,
泉水边上取名字，	By the spring, or
升斗当中取名字。	From the measure for grain.
杀了一只红公鸡，	A red rooster is killed
公鸡来祭树，	To sacrifice to the trees
公鸡来祭水，	And to the water.
祭完大家吃，	After that, it is eaten by all.
吃了长辈取名字，	Then the elders discuss the baby's name.
名字取出来，	When the name is decided on,
指望娃娃快长大。	People expect the baby to grow up fast.

梅葛 // Meige

七　安　家　　　　Ⅶ. Settling Down

两个娃娃会坐了，　　　The two babies can sit,
两双小手一样长；　　　Their little hands are of the same length.
两个娃娃会站了，　　　The two babies can stand,
站着个子一样高。　　　They are of the same height.

小哥小妹一处玩，　　　The little boy and little girl play together.
小哥玩白土，　　　　　The boy plays with clay.
小妹玩黄土，　　　　　The girl plays with loess.
白土当白饭，　　　　　They use clay as rice,
黄土当黄饭。　　　　　And loess as corn,
烂瓦做小锅，　　　　　Broken tile as a pot.
切肉切两块，　　　　　They cut the meat in halves,
一块小哥吃，　　　　　One for the girl,
一块小妹吃。　　　　　One for the boy.
舀饭舀两碗，　　　　　They serve two bowls of rice,
一碗小哥吃，　　　　　One for the girl,
一碗小妹吃，　　　　　One for the boy.
他们两个呵，　　　　　The two of them
要永远相好。　　　　　Will love each other forever.

第三部　婚事和恋歌
Book Three　Marriage and Love Songs

小妹做什么，	Whatever the girl does,
小哥跟着做，	The boy follows suit,
盘田哥妹一起去，	Doing farm work together,
放牛放羊一起去。	Grazing cattle together.
小妹走哪条路，	Wherever the girl goes,
小哥跟着走。	The boy follows her.
脚迹合脚迹，	Their footprints overlap.
甩手一个样。	They swing their arms in the same manner.
把羊放到山坡上，	They graze sheep on the hillside,
扯把树叶垫着坐，	And take a handful of leaves as cushions.
坐过的树叶，	Leaves on which they have sat
永远留在山坡上。	Will always remain by the hillside.
盘田去到大河边，	They go to the riverside to do farm work,
搬块石头垫着坐，	Taking stones as cushions,
坐过的石头，	Stones on which they have sat on
永远留在大河边。	Will always remain on the riverside.
用米来煮饭，	They cook rice for food.
生米会煮烂。	The rice turns soft.
哥妹情意好，	The boy and girl love each other,
永远不分散。	And will never be apart.

梅葛 // Meige

被窝里子白布做，
被窝面子青布做，
白布青布会盖烂，
哥妹的心永不变。

男：
对面望妹家，
房子真是矮，
走起路来实在长，
你家的地方住得远。
有了情妹在，
不嫌路遥远。
小哥来到妹门前，
房前"噢啊"喊三声，
房后"噢啊"喊三声，
打过口哨吹笛子，
小妹可听见。

女：
听是听见了，
就是出不来，
跑到大门边，

One side of a quilt is made of white cloth,
The other side is made of blue cloth.
White cloth and blue cloth will rot,
But the hearts of the two will never change.

Man:
Your home is across the plain.
The house is really low.
It takes a long time to walk there.
Your home is so far away.
But my love for you
Shortens the way.
Now I come to your door,
Shouting "Uh-oh" three times in front of the house,
Three times behind the house,
Whistling and fluting,
My dear girl, do you hear that?

Woman:
I hear it,
But I can't come out.
Now I come to the door,

第三部　婚事和恋歌
Book Three　Marriage and Love Songs

一口唾沫吐出来①，
小哥可听见。

And spit①,
My dear boy, do you hear that?

男：
听是听见了，
小妹家里有爹娘，
小妹家里养着狗，
小哥不敢进你家。

Man:
I hear it all right,
But your parents are at home,
Your dog is at home.
I dare not go in.

羊羔"呃呃"叫，
你没有说不喜欢的话，
母牛"啊啊"叫，
你真的答应了？
母鸡领小鸡，
小哥要领妹，
小妹啊！
你能不能自己做主？

Lambs are bleating.
You never say you don't like me.
Cows are mooing.
Is it true that you agreed?
Hens take care of chicks,
I take care of you.
My dear girl!
Can you decide your own fate?

女：
小哥啊！
我爹把我嫁了，
我妈把我嫁了，

Woman:
My dear boy!
My dad married me off,
My mom married me off.

---

① 这里吐唾沫是相约的暗号，并无厌弃之意。

① Here spitting is an agreed signal between the two lovers, not a sign of contempt.

- 197 -

梅葛 // Meige

我两个都不晓得,	We knew nothing about that,
我两个都不知道。	We had no idea about that.

我爹我妈说: My mom and dad said,
　"天上黑云嫁白云, "Black cloud marries white cloud,
天山绿云嫁黄云, Green cloud marries yellow cloud,
七星姊妹嫁星星, The Big Dipper marries stars,
天亮星嫁过天星, Venus marries Jupiter,
天虹嫁地虹, The rainbow above marries the rainbow below,
爸妈的女儿也得嫁。 Our daughter has to get married."

"天上的龙要出嫁, "The dragon in heaven will get married,
龙冠亮闪闪, Its crown is shining bright,
龙尾摆又摆。 Its tail is swinging hard.
背阴林里八哥也要嫁, The parrot in the forest also has to get married,
乌鸦嫁老鹰, The crow marries the eagle,
鹧鸪嫁斑鸠, The partridge marries the dove,
野鸡嫁竹鸡, The pheasant marries the bamboo partridge,
野鸭嫁雁鹅, Wild duck marries the goose,
禽鸟嫁禽鸟, Birds marry birds,
爹妈的女儿也得嫁。 Our daughter has to get married."

"豹子嫁给老虎, "The leopard marries the tiger,
老熊嫁给野猪, The bear marries the wild boar,

第三部　婚事和恋歌
Book Three　Marriage and Love Songs

黄鼠狼嫁麂子，
香獐嫁狐狸，
松鼠嫁白鼠，
恶狗嫁白狼，
爹妈的女儿也得嫁。

"黑水嫁白水，
波浪嫁暴风，
急水嫁弯河，
爹妈的女儿也得嫁。

"小木嫁大水，
绿水嫁红水，
慢水嫁快水，
爹妈的女儿也得嫁。

"黑鱼嫁白鱼，
蜻蜓嫁黑蛇，
白蚁嫁黑蚁，
爹妈的女儿也得嫁。

"银葫芦蜂嫁金葫芦蜂，
家蜂嫁土蜂，
苍蝇嫁毛虫，

The weasel marries the muntjac,
The musk deer marries the fox,
The squirrel marries the white rat,
The barking dog marries the white wolf,
Our daughter has to get married."

"Black water marries white water,
Wave marries storm,
Rushing water marries curved river,
Our daughter has to get married."

"Small wood marries big flood,
Red water marries green water,
Slow water marries fast water,
Our daughter has to get married."

"Black fish marries white fish,
The dragonfly marries the black snake,
The termite marries the black ant,
Our daughter has to get married."

"Silver wasps marry golden wasps.
The honey bee marries the bumblebee,
The fly marries the caterpillar,

梅葛 // Meige

爹妈的女儿也得嫁。 Our daughter has to get married."

"大金蝴蝶要出嫁, "The golden butterfly gets married,
红花蝴蝶要出嫁, The red butterfly gets married,
金头蜻蜓要出嫁, The golden-head dragonfly gets married,
爹妈的女儿也得嫁。 Our daughter has to get married."

"双尾虫虫要出嫁, "The double-tailed worm gets married,
单尾虫虫要出嫁, The one-tailed worm gets married,
多脚虫虫要出嫁, The multi-feet worm gets married,
独脚虫虫要出嫁, The single-foot worm gets married,
爹妈的女儿也得嫁。 Our daughter has to get married."

"世间的虫虫都要出嫁, "All insects in the world get married,
世间万物都要出嫁, All things on the earth get married,
爹妈的女儿也得嫁。 Our daughter has to get married."

"岩上'伯么'① 有三对, "Three pairs of insects are mating on the rock.
河坝'山灵'② 有二对, Two more pairs are doing it by the river.
人人见了都喊打。 Everyone wants to see them dead.
要是我的女儿, If my daughter
像'伯么'一样, Is like the insects,

---

① 伯么:系昆虫,性淫。
② 山灵:系昆虫,性淫。

第三部　婚事和恋歌
Book Three　Marriage and Love Songs

像'山灵'一样，	Doing the same thing,
她就别想活在世上。"	She will not live in the world."
自从那天和你相会后，	Since the day we met,
找柴煮饭别人做，	House chores have been done by others.
我被关在屋子里，	I have been locked up in the room.
太阳没有晒过我的脸，	The sun hasn't touched my face
太阳没有晒过我的脚，	Or my feet.
我的小哥啊！	My dear boy!
快快替我出主意。	You have to give me an idea.

男： **Man:**

小妹啊！	My dear girl!
只要你愿意，	As long as you need it,
我来想办法，	I'll find a method.
我去捉麂子，	I will catch a muntjac,
我去捉狐狸，	I will catch a fox,
把兽肉送给你爹妈。	And give the meat to your parents.
小哥用真心，	With my sincerity,
小哥用金银，	With my gold and silver,
小哥一定要赎你。	Your dear boy will get you out.

你的婆家来说亲，	If the matchmaker from your parents-in-law
费了三杯酒，	Brought three glasses of wine to propose,
我还他三坛。	I will return him three jars.

梅葛 // Meige

费了三块羊肉，	If he brought three pieces of lamb,
我还他三只羊。	I will return him three sheep.
费了三升米，	If he brought three kilograms of rice,
我还他三斗米。	I will return him thirty kilograms.
你爹妈接了三钱金子，	If your parents received three grams of gold,
我还他三两。	I will return him thirty grams.
你爹妈接了五钱银子，	If they received five grams of silver,
我还他五两。	I will return him fifty grams.
接了三钱还三两，	Receiving three, returning thirty,
接了五钱还五两；	Receiving five, returning fifty,
戥子旺旺地称，	I will compensate them,
戥尾翘上天地称；	And compensate them generously.
你婆婆心喜欢，	Your mother-in-law will be happy,
你婆婆心快乐，	Your mother-in-law will be satisfied.
我们两个就能成一家。	The two of us will be able to get married.

女： **Woman:**

小哥用真心来赎小妹，	My dear boy, you ransomed me with sincerity,
小哥用金银来赎小妹。	You ransomed me with gold and silver.
婆家答应了，	My husband's family has agreed.
爹妈也答应了。	My mom and dad have agreed.

第三部　婚事和恋歌
Book Three　Marriage and Love Songs

男：

小妹啊！

小哥讨小妹，

小妹嫁小哥，

从此我们成一家。

鱼儿跟着水走，

水顺笕槽流，

竹鸡跟着野鸡走，

小妹快跟小哥走。

女：

家里有爹妈，

小妹舍不得。

男：

送你爹爹三升马蹄金，

送你妈妈三升驴蹄银。

女：

家里亲哥亲兄弟，

小妹舍不得。

男：

送你阿哥三把刀，

Man:

My dear girl!

The boy will marry the girl.

The girl will marry the boy.

We will be happily together.

Fish follows the water,

Water flows the tunnel,

The bamboo partridge follows the pheasant,

The girl follows the boy.

Woman:

I hate to part with my mom,

I hate to part with my dad.

Man:

I'll give your dad three kilograms of gold,

And your mom three kilograms of silver.

Woman:

I hate to part with my elder brother,

I hate to part with my younger brother.

Man:

I'll give your elder brother three knives,

梅葛 // Meige

送你阿弟三把锄。 And your younger brother three hoes.

女：
家里阿姐和阿妹， I hate to part with my elder sister,
小妹舍不得。 I hate to part with my younger sister.

男：
送你阿姐三对银耳环， I'll give your elder sister three pairs of silver earrings,
送你阿妹三副银镯头。 And your younger sister three pairs of silver bracelets.

女：
还有亲戚和朋友， I hate to part with my relatives,
小妹舍不得。 I hate to part with my friends.

男：
杀猪宰羊请他们， I'll butcher hogs and sheep to treat them,
煮肉打酒请他们。 I'll cook meat and buy wine to treat them.

女：
还有家禽和家畜， There are poultry and livestock,
小妹舍不得。 I hate to part with them.
家里红公鸡， There is a red rooster,
小妹舍不得。 I hate to part with it.
家里大白鹅， There is a white goose,

第三部　婚事和恋歌
Book Three　Marriage and Love Songs

小妹舍不得。	I hate to part with it.
家里老灰鸭，	There is an old gray duck,
小妹舍不得。	I hate to part with it.
家里水牛和黄牛，	There are buffalo and cattle,
小妹舍不得。	I hate to part with them.
家里大肥猪，	There is a fat pig,
小妹舍不得。	I hate to part with it.
家里大黄狗，	There is a big dog,
小妹舍不得，	I hate to part with it,
家里小花猫，	There is a little kitten,
小妹舍不得。	I hate to part with it.
小妹若要走，	If I have to go,
猪鸡牛羊也要跟着走。	All of them must follow.

男： **Man:**

小哥想办法，	I have an idea to coax poultry
把猪鸡牛羊哄在家；	And livestock to stay at home.
喂鸡三升谷，	We'll feed the rooster three kilograms of grain,
喂鹅三升豆，	Feed the goose three kilograms of beans,
喂鸭三升米，	Feed the duck three kilograms of rice,
喂牛三把草，	Feed the cattle three bundles of grass,
喂羊三枝叶，	Feed the sheep three bundles of leaves,
喂猪三升糠，	Feed the pig three kilograms of bran,
喂狗三个骨头，	Feed the dog three bones,

梅葛 // Meige

糯米饭舀三碗，
喂给小花猫。

And scoop up three bowls of sticky rice,
To feed your kitten.

女：
家里正房后房各三间，
小妹舍不得。

Woman:
We have three living rooms and three back rooms,
I hate to part with them.

男：
正房里烧下三堆火，
后房里堆下三把草。

Man:
You can make three fires in the three living rooms,
And put three piles of grass in the three back rooms.

女：
家里粮仓和水槽，
小妹舍不得。

Woman:
There is the barn and the sink,
I hate to part with them.

男：
粮仓头装下三斗粮，
水槽里挑下三挑水。

Man:
I'll fill the barn with thirty kilograms of grain,
And put thirty kilograms of water in the sink.

女：
家里箱子和柜子，
小妹舍不得。

Woman:
There is the chest and the cabinet,
I hate to part with them.

第三部　婚事和恋歌
Book Three　Marriage and Love Songs

男：
箱子里装下三丈布，
柜子头装下三件衣。

Man:
I'll put three feet of cloth into the chest,
And three pieces of clothes into the cabinet.

女：
家里装碗筷的篮子，
小妹舍不得。

Woman:
There is a basket for bowls and chopsticks,
I hate to part with it.

男：
篮子头装下白碗三个，
篮子头装下筷子三双；
样样安排好，
小妹走得了。

Man:
You can put three white bowls
And three pairs of chopsticks into the basket.
When all these have been done,
You can hit the road.

女：
小哥啊！
小妹头上无新帽，
身上无新衣，
脚上无新鞋，
穿的破烂出不来，
戴的破烂出不来。

Woman:
But my dear boy!
I don't have new hats,
I don't have new clothes,
I don't have new shoes.
I cannot go out in rags.
I cannot go out in an old hat.

男：
小妹啊！

Man:
Oh, my dear girl!

梅葛 // Meige

穿的不好不要怕，	Don't worry about your clothes,
戴的不好不要愁；	Don't worry about your hat.
小哥想办法，	I have an idea.
街头有花帽，	Hats are sold on the east end of the street,
街中有花布，	Fabrics are sold in the middle of the street,
街尾有花鞋。	Shoes are sold on the west end of the street.
马蹄金子我背着，	I have gold with me,
驴蹄银子我背着，	I have silver with me.
哥妹欢欢喜喜去赶街。	Happily, you and I will go shopping together.
街头买花帽，	We'll buy hats on the east end of the street,
街中买花布，	Fabrics in the middle of the street,
街尾买花鞋，	And shoes on the west end of the street,
小妹头上戴花帽，	Hat on head,
手上戴银镯，	Silver bracelets on hands,
脚上穿花鞋，	Shoes on feet,
浑身上下银花开，	You are shining all over,
从头到脚打扮好，	You are dressed up all over.
小妹走得了。	Now you can hit the road.

女： **Woman:**

小哥啊！	But my dear boy!
小妹没有好花戴，	I don't have a flower to wear.
没有花戴不出来。	Without a flower, I cannot go out.

第三部　婚事和恋歌
Book Three　Marriage and Love Songs

男：
小妹啊！
没有花戴不要怕，
小哥上山坡，
采来二月红山花，
茶花头上戴，
茶花腰上挂，
茶花脚上插。
小妹从头红到脚，
小妹从头亮到脚。
这回走得了。

女：
有心跟哥走，
就是路没有。

男：
大理生铁好，
打把好条锄，
打把好腰斧，
打把好钩刀，
小哥来开路。

Man:
My dear girl!
Don't worry about the flower.
I will go to the hillside
To pick some red February flowers,
Wearing a camellia on your head,
Hanging a camellia on your belt,
Plugging a camellia to your shoes.
You are red from head to toe,
You are bright from toe to head.
Now you can hit the road.

Woman:
I want to go with you,
But there is no road to follow.

Man:
Cast iron in Dali is good,
Let's use it to make a good hoe.
Let's use it to make a good waist ax.
Let's use it to make a good hook knife.
I will hew a way out.

梅葛 // Meige

女：
小哥来开路，
越挖路越长，
越挖路越窄，
路长路窄难走过，
只有乌鸦喜鹊才能走，
小妹不能走。

男：
小妹不能走，
小哥从头挖。
挖路到松林，
松树哪个砍？

女：
挖路到松林，
请啄木鸟来啄。

男：
挖路到石岩，
石岩哪个挖？

女：
挖路到石岩，

Woman:
My dear boy wants to open a road,
The road grows longer as you hew,
The road turns narrower as you hew.
Long and narrow, it is a hard road,
Only crows and magpies can go,
But I cannot.

Man:
You cannot go.
Then I'll hew out another road.
When the road reaches the pinewood,
Who will remove the trees?

Woman:
When the road reaches the pinewood,
Ask the woodpeckers to remove the trees.

Man:
When the road meets rocks,
Who will remove them?

Woman:
When the road meets rocks,

第三部　婚事和恋歌
Book Three　Marriage and Love Songs

请古字子①来挖。　　　　　Ask the bird guzizi to remove them.

男：
路也挖通了，　　　　　　　The road is opened up.
小妹快快走。　　　　　　　Let's hurry away.

女：
小妹出嫁有了路，　　　　　The road to your home is opened up.
老牛前面走，　　　　　　　Old cows go first,
哥妹跟后头。　　　　　　　You and I follow in the rear.
来到十一条河，　　　　　　We come across the eleventh river,
来到十二条河，　　　　　　We come across the twelfth river.
忽见洪水涨，　　　　　　　The rivers are rising,
波浪滚滚来，　　　　　　　Waves are roaring.
小妹不敢过河去。　　　　　I dare not cross the rivers.

男：
小妹不要怕，　　　　　　　Don't be afraid, my little girl.
小哥上山砍棵树，　　　　　I will cut down a tree,
搭上一座桥，　　　　　　　Make you a bridge
扶妹过桥去。　　　　　　　And help you cross the rivers.

---
① 古字子：鸟名。

梅葛 // Meige

女：
路上有老虎，
路下有豹子，
路心头有大麻蛇。
小妹最怕老虎，
小妹最怕豹子，
小妹最怕大麻蛇。

男：
人说小米小，
小妹的胆子比小米小。
路上不是虎，
是个大石头。
路下不是豹，
是个老树根。
路心不是大麻蛇，
放羊娃娃掉下一根赶羊鞭。

女：
路过青草上，
为何有油水？
小妹心害怕。

Woman:
There is a tiger on the road,
There is a leopard by the road,
There is a snake in the middle of the road.
I am afraid of tigers,
I am afraid of leopards,
I am afraid of snakes.

Man:
My dear girl,
You are so timid.
It's not a tiger on the road:
It's a big rock.
It's not a leopard by the road:
It is an old root.
It's not a snake on the road,
It is a whip left by the shepherd.

Woman:
I see oil
On the grass.
I am so scared.

第三部　婚事和恋歌
Book Three　Marriage and Love Songs

男：

不是草上有油水，

露水露到青草上。

太阳出来晒一晒，

露水就干了。

女：

一面走来一面听，

路上路下有声音。

小妹不敢走。

男：

小妹不要怕，

路上有声音，

是小貂鼠在跑；

路下有声音，

是小雀飞起来。

女：

小哥啊！

怎么树上挂篮子？

怎么路心头垫虎皮？

小妹没见过。

Man:

There is no oil on the grass.

It is the morning dew.

When the sun comes out,

It will evaporate.

Woman:

I listen while we move on.

I hear some sound.

I am so scared.

Man:

Don't be afraid, my girl.

The sound you hear

Comes from running martens.

The sound you hear

Comes from flying sparrows.

Woman:

My dear boy,

Why is there a basket on the tree?

Why is there tiger skin on the road?

I never see that.

梅葛 // Meige

男：
树上没有挂篮子，
那是小雀窝。
路心没有垫虎皮，
那是树影子。
小妹莫胆小，
只管放心走。

女：
走到小哥家门前，
小妹抬头看一看，
有些飞鸟来卖针，
小妹胆子小，
不敢走门槛。

男：
小妹不要怕，
飞的不是鸟，
我家蜜蜂采花回；
不是鸟卖针，
蜜蜂身上有蜂刺。

女：
来到小哥家，

Man:
It is not a basket on the tree,
It's a bird's nest.
It is not a tiger skin on the road,
It is the shadow of trees.
My dear girl, don't be afraid.
You can rest assured.

Woman:
Arriving at your door,
I look up and see some birds.
They are selling needles.
I am too timid
To go inside.

Man:
Don't be afraid, my dear girl.
They are not birds.
They are honey bees coming back.
They are not birds selling needles:
Bees have stingers.

Woman:
Arriving at your home,

第三部　婚事和恋歌
Book Three　Marriage and Love Songs

小哥家里老虎叫，
小哥家里豹子吼，
小妹很害怕。

男：
小妹不要怕，
不是老虎叫，
不是豹子吼；
亲戚朋友接小妹，
吹着唢呐接小妹，
敲锣打鼓接小妹。

I hear roaring of tigers,
I hear roaring of leopards.
I am so scared.

Man:
My dear girl, don't be afraid,
It's not the roaring of tigers,
It's not the roaring of leopards.
They are my relatives and friends,
Welcoming you by playing the suona,
Welcoming you by beating drums.

女：
妹跟小哥进了门，
院头开银花，
院中栽虎骨，
院尾开金花。

Woman:
I follow my dear boy into the house
And see silver flowers blooming to the north side,
Tiger bones planted in the middle of the yard,
Gold flowers blooming to the south side.

男：
院头不是开银花，
要办喜事搭彩棚；
院中不是栽虎骨，
搭棚用的松树桩；
院尾不是开金花，

Man:
It's not silver flowers blooming to the north side.
It is our wedding shed.
It's not tiger bones planted in the middle of the yard.
It's pine stumps for building the shed.
It's not gold flowers blooming to south side.

- 215 -

梅葛 // Meige

院尾搭起锥栗架。	It is a frame for castanea henryi.

女：
进了哥家门，
小妹无房住。

Woman:
Entering your home,
I have no room to live in.

男：
小妹无房住，
小哥挖地基。

Man:
You have no room to live in,
I will lay the foundation.

女：
地基挖好了，
哪个量地基？
哪个看地基？
哪个滚地基？

Woman:
The foundation is laid,
But who will measure it?
Who will guard it?
Who will roll it?

男：
公鸡量地基，
公鸡看地基，
公鸡滚地基。

Man:
The rooster will measure it.
The rooster will guard it.
The rooster will roll it.

女：
地基量好了，
怎么盖房子？

Woman:
The foundation is measured,
But how to build a house?

第三部　婚事和恋歌
Book Three　Marriage and Love Songs

男：

哥妹来商量：

小哥翘起拇指好算年，

小妹掐着食指好算月。

到了正二月，

上山砍木料，

松头做椽子，

松杆做过梁，

松根做柱子。

到了三四月，

木头晒干了，

小哥上山抬木头。

女：

木头抬回来，

哪个钻木头？

男：

木头抬回来，

请啄木鸟钻木头。

女：

用什么量木头？

Man:

Let's talk it over:

I count years with my thumb,

You count months with you forefinger.

In January and February,

We go to the mountains to cut down trees.

Pine branches are used to make rafters,

Pine trunks are used to make beams,

Pine roots are used to make pillars.

When it comes to March and April,

The wood are dried up,

I will go to the mountains to carry it back.

Woman:

When the logs are carried home,

Who will drill them?

Man:

When the logs are carried home,

Woodpeckers will be invited to drill them.

Woman:

What tool will be used to measure the logs?

梅葛 // Meige

用什么弹墨线?

What tool will be used to make ink markers?

男：
尺子量木头，
墨斗弹墨线。

Man:
Ruler will be used to measure the logs,
Ink fountain will be used to make ink markers.

女：
哪个合木头？
哪个竖过梁？

Woman:
Who will assemble the logs?
Who will set up the beams?

男：
木匠合木头，
木匠竖过梁。

Man:
Carpenters will assemble the logs,
Carpenters will set up the beams.

女：
木头合好了，
过梁竖好了，
哪个盖房子？

Woman:
Logs are assembled,
Beams are set up,
But who will make the roof?

男：
房架竖好了，
木匠来盖房。

Man:
When the frame is set up,
Carpenters will make the roof.

第三部　婚事和恋歌
Book Three　Marriage and Love Songs

女：
割草盖草房，
烧瓦盖瓦房，
小妹进了房，
房里没有床。

Woman:
They cut grass to build a straw roof,
And bake tiles to build a tile roof.
When I get into the room,
I can't find a bed.

男：
松板来做床，
竹席做垫子。

Man:
I'll make a bed with pine board,
Plus a bamboo woven-mat.

女：
飞蚊做了窝，
鸳鸯鸟成双，
我们两个安家了。

Woman:
Mosquitoes have their nests,
Mandarin ducks are in pairs,
We are finally married.

男：
哥妹去赶街，
二十二两白银买水牛，
二十二两白银买驮马；
买了绵羊买山羊，
样样买齐全。

Man:
You and I go shopping together,
Paying twenty-two taels of silver for a buffalo,
Another twenty-two taels of silver for a workhorse.
We buy sheep and goats.
We buy everything we need.

女：
鸡猪牛羊关满圈，

Woman:
Our pens are crammed with domestic animals,

梅葛 // Meige

我们两个啊，
养的牛多起来了，
养的羊多起来了！

男：
小妹在家放牛羊，
小哥上街买种子，
走到街上看粮食，
粮仓十二间，
一间装谷子，
一间装荞子，
一间装苞谷，
一间装麻子，
一间装麦子，
一间装豆子，
样样都齐全。
好的种子给三文，
坏的种子给两文，
谷子买三箩，
荞子买三箩，
苞谷买三箩，
麻子买三箩，
麦子买三箩，
豆子买三箩，

The two of us
Have more and more cattle,
And more and more sheep!

Man:
You stay at home to graze the cattle and sheep,
I go to town to buy
Seeds and grain.
There are twelve barns.
One for millet,
One for buckwheat,
One for corn,
One for hemp seeds,
One for wheat,
One for beans,
They have all sorts of grain there.
Three pence for good seeds,
Two pence for bad seeds,
I buy three baskets of millet,
Three baskets of buckwheat,
Three baskets of corn,
Three baskets of hemp seeds,
Three baskets of wheat,
And three baskets of beans,

第三部　婚事和恋歌
Book Three　Marriage and Love Songs

样样种子买齐全。　　　　　I buy everything we need.

女：**Woman:**
小哥小妹开了田地，　　　　You and I plow the field.
小哥小妹找到放牛羊的地方，You and I find a grazing place.
照着年月节令盘庄稼，　　　We plant crops according to the season.
照着年月节令放牛羊。　　　We graze livestock according to the season.

男：**Man:**
正月初二到，　　　　　　　The second day of January
动手撒秧了，　　　　　　　Is the time to sow rice seeds,
犁头犁架动起来，　　　　　Ploughshare and plow frames are busy,
先盘河边有水田。　　　　　Let's start with riverside fields.

女：**Woman:**
小妹筛出种子来，　　　　　I sift the seeds.
小妹簸出种子来，　　　　　I toss the seeds.
小哥背去河里泡。　　　　　You soak them in the river.

男：**Man:**
正月初二撒小秧，　　　　　Rice seeds are sowed on the second day of January.
二月初二秧出土，　　　　　Seedlings sprout on the second day of February.
三月初二秧长大，　　　　　Seedlings grow up by the second day of March.
到了五月间，　　　　　　　When May comes,

- 221 -

梅葛 // Meige

栽秧季节到，
头棵秧苗哥来栽，
秧苗长得绿茵茵，
草也长得秧样高，
小妹你快薅秧去。

It's time to plant seedlings.
I'll plant the first one.
Seedlings are green and verdant.
Weeds are as high as the seedlings.
My dear girl, go and pull the weeds.

女：
小妹力气小，
抓不了稗子拔不起草。
薅秧薅到五月间，
紧薅薅不完。
小哥啊！
你不是撒秧是撒草。

Woman:
I have little strength,
I cannot pull up barnyard grass and weeds.
I cannot finish in May.
I can never finish it.
My dear boy!
What you planted are not seedlings, but weeds.

男：
小妹啊！
抓不到的草有十二种，
抓得动的草有十二种；
拔不动的草有十二种，
拔得动的草有十二种；
硬的草有十二种，
软的草有十二种。
小哥力气大，
抓不到的草哥去抓，

Man:
My dear sister!
There are twelve sorts of grass you can't weed,
There are twelve sorts of grass you can weed.
There are twelve sorts of grass you can't pull,
There are twelve sorts of grass you can pull.
There are twelve kinds of hard grass,
There are twelve kinds of soft grass.
I am strong.
I can weed the grass that you can't.

第三部　婚事和恋歌
Book Three　Marriage and Love Songs

拔不动的草哥去拔，	I can pull the grass that you can't.
小妹力气小，	You have little strength.
抓得动的草妹去抓，	You weed the grass that you can.
拔得动的草妹去拔。	You pull the grass that you can.
杂草稗子小哥分不清，	I can't tell barnyard grass from weeds.
要请小妹教小哥。	Teach me please.

女： **Woman:**

小哥听妹说：	Listen to me carefully:
抓不动的是牙齿草，	What you can't weed is teeth grass,
拔不动的是稗子。	What you can't pull up is barnyard grass.

男： **Man:**

正月接二月，	February follows January.
正合撒麻子，	It's time to sow hemp seeds.
麻子出得绿油油；	Hemps grow green and verdant.
三月接四月，	April follows March.
正合撒荞子，	It's time to sow buckwheat seeds.
荞子出得绿又嫩；	Buckwheat grows green and tender.
六月屋后撒萝卜，	In June turnips are planted behind the house.
萝卜长得粗又长；	Turnips grow thick and long.
七月割甜荞，	In July common buckwheat is harvested.
甜荞装满袋，	Bags are full, bags are filled.
七月十四尝新荞；	New buckwheat is served on the fourteenth day of July.

梅葛 // Meige

八月谷子低着头，	In August the ears of millet grow heavy,
谷穗像马尾，	Bowing like a horsetail.
拿起镰刀下田去，	I work in the fields with a sickle.
割谷晒谷忙。	Harvested and dried,
谷子背回家，	Millet is carried home.
属蛇日来尝。	On the Day of the Snake, we'll eat them.

女： **Woman:**
哪个来割麻？ Who will cut the hemp?
哪个来刷麻？ Who will brush the hemp?

男： **Man:**
小妹来割麻， You will cut the hemp,
小哥来刷麻， I will brush the hemp.
小妹拿起镰刀来割麻， You cut the hemp with a sickle,
小哥拿起梨树板子来刷麻。 I brush the hemp with a pear tree board.

女： **Woman:**
哪个抱麻秸？ Who will carry the stalks?
哪个掰麻枝？ Who will break off the branches?

男： **Man:**
小哥抱麻秸， I will carry the stalks,
小妹掰麻枝。 You will break off the branches.

第三部　婚事和恋歌
Book Three　Marriage and Love Songs

女：
麻皮哪里晒？
麻皮哪里泡？

Woman:
Where to dry the stem-fibre?
Where to soak the stem-fibre?

男：
松树杆上晒，
河水深处泡。

Man:
Dry it on the pine tree,
Soak it in the river.

女：
麻皮哪里洗？

Woman:
Where to wash the stem-fibre?

男：
河里青石板上洗。

Man:
On the riverside slate.

男：
哪个来绩麻？

Man:
Who will twist hemp fibers?

女：
小妹来绩麻。
二指把麻绕，
大指把麻分。

Woman:
I will twist hemp fibers,
Winding them with the forefinger,
Separating them with the thumb.

梅葛 // Meige

男：
哪个来纺线？

女：
小妹来纺线。
大锅来煮线，
煮线煮出来，
青石板上洗，
房前屋后晒。

男：
哪个来织布？

女：
小妹来织布。
麻布织出来，
拿去街上换，
麻布换细布，
两丈换一丈。
麻布换花布，
三丈换一丈。
青布白布夹杂缝，
花衣装满箱。

Man:
Who will spin thread?

Woman:
I will do it,
Cooking the thread in a cauldron.
Cooked thread will be washed,
Washed on the slate,
And dried around the house.

Man:
Who will weave?

Woman:
I will weave.
Woven linen
Will be taken to town
To exchange for muslin,
Two feet of linen for one foot of muslin.
When exchanging for printed cloth,
Three feet of linen for one foot of printed cloth.
These are woven with green cloth and white cloth.
Boxes are filled with beautiful clothes.

第三部　婚事和恋歌
Book Three　Marriage and Love Songs

男：
楼上谷子堆满仓，
楼下荞子装满囤，
养牛牛满圈，
养羊羊满圈，
养马马满圈，
养猪猪满圈，
养鸡鸡满圈。
小妹啊！
日子过得好，
日子过得长；
生了好儿子，
生了好姑娘；
儿子长大放牛羊，
姑娘长大织布缝衣裳。

Man:
The upstairs warehouse is filled with millet,
The downstairs bins are full of buckwheat,
Cattle are thriving,
Sheep are thriving,
Horses are thriving,
Pigs are thriving,
Chickens are thriving.
My dear girl!
Our life is good,
Our life is long.
We have a good son,
We have a good daughter.
Our son grows up to raise cattle and sheep,
Our daughter grows up to weave and sew.

第四部 丧葬
Book Four   Funerals

梅葛 // Meige

一 死 亡　　　　I. Death

天王撒下活种子，　　　　The king of the sky sows the seeds of life,
天王撒下死种子。　　　　The king of the sky sows the seeds of death.
活的种子筛一角，　　　　Life seeds are sifted once,
死的种子筛三筛。　　　　But death seeds are sieved three times.
活的种子撒一把，　　　　The king casts one handful of life seeds,
死的种子撒三把。　　　　But three handfuls of death seeds.

死种撒出去，　　　　　　When the death seeds are cast,
会让的就能活在世上，　　Those who know how to dodge will live,
不会让的就死亡。　　　　And those who don't will die.

六月七月间，　　　　　　In June and July,
死种撒到白云上，　　　　Death seeds are cast onto white clouds,
死种撒到黑云上，　　　　Death seeds are cast onto black clouds,
白云黑云都会让。　　　　Which know how to dodge.

八月九月间，　　　　　　In August and September,
死种撒到月亮上，　　　　Death seeds are cast onto the moon,
月亮也会让。　　　　　　Which knows how to dodge.

第四部　丧葬
Book Four　Funerals

十冬腊月天，	In October, November and December,
死种撒到星星上，	Death seeds are cast onto the stars,
星星也会让。	Which know how to dodge.
正二三月春天来，	In January, February and March,
死种撒到节令上，	Death seeds are cast onto the seasons,
节令也会让。	Which know how to dodge.
死种撒地上，	Death seeds are cast onto the earth,
大地不会让，	Which doesn't know how to dodge,
地会裂成缝。	So it cracks.
死种撒到山头上，	Death seeds are cast onto the mountains,
山也不会让，	Which don't know how to dodge,
山会塌下来。	So they collapse.
死种撒到石岩上，	Death seeds are cast onto rocks,
石岩不会让，	Which don't know how to dodge,
石岩会裂开。	So they break.
死种撒到树头上，	Death seeds are cast into trees,
树也不会让，	Which don't know how to dodge,
树子会死亡：	So they will die:
撒到橡子树头上，	Death seeds are cast into acorn trees,
橡子树就死了；	Acorn trees will die;
撒到柏枝树头上，	Death seeds are cast into cypress trees,

梅葛 // Meige

柏枝树就死了；	Cypress trees will die;
撒到赤松树头上，	Death seeds are cast into red pines,
赤松树也死了；	Red pines will die;
撒到梧桐树头上，	Death seeds are cast into plane trees,
梧桐树也死了；	Plane trees will die;
撒到杨柳树头上，	Death seeds are cast into willow trees,
杨柳树也死了；	Willow trees will die;
撒到马缨花树上，	Death seeds are cast into azalea trees,
马缨花树不开花；	Azalea trees won't blossom;
撒到橄榄树头上，	Death seeds are cast into olive trees,
橄榄树也死了；	Olive trees will die;
撒到花椒树头上，	Death seeds are cast into pepper trees,
花椒树也死了；	Pepper trees will die;
撒到竹子上，	Death seeds are cast into bamboos,
竹子会枯死。	Bamboos will wither and die.
地上树木都撒遍，	Death seeds are cast into all trees,
地上树木都会死。	All trees will die.
没有撒不到的树，	No tree will be spared,
没有不会死的树。	So there is no tree that will not die.
死种撒到草头上，	Death seeds are cast onto grass,
草不会让，	Which doesn't know how to dodge,
草会死亡。	And will die.

第四部　丧葬
Book Four　Funerals

撒在地面草尖上，	Death seeds are cast onto the earth,
地上的草会枯黄。	Grass will turn brown.

撒到芦苇上，　　　　　Death seeds are cast onto the reed,
芦苇会枯死；　　　　　Reed will die.
撒到山草上，　　　　　Death seeds are cast onto mountain grass,
山草就会死；　　　　　Mountain grass will die.
撒到艾草上，　　　　　Death seeds are cast onto wormwood,
艾草会枯死；　　　　　Wormwood will die.
撒到黄麻上，　　　　　Death seeds are cast onto the jute,
黄麻就会死。　　　　　The jute will die.

地上的草都撒遍，　　　Death seeds are cast onto all grass,
地上的草都会死。　　　All grass will die.
没有撒不到的草，　　　No grass will be spared,
没有不会死的草。　　　There is no grass that will not die.
死种撒到百兽头顶上，　Death seeds are cast onto the heads of animals,
百兽不会让，　　　　　Who don't know how to dodge,
百兽会死亡。　　　　　And will die.

撒到兔子头顶上，　　　Death seeds are cast onto the heads of rabbits,
兔子会被石头打死；　　Rabbits will be stoned to death.
撒到老虎头顶上，　　　Death seeds are cast onto the heads of tigers,
老虎会钻在猎人的木圈里；Tigers will be trapped in the hunters' wooden hens.

梅葛 // Meige

撒到野猪头顶上，	Death seeds are cast onto the heads of wild boars,
野猪会被猎人打死；	Wide boars will be killed by hunters.
撒到獐子麂子头顶上，	Death seeds are cast onto the heads of deer and muntjacs,
獐子麂子会跑进猎人的网里；	Deer and muntjacs will fall into hunters' nets.
撒到狐狸头顶上，	Death seeds are cast onto the heads of foxes,
狐狸会跑进猎人网里；	Foxes will run into hunters' nets.
撒到大熊小熊头顶上，	Death seeds are cast onto the heads of bears,
大熊小熊会跳进陷阱里。	Bears will jump into traps.
百兽都撒遍了，	Death seeds are cast onto all animals,
百兽都会死。	All animals will die.
没有撒不到的兽，	No animal will be spared.
没有不会死的兽。	There is no animal that will not die.
死种撒到百鸟头顶上，	Death seeds are cast onto the heads of birds,
百鸟不会让，	Which don't know how to dodge,
百鸟会死亡。	And will die.
撒到凤凰头顶上，	Death seeds are cast onto the heads of phoenixes,
凤凰飞进网里死；	Phoenixes will fly into the net and die.
撒到大雁头顶上，	Death seeds are cast onto the heads of wild geese,
大雁到高山顶上死；	Wild geese will die on the mountain top.
撒到野鸡头顶上，	Death seeds are cast onto the heads of pheasants,
野鸡踩着扣子死；	Pheasants will be trapped.

第四部　丧葬
Book Four　Funerals

撒到啄木鸟头顶上，	Death seeds are cast onto the heads of woodpeckers,
啄木鸟折断脖子死；	Woodpeckers will break their necks.
撒到画眉头顶上，	Death seeds are cast onto the heads of thrushes,
画眉也会死；	Thrushes will die.
撒到杂雀头顶上，	Death seeds are cast onto the heads of sparrows,
杂雀都会死。	Sparrows will die.

百鸟都撒遍了，　　　　Death seeds are cast onto all birds,
百鸟都会死。　　　　　All birds will die.
就连春天布谷鸟，　　　Even the spring cuckoos,
就连河中洗衣鸟，　　　And the laundry birds in the rivers,
也都撒到了。　　　　　Are all doomed.
没有撒不到的鸟，　　　No bird will be spared.
没有不会死的鸟。　　　There is no bird that will not die.

死种撒到百虫头顶上，　Death seeds are cast onto the heads of insects,
百虫不会让，　　　　　Which don't know how to dodge,
百虫会死亡。　　　　　And will die.

撒到大马蜂头顶上，　　When death seeds are cast onto the heads of wasps,
大马蜂在风雪中冻死；　Wasps will freeze to death in snowstorms.
撒到蚂蚱头顶上，　　　When they are cast onto the heads of grasshoppers,
蚂蚱会被火烧死；　　　Grasshoppers will be burned to death.
撒到苍蝇蚊子头顶上，　When they are cast onto the heads of mosquitoes and

梅葛 // Meige

苍蝇蚊子会被药毒死；
撒到蚯蚓头顶上，
蚯蚓会被锄头挖死。

flies,
Mosquitoes and flies will be poisoned to death.
When they are cast onto the heads of earthworms,
Earthworms will be cut dead.

百虫都撒遍了，
百虫都会死。
没有撒不到的虫，
没有不会死的虫。

Death seeds are cast onto all insects,
All insects will die.
No insect will be spared.
There is no insect that will not die.

死种撒到鱼儿头顶上，
鱼儿不会让，
鱼儿会死亡。

Death seeds are cast onto the heads of fishes,
Which don't know how to dodge,
And will die.

撒到鱼儿头顶上，
鱼儿跳进渔网死；
撒到石蚌头顶上，
石蚌也会跳进网里死。

When they are cast onto the heads of fishes,
Fishes will jump into fishing nets.
When they are cast onto the heads of frogs,
Frogs will also jump into nets.

鱼儿都撒遍了，
鱼儿都会死。
没有撒不到的鱼，
没有不会死的鱼。

Death seeds are cast onto all fishes,
All fishes will die.
No fish will be spared.
There is no fish that will not die.

第四部　丧葬
Book Four　Funerals

死种撒在家畜头顶上，	Death seeds are cast onto the heads of livestock,
家畜不会让，	Livestock don't know how to dodge,
家畜会死亡。	And will die.
撒到黄牛头顶上，	When they are cast onto the heads of cattle,
黄牛犁地会累死；	Cattle will work to death.
撒到肥猪头顶上，	When they are cast onto the heads of pigs,
肥猪过年要杀死；	Pigs will be killed to celebrate the New Year.
撒到绵羊头顶上，	When they are cast onto the heads of sheep,
绵羊在山上跌死。	Sheep will run off the cliff and die.
家畜都撒遍了，	When they are cast onto all livestock,
家畜都会死。	All livestock will die.
没有撒不到的家畜，	No livestock will be spared.
没有不会死的家畜。	There is no livestock that will not die.
四月撒死种，	Death seeds are cast in April,
八月会死完。	All creatures will die by August.
鸟兽鱼虫都撒遍，	Death seeds are cast onto all creatures,
鸟兽鱼虫都会死。	All creatures will die.
撒也撒完了，	All death seeds are cast,
死也死完了。	All creatures are dead.
没有撒不到的东西，	Everything is doomed,
没有不会死的东西。	Everything will die.

梅葛 // Meige

早晨太阳出，	The sun rises in the morning,
晚上太阳落，	And sets in the evening,
太阳会出也会落，	Like the sun,
人和太阳一个样，	Which rises and sets,
会生也会死。	People live and die.

高山长树木，　　　　　　　Trees grow on high mountains,
发出嫩芽绿又旺，　　　　　Their buds are green,
长出叶来也很稳。　　　　　Their leaves are prosperous.
只说高山树木不落叶，　　　It is said that alpine trees are indeciduate,
哪知九月叶会黄，　　　　　But leaves turn yellow in September.
风吹黄叶叶就落。　　　　　The wind blows and the leaves fall.
人死就像落叶样，　　　　　Like fallen leaves,
到死时候也会死。　　　　　People die when it's time to die.

灶洞烧火要有风，　　　　　To light a fire in the stove needs wind.
没风烧火火褪色，　　　　　When wind abates, the fire fades,
没风烧火火会灭；　　　　　When wind stops, the fire extinguishes.
人死就像火褪色，　　　　　People die like the fire fades.
人死就像火会灭，　　　　　People die like the fire extinguishes.
到死时候也会死。　　　　　People die when it's time to die.

田头梨子树，　　　　　　　The pear trees on the farms

第四部　丧葬
Book Four　Funerals

二月开花长出叶，	Blossom and come into leaf in February.
三月四月会结果，	They bear fruits in March and April.
五月六月果子稳，	Fruits stabilize in May and June,
七月八月果子熟，	Mature in July and August,
籽饱果熟就掉下，	And fall when their seeds and pulp are ripe.
人死就像果子掉，	People die like fruits fall.
到死时候也会死。	People die when it's time to die.
世人都会死，	Everyone dies,
一百岁的人会死，	One-hundred-year-olds die.
三十多岁的人也会死，	People in their thirties die.
几岁的人也会死，	Little kids may die.
生下地的娃娃也会死；	Newborns may die.
男人会死，	Men will die.
女人会死；	Women will die.
做大官的人会死，	High officials will die.
做小吏的人也会死；	Functionaries will die.
穷人会死，	The poor will die.
发财的人也会死。	The rich will die.
死种撒下来，	Death seeds are cast down,
撒到病人头顶上，	Onto the heads of the sick,
病人不会让，	Who don't know how to dodge.
就会病死掉。	They will die of disease.

梅葛 // Meige

阿爹生了病，	Dad got sick,
要找不死药，	Medicine could not be found.
找到昆明去，	I went to Kunming,
找到禄丰去，	I went to Lufeng,
找到大理去，	I went to Dali,
找到白井去，	I went to Baijing,
又到姚安找，	I went to Yao'an,
又到牟定找，	I went to Mouding,
找过了许多地方。	I went to many places.
医疼的药倒有，	There are pain killers,
医死的药没有。	But no death killers.
没有办法了！	There was no way out!
只好背爹去躲病。	So I had to carry dad away
背到哪里躲？	To hide from disease. But where to hide?
背到大山上，	In the mountains,
松树根边躲。	Hiding beside pine roots.
只说松树万古不会死，	They say that pines live forever,
哪知松树也会死。	But pines die, too.
松树咋个死？	How did these pines die?
打柴人来劈明子，	People needed firewood.
劈开松树当火把；	They cut pines for torches.
松树被劈死，	The pines were hacked to death.

第四部　丧葬
Book Four　Funerals

还是躲不脱。	There was no way to hide.
山上躲不脱，	We could not hide in mountains,
背去大箐里，	So I carried dad into the valley,
锥栗树根边躲，	Hiding beside chestnut roots,
哪知锥栗树也会死！	But chestnut trees die!
锥栗树咋个死？	How did these die?
寸水糟树心，	Water rotted their piths,
风刮腰断死，	Wind broke their waists.
还是躲不脱。	There was no way to hide.
大箐躲不脱，	We could not hide in the valley,
背去山岩边，	So I carried dad to the rock,
石岩底下躲。	Hiding under it.
只说石岩下雨不会死，	They say that rocks will not die from rain,
日晒不会炸，	And that rocks will not crack in the sun,
哪知石岩也会死！	But rocks die!
石岩咋个死？	How did these rocks die?
石岩崩裂死，	They cracked to death.
还是躲不脱。	There was no way to hide.
石岩躲不脱，	We could not hide under the rock,
背回家里去，	So I carried dad back home,
柜子里头躲。	Hiding inside the cabinet.

梅葛 // Meige

只说柜子里头不进风，	It is said that cabinets are
日晒不着，	Windproof, sunproof,
雨打不着，	And rainproof,
哪知柜子也会死！	But cabinets die!
柜子咋个死？	How did this cabinet die?
蛀虫来蛀死，	Moths ate it to death.
还是躲不脱。	There was no way to hide.
吃药吃不好，	Medicine failed,
躲病躲不好，	Hiding places failed.
阿爹死掉了！	Dad was dead!
高山石头最稳当，	Alpine stones are the most secure,
七月下雨也会垮，	But they collapse in July rains.
石头垮了滚下箐，	Collapsed stones roll down,
滚到箐底不回头。	Down to the valley and never go back.
阿爹也像石头滚下箐，	Like a stone rolling down,
阿爹救不活，	Dad could not be saved.
阿爹死掉了！	Dad was dead!
水在秧田里面很稳当，	Water is stable in seedling bed,
坝头泥裂不会垮，	Soil cracks but seedling bed doesn't.
种田人来翻埂子，	Cultivators come to turn the soil,
只见水浪滚出去，	Water waves roll out,
不见水浪折回来。	And never come back.
阿爹也像水浪滚出去，	Like water waves,

第四部　丧葬

Book Four　Funerals

阿爹救不活，	Dad could not be saved.
阿爹死掉了！	Dad was dead!

二　怀亲

II. Memory of Loved Ones

我爹我妈来兴家，	Mom and Dad brought prosperity to our family.
松头做椽子，	Rafters were made of pine branches,
松腰做过梁，	Beams were made of pine trunks,
松根做柱子，	And pillars were made of pine roots.
房子盖得好，	The house was well built,
房子修齐了。	The rooms were well equipped.
家里有儿子，	There were boys at home,
村里有嫁出去的姑娘。	There were girls who married out.
有满圈的牛，	Cattle were thriving,
有成百匹的马，	Horses were thriving,
成千的公羊，	Rams were thriving,
成百的母羊，	Ewes were thriving,
满槽的黑猪，	Black pigs were thriving,
满村的家狗，	Dogs were thriving,
满院的鸡。	Chickens were thriving.
我爹我妈来管家，	When mom and dad managed our family,

- 243 -

梅葛 // Meige

事事有头绪，	Everything was well-thought-out,
样样都顺利。	Everything was well settled.
一年有四季，	There are four seasons in a year,
一季三个月；	And three months in a season.
我爹和我妈，	My Mom and Dad,
大拇指算年，	Counted years with their thumbs,
小拇指算月，	Counted months with their little fingers,
算着年月盘庄稼，	Planted crops according to the season,
正月撒小秧，	Sowed rice seeds in January.
二月三月到，	In February to March,
山坡上面撒荞子，	Buckwheat seeds were sowed on the hills,
山腰上面撒小米；	Millet seeds were sowed on the hillside;
四月栽秧忙，	April was for transplanting seedlings.
山脚河边栽小秧，	At the mountain foot and by the riverside,
苞谷撒在房后头，	Corn seeds were scattered behind the house,
麦瓜黄瓜房前种。	Pumpkins and cucumbers were planted in front.

庄稼长得好，	Crops grew well,
荞子像葡萄，	Buckwheat was like grapes,
小米穗像团白麻线，	The ears of millet were like white twine,
谷穗像马尾，	Ears of corns were like horsetails,
好麻像竹林。	Hemps were as high as bamboos.
麦瓜和黄瓜，	Pumpkin and cucumber vines
一棵发十棵，	Were heavily laden with fruits.

第四部　丧葬
Book Four　Funerals

瓜儿结得好，	Melons grew well,
瓜儿结得多。	Melons were many.
庄稼长得好，	Crops grew well.
粮食堆满仓。	Barns were full.
好家不出好事情：	Bad things happened to good families:
房顶上结了蜘蛛网，	Spiders span webs under the roof,
梁上挂着葫芦包，	Wasps combs hung on the beam,
马鬃被虫咬，	Horsehair was bitten by insects,
马尾被鼠咬，	Horsetail was bitten by rats,
公牛的角开了花，	The bull's horns cracked,
母牛下双儿，	The cow had twin calves,
母狗下独儿，	The female dog had one puppy,
牙狗半夜三更哭，	The male dog cried at night,
公鸡叫不出声来，	The rooster lost its voice,
母鸡下软蛋，	And the hen laid soft eggs.
花衣花布装满柜，	Cabinets were filled with cloth and clothes,
尽被虫吃老鼠咬，	Which were bitten by mice,
缝衣裳呵缝歪了，	Clothes were badly sewn,
麻团中间躲苍蝇。	And flies were hidden in thread reels.
好麻长得不像竹林，	Hemps did not grow as high as bamboos,
麻头成了蜘蛛网；	Spiders span webs in twines.
荞子长得不像葡萄，	Buckwheat did not look like grapes,

梅葛 // Meige

荞子开花不结子；	Buckwheat did not bear fruits.
小米长得不像白麻线，	Millet did not look like white twine,
成了白穗子；	It turned empty.
谷子长得不像马尾，	Foxtail millet did not look like horsetail,
变成了鸟窝；	It turned into a nest.
这些不是好事情。	These were not good things.
我爹属龙那天病，	My dad got sick on the Day of the Dragon,
我妈属蛇那天病。	My mom got sick on the Day of the Snake.
河里白鱼尾巴跳，	White fish were jumping in the river,
我爹病倒在床头，	My Dad was ill in bed,
我妈病倒在床尾。	My Mom was ill in bed.
左手拉我爹，	I held Dad's hand with my left hand,
右手扶我妈，	And Mom's hand with my right hand,
拉也拉不住，	Dad slipped,
扶也扶不稳。	Mom fell.
房前跟弟弟商量，	I discussed with my younger brother,
房后跟哥哥商量，	And my elder brother
替爹来送鬼，	How to drive away ghosts for Dad,
替妈来送鬼。	And for Mom as well.
拿红梨枝送鬼，	Red pear branches were used to drive ghosts,
拿白梨枝送鬼，	White pear branches were used to drive ghosts
把鬼送到松山头，	Away to the hilltop,
把鬼送到松山坡，	Away to the hillside.

第四部　丧葬
Book Four　Funerals

鬼已送过了，	Ghosts had been driven away,
我爹的病没有好，	But Dad's illness was not cured.
我妈的病没有好。	Mom's illness was not cured, either.

房前跟弟弟商量，	I discussed with my younger brother,
房后跟哥哥商量，	And with my elder brother
替爹来祭神，	About worshiping gods for Dad,
替妈来祭神。	And for Mom as well.
祭神没有跳神匠，	There was no shaman,
祭神要有跳神匠。	But we needed one to worship gods.
左手拿起三炷香，	Carrying three sticks of incense,
右手提起三升米，	Three kilograms of rice,
再拿三块白盐巴，	And three blocks of white salt with me,
去找跳神匠。	I went to fetch a shaman.

一找找着泥瓦匠：	I went to a brickie, who said,
"三炷香我不接，	"I won't take your three sticks of incense,
三升白米我不收，	Or your three kilograms of rice,
三块盐巴我不拿；	Or your three blocks of white salt.
我靠烧瓦罐卖瓦罐吃饭，	I make and sell crocks for a living.
不当跳神匠。"	I am not a shaman."

再找找到木匠家：	I then went to a carpenter, who said:
"三炷香我不接，	"I won't take your three sticks of incense,

梅葛 // Meige

三升白米我不收， Or your three kilograms of rice,
三块盐巴我不拿； Or your three blocks of white salt.
我靠做木桶卖木桶吃饭， I make and sell casks for a living.
不当跳神匠。" I am not a shaman."

去找养马人： I went to a horseman, who said,
　"三炷香我不接， "I won't take your three sticks of incense,
三升白米我不收， Or your three kilograms of rice,
三块盐巴我不拿； Or your three blocks of white salt.
我靠养马卖马吃饭， I raise and sell horses for a living.
不当跳神匠。" I am not a shaman."

去找弓弩匠， I went to a bowyer, who said,
　"三炷香我不接， "I won't take your three sticks of incense,
三升白米我不收， Or your three kilograms of rice,
三块盐巴我不拿； Or your three blocks of white salt.
我靠做弩弓卖弩弓吃饭， I make and sell bows for a living.
不当跳神匠。" I am not a shaman."

去找石匠家： We found a stonemason, who said,
　"三炷香我不接， "I won't take your three sticks of incense,
三升白米我不收， Or your three kilograms of rice,
三块盐巴我不拿； Or your three blocks of white salt.
我靠打石头卖石头吃饭， I cut and sell stones for a living.

第四部　丧葬
Book Four　Funerals

不当跳神匠。"　　　　　　　　I am not a shaman."

最后找到老朵觋①，　　　　　　Finally we found an old wizard,
三炷香他接去，　　　　　　　Who took the three sticks of incense,
三升白米他收下，　　　　　　The three kilograms of rice,
三块盐巴他拿去。　　　　　　And the three blocks of white salt.
老朵觋说：　　　　　　　　　The old wizard said,
"天神我会祭，　　　　　　　　"I know how to worship the God of Heaven,
地神我会祭，　　　　　　　　I know how to worship the God of Earth,
屋里的神我会祭，　　　　　　I know how to worship the god inside the house,
屋外的神我会祭。　　　　　　I know how to worship the god outside the house.

"要祭房后的山神地神，　　　　"To worship the Mountain God and the Earth God,
要用蜡烛白纸蔬菜来祭它，　　We need candles, white paper and vegetables,
要用青树叶来祭它，　　　　　We need green leaves,
要用松枝打卦祭它，　　　　　We need pine branches,
要用母鸡祭它，　　　　　　　We need hens,
要用鸡蛋祭它，　　　　　　　We need eggs,
要用老绵羊祭它，　　　　　　We need old sheep,
要用母羊和阉羊祭它。"　　　　We need ewes and wethers."

---
① 朵觋：即贝玛或西波，替人念经送鬼神的人，与汉族道士不尽相同，朵觋是彝族中有文化的人，是书面文学和口头文学的主要保存者之一。

梅葛 // Meige

祭也祭过了，	Gods had been worshipped,
我爹的病没有好，	Dad's illness was not cured,
我妈的病没有好。	Mom's illness was not cured.
再拿六棵青柏树枝祭它，	Another six cypress branches were used,
拿一棵大竹子祭它，	A large bamboo was used,
拿面团祭它，	A piece of dough was used,
拿三年的大公鸡祭它，	A three-year-old rooster was used,
拿酒饭来祭它，	And food and drink was all used.
山神地神祭过了，	The Mountain God and the Earth God were worshipped,
我爹的病没有好，	But Dad's illness was not cured,
我妈的病没有好。	Mom's illness was not cured, either.

又祭牲畜神，	Then we worshiped the Livestock God,
牲畜神祭过了，	The Livestock God was worshipped,
我爹的病没有好，	But Dad's illness was not cured,
我妈的病没有好。	Mom's illness was not cured, either.

又祭屋里灶君老爷，	We worshiped the Kitchen God,
灶君老爷祭过了，	The Kitchen God was worshipped,
我爹的病没有好，	But Dad's illness was not cured,
我妈的病没有好。	Mom's illness was not cured, either.

又祭过往神，	The God of the Past was worshipped,

第四部　丧葬
Book Four　Funerals

又祭喜丧神，	The God of Wedding and Funeral was worshipped,
又祭天上雷神，	The God of Thunder in the heaven was worshipped,
又祭河边龙神，	The God of Dragon on the riverside was worshipped,
又祭道路神，	The God of Road was worshipped
祭天神，	The God of Heaven was worshipped,
祭地神，	The God of Earth was worshipped,
又祭七姊妹神，	The God of the Seven Sisters was worshipped,
所有的神都祭过了，	All the gods were worshipped,
我爹的病没有好，	But Dad's illness was not cured,
我妈的病没有好。	Mom's illness was not cured, either.
又请朵觋来送鬼，	We sent for the wizard to drive away ghosts,
鬼也送过了，	Ghosts were driven away,
我爹的病没有好，	But Dad's illness was not cured,
我妈的病没有好，	Mom's illness was not cured, either.
爹妈越病越重了！	Their illnesses were even worse!
我爹死了，	My Dad died,
我妈死了！	My Mom died!
我爹死在床头，	My Dad died in bed,
我妈死在床尾。	My Mom died in bed.
找个聪明人，	We asked a wise man,
去请外家①来。	To bring the relatives of my parents.

---

① 外家：即外祖母家。

- 251 -

梅葛 // Meige

外家说：	The relatives said,
"你爹和你妈，	"Your Mom and Dad
没有帽子戴，	Have no hat to wear,
没有衣裳穿，	No clothes to wear,
没有鞋子穿，	No shoes to wear,
没有银子用。	And no money to spend.
街头买帽子，	You have to buy a hat,
街中买布匹，	You have to buy some cloth,
街尾买鞋子，	You have to buy shoes.
白纸锭像马蹄，	White paper ingots are like horse hooves,
黄纸锭像驴蹄，	Yellow paper ingots are like donkey hooves,
样样都要备办齐。"	Everything must be prepared."
样样都买来了，	Everything was bought,
我爹和我妈，	My Mom and Dad,
头上戴的有了，	Had hats to wear,
身上穿的有了，	Had clothes to wear,
脚上穿的有了。	Had shoes to wear.
挖苦葛藤给爹妈洗脸，	Kudzu vine was used to wash Mom and Dad's faces,
挖苦葛藤给爹妈洗身，	Kudzu vine was used to wash Mom and Dad's bodies,
外侄做的麻布包脸嘴，	Linen woven by nephews was used to cover their faces,
买来的金头鞋脚上穿，	Golden shoes were put on their feet.
请人去砍罗汉松，	People were asked to chop podocarpus,
砍来做棺材。	To make coffins for Mom and Dad.

第四部　丧葬
Book Four　Funerals

侄儿侄女来磕头，	Nephews came to kowtow,
大家哭一场。	There arose a loud weeping and wailing.
姑娘送来一只羊，	My daughter came with a sheep,
舅爷送来一只羊，	My uncle came with a sheep,
家里拉出两只羊，	Two sheep were pulled out,
杀了祭我爹，	To be killed to worship Dad,
杀了祭我妈。	To be killed to honor Mom.
棺材停在院里，	Their coffins were put in the yard,
棺材头上插花钱，	With joss paper on their tops.
两口棺材，	The two coffins were like
像两匹白马。	Two white horses.
什么当马鞭？	What would be used as whips?
松树杆当马鞭。	Pine branches.
什么当缰绳？	What would be used as reins?
麻索当缰绳。	Hemp ropes.
什么当马掌？	What would be used as horse shoes?
钱纸纸锭当马掌。	Paper ingots.
两匹白马去到山坡上，	The two white horses went to the hillside,
不看松坡不吃草，	They didn't enjoy hill views or eat grass.
我爹住在石房里，	My Dad lived in a stone house,
我妈住在土房里。	My Mom lived in a mud house.
我的爹妈啊！	My dear Mom and Dad!

梅葛 // Meige

不再在家里住瓦房, You won't live in our tile-roofed house anymore,
不再在家里睡大床。 You won't sleep in our big bed anymore.

让爹住石房, Leaving Dad in stone house
我心里不愿, Made me sad.
让妈住土房, Letting Mom live in mud house
我心里不忍! Was beyond what I could bear!
作揖磕头把他们请回来。 I kowtowed to God to bring them back.

有人劝我说: People consoled me,
　"世上鸟兽虫鱼都会死, "All creatures on the earth will die,
　皇帝的独儿独女也要死, The emperor's only child will die,
　有生就有死, Death follows birth,
　你爹你妈也要死。" Your Mom and Dad are not spared."

有人劝我说: Others consoled me,
　"你爹没有死, "Your Dad isn't dead,
　你妈没有死, Your Mom isn't dead.
　你爹妈到红杨树林里去了。" They've just moved to the red woods."

我想爹, I miss my Dad.
我想妈, I miss my Mom.
没有父母的儿女, Children without parents
就像葫芦打水, Are like a water ladle,

第四部　丧葬
Book Four　Funerals

一打底就通。	With a hole in the bottom.
没有父母的儿女，	Children without parents
舂面不成团，	Cannot pound flour into a dough,
舂米不成团。	Or rice into a ball.
我要把爹找回来，	I want to bring my Dad back,
我要把妈找回来。	I want to bring my Mom back.

三月十五，	On the fifteenth day of March,
三月二十，	On the twentieth day of March,
舂好面团团，	I made a rice ball,
舂好米团团，	And some dough.
背起面团团，	Taking my dough,
背起米团团，	And my rice ball,
找我爹去，	I went to find my Dad
找我妈去。	And my Mom.

找到大河边，	I went to the riverside,
找到刺棵里，	I went to the thorn bush.
河水哗哗响，	The river was rushing,
刺棵太戳人。	The bush was thorny.
找到红梨树林里，	I went to red pear orchard,
找到锥栗树林里，	I went to chestnut woods.
没有爹的影子，	Dad was not there,
没有妈的影子。	Mom was not there.

梅葛 // Meige

太阳快落山了，	The sun was setting.
端起碗吃饭，	It was time to have supper.
吃的什么菜？	What did I eat?
吃的河里长的蒿枝菜，	Artemisia in the river.
苦得不得了。	It tasted bitter.
带的面团团吃完了，	The dough was eaten up,
带的米团团吃完了，	The rice ball was eaten up,
只好转回家，	I decided to go home,
另外找盘缠。	To get more money to travel.
到了五月间，	When May came,
小麦割回来，	Wheat was harvested,
舂出面团团，	I made dough with flour.
背起面团团，	Carrying the dough on the shoulder,
到处找我爹，	I went to find my Dad
到处找我妈。	And my Mom.
找到大河边，	I went to the riverside,
找到荨麻窝，	I went to the nettle cluster.
河水哗哗响，	The river was rushing,
荨麻辣得很。	The nettle was stinging.
找到白杨树林里，	I went to the aspen forest.
没有爹的影子，	Dad was not there,
没有妈的影子，	Mom was not there.

第四部　丧葬

Book Four　Funerals

太阳快落山了，	The sun was setting,
口渴想喝水。	And I was thirsty.
喝的什么水？	What did I drink?
喝老树心里的水，	Water from the trees.
臭得不得了，	It stunk.
带的面团吃完了，	The dough was eaten up,
只好转回家，	I decided to go home,
另外找盘缠。	To get more money to travel.
到了七月间，	When it came to July,
苦荞割回家，	Buckwheat was harvested,
舂成面团团，	I made dough with flour.
背起荞面团，	Carrying the dough on the shoulder,
到处找我爹，	I went to find my Dad
到处找我妈。	And my Mom.
找到大河边，	I went to the riverside,
找到刺棵里，	I went to the thorn bush.
河水哗哗响，	The river was rushing,
乱刺太戳人。	The bush was thorny.
找到楸木树林里，	I went to Catalpa bungei woods,
找到白木树林里，	I went to whitewood forest.
没有爹的影子，	Dad was not there,
没有妈的影子。	Mom was not there.

梅葛 // Meige

太阳落山了，	The sun was setting.
烧起火堆来过夜，	I made a fire to warm my night.
烧的什么柴？	What was used as firewood?
烧的白樱桃树枝。	White cherry branches.
烧得火星炸，	There were sparks,
睡也睡不着，	I could not fall asleep.
眼泪像水流，	My tears were running like water.
鼻涕像蜜淌。	Snot was dripping like honey.
爹妈没找着，	Mom and Dad were not found.
盘缠没有了，	I had no money left.
再回家来找盘缠。	I had to go home to get more money to travel.
到了九月间，	When it came to September,
下到坝里找苞谷，	I went to the field to look for corn.
舂成面团团，	I made dough with corn flour,
背起苞谷面团团，	Carried the dough on the shoulder,
到处找我爹，	I went to find my Dad
到处找我妈。	And my Mom.
找到大河边，	I went to the riverside,
遇着放牧人，	And met a shepherd.
问问放牧人，	I asked him about my parents,
牧人对我说：	The shepherd then said,
"来帮我放牛，	"Come and help me pasture my cattle,

第四部　丧葬
Book Four　Funerals

来帮我放羊，	Come and help me pasture my sheep,
你爹在什么地方，	Then I will tell you
我告诉你，	Where to find your Dad.
你妈在什么地方，	Then I will tell you,
我告诉你。"	Where to find your Mom."
牛羊满山坡，	Cattle and sheep were all over the mountain,
放到太阳落山了，	Not until the sun was setting,
放牧人才说：	Did the shepherd tell me,
"我没有看见你爹，	"I haven't seen your Dad,
我没有看见你妈，	I haven't seen your Mom.
你要快点走，	You have to leave now.
怕牛要触你，	The cattle may hurt you,
怕羊要触你。"	The sheep may hurt you."
放牛人的哄我，	The shepherd lied to me,
放羊的人哄我，	The herdsman lied to me.
放牛的人心不好，	The shepherd was evil,
放羊的人心不好。	The herdsman was bad.
我找爹妈没找到，	Mom and dad were not found.
盘缠没有了，	I had no money left.
再回家去找盘缠。	I had to go home to get more money to travel.
到了十月间，	When it came to October,
下坝找谷子，	I went to the field to look for millet.
春成饭团团，	I made dough with flour.

- 259 -

梅葛 // Meige

背起饭团团，	Carrying the dough on the shoulder,
到处找我爹，	I went to find my Dad
到处找我妈。	And my Mom.

找到石房里，	I went to a stone house,
遇着一位织布老妈妈，	And met an old weaver.
进屋问问老妈妈，	I went in to ask her about my parents,
老妈妈忙答话：	She quickly answered,
"你爹，我晓得，	"I know where your Dad is,
你妈，我晓得。	I know where your Mom is.
你来帮我织麻布，	Come and help me weave linen.
麻布织好了，	When the linen is done,
我就说给你。	I will tell you.
给你一个麻团团，	Here is a thread reel,
麻团前面滚，	It rolls in front of you,
你在后面跟。	And you have to follow.
麻团横处滚，	If it rolls horizontally,
你往横处找，	You have to look for it horizontally.
麻团滚下坡，	If it rolls downhill,
你往坡下找，	You have to look for it down the hill.
麻团滚完了，	When the linen is done,
你爹找到了，	Your dad will be found,
你妈找到了。"	Your mom will be found."

第四部 丧葬
Book Four Funerals

麻团前面滚，	The reel rolled in front of me,
顺着麻线找，	I followed it to look for my parents.
找到石岩下，	I stopped under the cliff,
石岩下边江水淌，	Looking at water running under,
麻团滚在江心中，	The reel was rolling in the river,
看爹爹不在，	I didn't see my Dad,
看妈妈不应。	I didn't see my Mom.
江边两岸上，	On both sides of the river,
松树长得直又密，	Pines were straight and dense,
青冈树长得直又密。	Beech trees were straight and dense.
找到松树林里，	I went to the pine forest,
找到青冈树林里，	I went to the beech woods.
山顶松树像我爹，	The pine on the hilltop was like my Dad.
山顶青冈树像我妈。	The beech tree on the hilltop was like my Mom.
松木砍回来，	I cut down the pine,
青冈木砍回来，	I cut down the beech tree.
松木刻成爹的像，	I carved the pine into the figure of my Dad,
青冈木刻成妈的像。	I carved the beech wood into the figure of my Mom.
后亲来点眼，	Relatives came
亲戚来点眼，	And painted the eyes.
爹妈的像刻好了，	Mom and dad were carved,
供在家堂上。	And enshrined on the family altar.
我爹回来了！	My Dad is back!

梅葛 // Meige

我妈回来了！	My Mom is back!
阿爹啊阿妈！	Dear Mom and Dad!
一月一节令，	There is a festival each month,
每逢节令要祭你。	I will offer sacrifices to you every month.
正月初一来祭你，	I will offer sacrifices to you on the first day in January,
二月初八来祭你，	On the eighth day in February,
三月二十八，	On the twenty-eighth day in March,
四月栽种节，	On the Planting Day in April,
五月端阳节，	On the Dragon Boat Festival in May,
六月火把节，	On the Torch Festival in June,
七月十四，	On the fourteenth day in July,
八月中秋，	On the Mid-Autumn Day in August,
九月土黄天，	During the Tuhuang Days in September,
十月初十日，	On the tenth day in October,
冬月冬至节，	During Winter Solstice in November,
腊月二十五，	And the twenty-fifth day in December.
一月一节令，	There is a festival each month,
月月逢节都祭你。	I will offer sacrifices to you every month.
阿爹啊阿妈！	My dear Mom and Dad!
生前你们说：	You told me,
"人家犁地你就犁，	"Plow when other people plow,

第四部　丧葬
Book Four　Funerals

人家撒种你就撒，	Sow when other people sow,
人家放羊你就放。	Pasture your sheep when others pasture their sheep.
人家撒种你不撒，	If you don't plow when others plow,
地里就会生野草；	Weeds will grow;
人家放羊你不放，	If you don't pasture your sheep when others pasture their sheep,
羊子小得兔儿样。"	Your sheep will be as small as rabbits."

"房后布谷鸟叫了，　　"Cuckoos are singing behind the house,
房前李桂秧叫了，　　Liguiyang birds are chirping in front of the house.
布谷鸟叫就撒种，　　Scatter your seeds when the cuckoos sing.
李桂秧叫就割荞，　　Reap your buckwheat when the liguiyang birds chirp.
按着节令种庄稼。"　Crops are planted according to the season."
阿爹啊阿妈！　　　My dear Mom and Dad!
照着你们说的做，　　I have done everything as you said.
五谷丰收，　　　　We have a bumper harvest.
人畜两旺。　　　　We have thriving livestock.

About the Translators

Chen Ping is an associate professor of English in the School of Foreign Languages and Literature at Yunnan Normal University. Her recent publications include three translations: *Outstanding Brands* (Yunnan University Press, 2002), *Board Secretary* (Huaxia Publishing House, 2004), *Unique Cultural Knowledge of Yunnan Ethnic Minorities* (Yunnan University Press, 2007), and more than twenty articles on translation strategies and translation teaching. Her research interests focus on stylistic translation, literary translation, news translation, conference interpretation, and cross-cultural communication and translation.

Liu Yi is a lecturer of English in the School of Foreign Languages and Literature at Yunnan Normal University. Her recent publications include: *Guide to Managerial Persuasion and Influence* (Posts & Telecom Press, 2010), *Winning the Battle for Sales* (China Renmin University Press, 2015), *The Future of Work* (Posts & Telecom Press, 2015), *How Great Leaders Think – the Art of Reframing* (Posts & Telecom Press, 2016), and *Supply Chain Management* (Posts & Telecom Press, 2017). Her research interests focus on translation and cross-cultural communication.

(Chen Ping translated Book One, Book Two and Part I of Book Three. Liu Yi translated Parts II to V of Book Three and Book IV.)

语文 九年级 下册
教科书

王宁、张联荣、柳士镇、方智范、谭邦和、梁捷、郑等审查专家提出了很多宝贵的修改意见，对教科书的修改和倾力帮助。在教育部的组织下，广大一线优秀教师反馈保证了教学的适切性。在试教试用过程中，我们得到了王南省、陕西省等省（市）教育科学研究院（所）、教研室及持，他们的意见和建议为教科书的进一步完善提供了保障。

人民教育出版社承担了教科书的编辑出版工作。在组织方面给予了全方位的协助。人民教育出版社中语室全体同的中坚力量。感谢吕敬人等为本套教科书的整体设计提供永康为本套教科书"读读写写"栏目书写了硬笔书法范字编写、出版提供过帮助的同仁和社会各界朋友还有很多，谢意。

期盼使用本套教科书的广大师生、家长提出宝贵意见不断修订，使教科书趋于完善。

联系方式

电　　话：010-58758959

电子邮箱：jctk@pep.com.cn